I0630627

THE DREAMT CHILD

EARTH'S PENDULUM

BOOK III

YVONNE HERTZBERGER

Website – www.newfantasyauthor.com

Twitter – YHERTZBE

Facebook author page -
www.facebook.com/EarthsPendulum.YvonneHertzberger.author

THE DREAMT CHILD

EARTH'S PENDULUM

BOOK III

YVONNE HERTZBERGER

ACKNOWLEDGEMENTS

I'd like to express my profound gratitude to all those who read and loved both Back From Chaos and Through Kestrel's Eyes and encouraged me to carry on and complete the Earth's Pendulum trilogy. You told me I am a writer, that I tell a good story and you wanted to see more. You helped me believe in this project and in myself.

To my spouse, Mark, who agrees that writing is 'real work' even though it adds little to the budget.

To Rosanne Dingli, who liked my work enough to endorse the cover.

To my beta readers; Carolyn, Denise, Lyrra and Ruth. Your feedback has made this a better book.

To Wendy Reis, editor and constant support. I am privileged to name you 'friend'.

And not least, to all my readers, those who took a chance on a new writer, and who have let me know they enjoyed my offering.

Thank you, all.

LIST OF CONTENTS:

GLOSSARY
Join – marry
Span – roughly an hour
Moon – 28 days
Eightday – eight days (instead of a week)
Demesne – an area ruled by a lord
Quire – a distance similar to a mile or kilometre

LIST OF CHARACTERS
Liannis – seer
Brensa – Liannis's mother
Merrist – her partner
Gaelen – lord of Bargia
Marja – Gaelen's wife
Lionn – Gaelen's son and heir
Sennia-Gaelen's daughter and wife of Dugal
Nairin – wife of Merlost, ousted lord of Lieth
Wartin – Nairin's son
Leyla – Nairin's daughter
Janest – elderly advisor to Gaelen
Dugal – lord of Gharn
Brynnell – member of council in Catania
Charest – interim governor of Catania
Joranna – Brynnell's daughter
Frellick – member of council in Catania
Grund – contender for lordship turned traitor
Strennock – guard turned traitor
Earth – goddess
Ayliss – the dreamt child

Other characters are minor and need not be listed separately

SPRING

Kira flew in excited circles overhead, emitting such a series of anxious klees and chirrups as Liannis had ever heard from her. Liannis opened her inner senses.

Man comes, the little kestrel sent to Liannis. *Wooden leg! Wooden leg comes on horse!*

Liannis had gone deeper into the forest in search of early greens and stood, bent over a patch of cress at the edge of the stream from which she took her water. The snows had almost all melted, leaving only a few dirty patches under the evergreens where the sun could not penetrate. *Merrist! It had to be.*

Wooden leg was the name Kira had given Merrist. She did this with all people. She could not understand names and referred to everyone by some identifying feature.

Liannis's head shot up in alarm, resulting in a painful crack as it met with an overhanging tree limb. She fell into the water with a splash and saw her precious harvest of cress and wild garlic float downstream. After pulling herself out by the same offending branch she wrung out her cloak and the hem of her gown, silently cursing herself for her clumsiness.

She looked up at Kira. *Are you certain, little one? Where is he now?*

Wooden leg comes! *On big horse! Come! Come see!*

Part of Liannis wanted to hide.

She had grown accustomed to the rhythm of life, alone in the forest all winter with only her horse Cloud and Kira for company. It demanded little of her, just the day to day practicalities of snaring rabbits for meat, gathering what greens she could find to supplement the meagre provisions she had brought with her and caring for Cloud. Kira hunted her own food. Liannis had found a measure of contentment here, away from the reminders of the death of her father or the demands of her mother and friends ... or the goddess, Earth.

She mused that perhaps her fall into the water was the goddess's way of making sure she returned to the cabin quickly.

Answering some unspoken call she must have sensed, Cloud appeared between the trees. *Go back now? Need ride?*

1

Liannis gave up on the idea of running. The cold from the icy water had chilled her skin and she began to shiver. She needed a change of clothes, and soon. *Thank you, Cloud. Yes, I need to get back to the cabin.*

Why are you wet?

Because I fell in the stream.

Hmph.

The disdain in Cloud's tone pricked Liannis. Yes, she had been careless to let herself be caught unprepared. But Cloud was a horse. She did not need to be chided by a horse.

Just get down so I can climb on. And hurry, I am freezing.

Chagrined by the rebuke, Cloud hurried to obey, and Liannis climbed onto her back. Ever since they had been isolated here Liannis had not bridled nor saddled her. There was no one here to question how she controlled a horse.

Kira had flown off when Cloud appeared and now returned. *Wooden leg close to cabin. Come!*

Thank you, little one. You may show yourself to him. It will let him know that I am coming.

I go. The little kestrel hurried away.

Liannis had no time to sort out how she felt about being found, or about seeing Merrist again. She knew it meant that her respite had ended. Was she ready? Just as she approached the last trees that sheltered her from view she heard his familiar voice.

"Kira? Is that you?"

Kira's excited answering klees left no doubt.

"It is you. I have found you. Where is Liannis? She must be near. There is a fire in the hearth. I see smoke. Is she coming?"

The eagerness in his voice awakened something in Liannis that had lain unacknowledged all winter. She no longer wondered if she ought to flee. She urged Cloud into the small clearing.

"Merrist! How did you find me?"

Merrist turned to meet her eyes. "Liannis! At last!" He stumped in her direction, his wooden peg leg causing a hitch in his step.

Liannis slid off Cloud's back so they stood face-to-face, each at a loss for words.

"How did you find me?" Liannis asked again when she found her voice.

2

A puzzled look came over his face. He opened his hands wide. "I do not know. I left as soon as the snows had melted enough to pass. I had to, though I could not tell you how I knew. I had no idea where to begin. And every time I chose a different direction, Warrior refused to budge so I finally gave him his head." He threw his arms wide in triumph, his mission accomplished. "And here I am." The last words brought the familiar grin that made him so dear to her.

At her answering grin the shyness fell away and he enveloped her in a great hug. Just as quickly he drew back, taking in her wet attire.

"Liannis, you are soaked! You need dry clothes!"

He grasped her hand and pulled her, laughing, into the cabin.

AWAKE

Seeing Merrist again, after a whole winter alone, woke a jumble of sensations and emotions that had lain dormant ever since the death of her father. Liannis had almost forgotten what feeling was. The winter had passed in a sort of half-trance and she had thought of friends and family only in a detached dream-like way. This fresh flood of sensation coursed into every part of her body and left it tingling, like a foot that has been sat on too long and suddenly receives blood again.

Now, her respite was clearly at an end. Merrist had found her.

She understood the time had come to re-enter the roles she had abandoned in order to rest and heal from the ordeals of the past two years. She needed, once again, to take up her duties as Earth's seer, however reluctant she might be.

Merrist's delight at finding her made him garrulous so she let him talk on while she got into dry clothes and he made tea. She needed those moments to gather her wits. While pulling a dry gown over her head Liannis looked at her arm. The wound there, the symbolic mirror of the one Earth bore from the strife in Lieth, had refused to heal since appearing the previous summer. She had not examined it since her arrival at the cabin four moons ago. In her perpetual stupor it had not occurred to her to do so. Now the scar, her reminder of the injuries Earth had sustained in the chaos that had befallen Lieth, showed a healthy pink. It had healed. She understood this to mean that Earth had also healed and now they were both ready to face the real world again. Part of her rejoiced at this. Another wanted to crawl back into her solitary cocoon and resume her dream existence where she needed no one and no one needed her.

The warmth from the fire gradually put an end to her shivering. She sat at the rough plank that served as a table and watched Merrist perched on the stool opposite, both with a hot mug cupped in their hands. Merrist had run out of things to tell her and now sat, regarding her.

Liannis met his eyes, suddenly speechless.

4

Merrist broke the silence, his voice unable to hide a slight quaver. "Liannis, I truly thought never to see you again." He stopped, seemingly unable to continue.

"Merrist, how ... what ...?" Words failed her.

She took a deep breath, looked away as she tried to regain her composure, and began again, choosing questions that would not challenge her so much.

"Merrist, how fares Mama? How have the people come through the winter with so little to eat? Is there still peace?" Underneath lay the unspoken question of what she must face now that Earth summoned her back.

"I do not know how I got here," he said, answering her unspoken question first. A look of puzzled awe gave way to his infectious grin, "But I am heartily glad I am!"

"As am I, though I know it means I must leave this peaceful place. I suppose it will no longer hold repose for me. Can you tell me more about what led you to search for me?"

Merrist sobered as he remembered. "Your last words to me before you left were 'look after Mama'. Liannis, I have never seen such grief. She never fully understood that you had no choice, that you followed a call from Earth. I admit, I, too, have wondered at this. Why could we not have helped you to recover your health? Could we not have aided each other better if we stayed together?"

The death of her father had stripped Liannis of the last bit of life force she had to offer in Earth's service. At that time Earth had placed a compulsion on her and led her to this cabin, to rest and recover while the land slept under its blanket of snow.

Merrist shook his head as if still trying to solve that puzzle. "But I came to accept that it must be so, else you would not have been called away. The others, too, Lord Gaelen, Lady Marja, Lionn – we have all made our peace with it ... but not your mother. She has aged ten years and barely speaks."

***

Mama sat in the small walled garden off Lord Gaelen's apartments. Her needlework lay untouched on the bench by her side. A warm blanket rested on her shoulders. She stared, unseeing, at the wall opposite.

Liannis saw a frail old woman, with unkempt grey hair, slumped shoulders and thin claws where she remembered warm strong fingers.

Her heart wrenched at the sight. "Mama!" Of course her mother did not hear.

Was this all her fault? Had she selfishly abandoned her mother?

***

As she came back to awareness, Merrist placed another mug of tea in her hands. "Here, drink; then tell me what you saw."

She gulped gratefully before speaking. "Merrist, we must hasten back! Poor Mama! Merrist, why did you not come sooner?"

He gaped. "Come sooner? Liannis, I did as you bade me. I have only found you now because Earth willed it."

Seeing his hurt and shock, Liannis realised how unjust her remark was and felt immediately contrite. "Forgive me. Of course this is none of your doing. Earth has her own ways." All her joy at seeing Merrist again eclipsed by her vision, she added, "We must leave immediately. It is clear Earth calls me back." She rose and made for the door but he put a restraining hand on her arm.

"Liannis, look outside. It is dark. We must wait until morning. Tell me what needs to be packed. We need some provisions. Those need to be carried as well. I am ready as I brought only what I could carry on Warrior. We can leave at dawn."

It took a moment for his words to reach her. "You are right. We cannot leave until then." She sagged and burst into tears, the first she had shed since beginning her apprenticeship with Liethis at age twelve. She felt as though she was that young girl again. "I want to see Mama."

"And we shall." He wrapped her in a gentle embrace. "We shall".

6

BACK TO BARGIA

Unlike the time Liannis had travelled from this cabin as Dugal's unwelcome guest, this journey to Bargia did not require stealth. And with almost all of the snow in the open gone, the path remained clear and easy to traverse.

The weather held calm and clear. Both Cloud and Kira welcomed the change. Kira stayed close, and during the quiet times when conversation stopped, Liannis let her sight join Kira's to view the familiar landscape. Soaring above with Kira, she surveyed the fields and the forest. She saw expanses of grass dotted with the new green of spring, pushing back the old brown of last year's growth. Snow had been plentiful through the winter leaving the soil ready to receive seeds and begin the new growing season. The trees that would be the first to show new growth, the willows and walnuts, wore a blush of pale green, bright against the starkness of bare branches. On sycamores tiny red buds still encased the blooms that would soon emerge, stood out on swaying limbs.

Crofts and villages had not fared so well. Here and there, Liannis saw fresh mounds of stones where families had buried their dead – more than ought to be there. When people emerged from their cabins they moved slowly, with heads bowed in what Liannis took to be grief, weariness or ill health. But they did not display anger, only resignation. She wondered how long that would last. Would Earth and her people have time to bring back the Balance before the next chaos injured the goddess again and prevented its full return?

No one could tell she was a seer as she did not wear her white robes on this journey and so did not accost her to ask for predictions for the future. She could observe freely. She had mixed feelings about what she saw. The signs of new growth gave her hope but that was offset by the sadness she felt for the condition of the people they passed.

She probed Merrist about what he knew. How had Lieth City passed the winter? Had Gaelen been successful in gathering enough food to feed the people there? And what of Gharn, Catania, even Bargia? Those were the topics of conversation as they took their meals by a fire in the evening. By the time they reached

Bargia Liannis felt she had a good grasp of all she needed to know before she met with Gaelen again.

She observed no signs of rebellion. Perhaps starvation had sapped the people of the will to fight. Now, with planting time almost upon them, Liannis hoped that the need to tend to the next season's food would prevent any uprising against Lord Gaelen, Lord Dugal or the rulers of the other demesnes. Questions for Gaelen whirled in her mind and she grew more anxious as they neared Bargia.

Earth sent her no dreams while they travelled and showed her nothing of what would come. She asked Merrist no more about her mother, Brensa, having seen all she needed in her vision. The sense of urgency to be with her mother never left, but she trusted that Earth had sent Merrist so that she might reach her before it was too late. It did not occur to her that Earth might have more important reasons for calling her back.

She and Merrist fell easily into their old, comfortable rhythms. Liannis did not think to question this until much later. His efficient, calm presence lent an air of rightness that helped her make the transition back into active life smoothly. She had time to gather about her with little effort the abilities and barriers she had not needed all winter. By the time they neared the gates of Bargia she knew she could resume her place without undue pain, her recovery almost complete.

When the walls and gate of Bargia came into view Liannis could hold back no longer. She urged Cloud into a gallop, ahead of Merrist on Warrior. Kira flew close and they were almost at the gate before Liannis remembered to remind Kira to stay out of sight. This was the first time since leaving home that Kira had not been permitted to stay close by her. At first Kira protested, so Liannis mind-spoke her. *Kira, you remember when you got caught by the falconer?* She sensed a frisson of fear from the bird.

Leg caught. Dark. Afraid.

Yes. So you must stay out of reach.

When Kira mind-spoke her agreement Liannis let out the breath she had been holding, confident that Kira would remain safe.

In her gallop to the gate, the blanket that had hidden her from view slipped off her shoulders, so the guards at the gate recognised her, or perhaps recognized Cloud. One hurried off,

8

likely to send a messenger to Lord Gaelen with the news of her return. By the time Merrist caught up with her the other guard had hailed a stable hand to receive their mounts. Cloud never liked being handled by anyone but her or Merrist, so Liannis had to admonish her to behave as well. *Cloud, we are back in the city now. You must allow the groom to take you. I cannot be there.*

By the time their horses were led away a welcome figure came running to greet them.

"Lionn!" Liannis hurried to meet her childhood friend, heir to Lord Gaelen, and soon found herself out of breath from a great hug.

"Liannis, you live!" He pushed her out to arms' length to examine her, grinning like a fool. Then, more serious, he added, "We had begun to believe we would not see you again. Liannis, where have you been all winter?" He caught himself and grinned again, relief warring with joy for a place on his face. He grasped Merrist's forearm and clapped him on the shoulder with his other hand in greeting. "Come." The sweep of his arm included them both. "Father will wish to see you right away."

Lionn took Liannis's one arm in his grasp and began to tug her in the direction of the weapons practice field.

She wrenched her arm free. "No, Lionn. I must see Mama first. Surely Lord Gaelen can wait a span longer."

Lionn spun back to face her, chagrined.

"Yes, Brensa needs you Liannis. She is not well. Go to her. I will fetch Father to meet you in his chambers." His face cleared again. "What a dinner we shall have tonight. Oh, I am glad to see you again."

With that, a grin still splitting his face, he turned on his heel and strode toward the practice field. From the corner of her eye Liannis could see that Gaelen had already received the news and marched toward them, the messenger close behind. She paid no mind, wanting only to see her mother.

9

MAMA

Word of Liannis's return had already reached Lady Marja, who flew down the stairs of the Great Hall to embrace her. Then her face took on a worried look. "Liannis, you have arrived none too soon. Come. I have not told Brensa you are here." She turned and led the way back up the stairs to the chambers she shared with Lord Gaelen. Along the way she called out to a passing maid. "Telsa, bring tea and food to our chambers. We have guests."

Liannis hurried after Marja, Merrist not far behind. "My lady, I know she is not well, but how badly fares Mama? I wish to be prepared."

Marja stopped at the top of the stairs and turned to face her. "Liannis, she has pined since you left. She does not accept that you were called by Earth, that you needed solitude to recover from the effects of the devastation in Lieth. She has withdrawn, barely eats or speaks, sleeps only fitfully. She is very frail. Nothing we do comforts her." She hesitated then added, "You may be the only one who can bring her back. She seems determined to join your father."

Her words added a chill to the fear Liannis already felt. *Earth, do not let me be too late.* But she said nothing aloud, merely nodded and followed Marja down the hall.

"She rests by the hearth in the sitting chamber." Marja opened the door and, her hand still on the latch, looked at Liannis. "I will wait in Lionn's chambers. I think it best you see her alone." Leaving the door ajar Marja stood back, pressed Liannis's arm in support, and headed to Lionn's chamber. She turned back only to say, "Merrist, please wait for the maid and tell her to bring the tea into Lionn's chamber."

"As you wish, my lady."

Liannis barely heard. Immobile, she sent her senses into the room to search for her mother's aura, afraid to enter without that knowledge. Later, when she reflected back on that moment, she realised that her fear came from guilt at having left her mother when she most needed her. While she had had no choice, she knew her mother could not understand, that she would think Liannis had willingly abandoned her. A guilty part of Liannis agreed that she ought to have found a way to remain with her, even though her

10

mind told her it had not been possible. She had had no choice in obeying Earth's command.

Even so close, Brensa's aura appeared dim, overshot with a grey pall, some red sparks of anger showing here and there. Anger at whom … Papa, Liannis, Earth? Liannis hoped her mother would be able to tell her. She wondered if her mother even knew she was angry. It was more Brensa's nature to transform anger into hurt.

Liannis let the aura go. Knowing she could delay no longer, she pushed the door gently open and slipped into the chamber.

Brensa sat with her back to Liannis, facing the hearth, in the rocking chair that Klast had commissioned for her when they first joined and moved to their cabin by the forest. Apparently someone had moved it here for her, possibly to help her feel connected to him. In spite of the comfortable warmth of the chamber, a wool blanket lay wrapped about her shoulders.

Brensa's hair, with the stubborn curls she had always taken efforts to control, now spilled over the edge of the blanket, loose and wild. Liannis remembered its dark, chestnut sheen from when she was a girl, and how her father would so often take an errant curl and finger it behind her ear in a gesture of affection. Now, since his death, chestnut had turned pure white.

Liannis swallowed back tears, gathered her courage and approached the chair in silence, not wanting to wake Brensa suddenly if she slept, or to shock her with her presence until she could face her and take her hand.

Brensa must have been awake. She stirred and turned her head to face Liannis, recognition dawning, as Liannis knelt beside her.

"Mama." Liannis took one hand in both of her own, unable to say more.

"You left me."

The whispered accusation hung between them. Liannis had never seen such hurt in her mother's eyes. It stung more than she could say. Papa had been taken from her by a stranger's hand, but she … Brensa thought Liannis had left of her own accord when she needed her most. Her pain would not allow her to consider otherwise.

11

Liannis could sense this all from her mother's eyes and from the touch of her hand. "I know, Mama. I could not stay. Earth called me. I could not act otherwise. I hope one day you will be able to forgive me."

She knew she could not explain, not yet, that if she had not obeyed Earth's call she would not now be alive to return to her. Nor that she had been under a compulsion she could not resist. In her state of grief her mother could not think beyond her own need enough to understand. Liannis could only hope that one day her mother would be able to. Now her pain was too great.

Two fat, silent tears tracked down the sides of her Brensa's nose and dripped silently onto her blanket.

Mother and daughter remained like that for some time, neither speaking, just looking into each other's eyes, both searching for what they had lost. Then Brensa reached for Liannis and they found themselves in a long, wordless embrace. Liannis could sense a spark of renewed life in her mother and hoped it would be enough to begin to pull her back from her despair. She finally allowed the tears she had held back to flow onto the blanket where they mingled with her mother's.

REPRISE

Earth sent Liannis no dreams or visions for the next eightday. She spent time with her mother and friends - Lord Gaelen, Lady Marja, Lionn, and of course, Merrist. She asked that another bed be set up in her chamber, deep within the stone heart of the castle, so that she could be with Brensa at night as well as during the daytime. That chamber had served both her old mentor, Liethis, and herself whenever they had to stay within the city. Its thick stone walls and relative isolation from the activities in the castle allowed a measure of peace by blocking the constant press of emotions and thoughts from the people around her. Her barriers quickly returned to their full strength, after they had not been needed all winter.

Having her mother with her while she slept made it more difficult to find peace at night but the improvement Brensa showed made it worthwhile. Liannis thought Brensa viewed that gesture as a way of making up for her long absence, as her mother knew how much Liannis needed solitude to stay strong.

Brensa said little but began to eat more. Her colour and strength improved and some life returned to her eyes.

On the afternoons, when some sun fell on the small walled garden outside the lord's chambers, they sat together over tea while Liannis tried to tell her how she had spent the winter, hoping that Brensa would begin to understand how necessary her isolation had been for her.

"Mama, Merrist wanted to come with me, but I told him to stay with you. Earth commanded that I go alone. But now I believe that when Earth saw how much you needed me, she sent Merrist to find me so that I might return to you." Liannis said this in different ways many times, though her mother seemed not to take it in until the seventh day when they once again sat alone in the garden.

Her mother looked directly at her for the first time, profound sadness in her eyes.

"Liannis, I do not have your strength. You get that from your father. I relied on him so much. I believed he was the only one who truly understood what I went through in that cave when those men used me. When Earth took him from me I thought she must leave you with me. But you did not stay. So when you left I

13

placed the blame for my pain and loneliness on you. You were all I had and you went away."

Her voice cracked on those last words. Unable to say more she fell silent, tears brimming unshed in her eyes.

Words failed Liannis. All she could do was nod and put her arms around her mother to draw her into her embrace. After some time she managed to whisper, "I am sorry, Mama. Can you forgive me?"

Her mother reached up one frail hand to caress Liannis's cheek, now wet with tears. "You are not mine, Liannis. You belong to Earth. I see that now. I have no claim on you."

Liannis knew then that her mother understood, though it was not what either of them wanted. "Oh, Mama ..." How she wished she could contradict her, but Brensa spoke true and they both knew it. Liannis's only consolation lay in knowing that, though Brensa had not said so in words, her mother had, indeed, forgiven her and now gave her permission to follow her destiny - not the destiny she chose but the one she was called to.

"I love you, Mama," she finally managed.

"I know, Liannis. And I love you, perhaps too much." She patted Liannis's cheek once more, before her face took on a far away expression. "Liannis, I have no wish to remain here without Klast. I wish Earth would let me join him."

Fear gripped Liannis. "No, Mama. I need you still."

Her mother drew herself away slightly to hold Liannis in her gaze with a new intensity.

"No, Liannis. You are mistaken. You have no need of me. Earth provides what you need just as she did when she took you away from me. I can lay no claim on you. I know that now."

Though Liannis knew, deep inside, that what she said was true she did not want to accept it. "No, Mama ..."

"Liannis, you never belonged to us. We knew that from the beginning." Her eyes softened. "We loved you so much, but you are a woman now and our duty to you is done. You have given me so much. I am grateful for your presence even now, and your love, but I release all claim on you. Let it be, Liannis. Let me be."

"Please do not leave me yet, Mama. Please."

"No, not yet, Liannis. But not so long. I feel it ... the pull. And I will not be sorry to leave this life. Klast waits for me. He can wait a little longer ... but not too long." Her eyes again took on that

14

far away look, as if she saw someone in the distance who called to her. A tiny smile played on her lips and Liannis knew she no longer saw her.

The next day Liannis could see that some spark had returned to Brensa and she smiled for the first time when they all took their evening meal in Lord Gaelen's chambers. Marja noticed it, too.

"Brensa seems better, Liannis. Will she recover, do you think?"

Liannis studied her mother before answering, trying to find the right words.

"For a time perhaps, though I do not think she will remain long." She turned back to see the hope fade from Marja's eyes and placed a hand on her arm. "She misses Papa. And she understands that I can not be here with her all the time. I think she is tired and feels Earth calling her back. But her time is not yet."

"I see." The sadness in Marja's voice belied her words. Brensa had been her best friend ever since they had been young girls together. Liannis thought, too, that Marja had not completely forgiven herself for Brensa's capture and rape so long ago. Lady Marja had been the intended target and Brensa had been taken by mistake. Brensa had never been the same after that ordeal.

15

CATANIA

Liannis had enticed her mother out for a stroll in hopes of bringing some colour back to her cheeks. The sun shone on the cobblestone path and warmed their faces as they walked outside the castle.

Just as they were about to turn back from the city wall to return to the castle they spied a messenger riding in through the gate that opened in the direction of Catania.

He rode bent over his horse as though having no strength with which to hold himself upright. His horse's flanks were lathered with foam. Though the horse approached at a slow walk Liannis could tell it had been ridden hard for some time.

A young castle guard saw the man at the same instant and ran toward the gate at a brisk trot to meet the rider. Liannis knew that Gaelen would be informed immediately as well, and said to Brensa, "We had best return to our chambers. Gaelen will wish to see me after he has spoken to the messenger."

She hailed a guard and asked him to find Merrist, sensing they would both be needed. "Mama, I fear I will be called away from Bargia. I do not wish to leave you again … but…"

Brensa gave her a wan smile. "Liannis, have you not heard what I said? I knew this time would come soon."

"What do you mean?"

"First, I will not die … not yet. And second, I have no claim on you. You belong to Earth. I will be waiting here until you return, this time at least."

Liannis felt a great weight lift from her shoulders. "I will return as soon as I can, Mama."

Brensa nodded acknowledgement. Liannis led her to their shared chamber and helped her to lie down before hurrying to meet Gaelen.

It did not take long before Gaelen strode into his chambers, where she waited for him by the hearth-fire. A maid bearing a tray of tea, bread and cheese followed close behind and set the tray down on the round table to one side of the hearth and hurried out again. Marja and Lionn joined them in the room, rounding out the group.

Gaelen wasted no time. "Has Merrist been summoned?"

Liannis nodded. "He has, my lord."

"Good. I will wait, then."

Marja placed a mug of hot sage tea into his hands. A knock came at the door and she hurried to admit Merrist.

As the rest of them took their accustomed chairs Gaelen remained standing.

"As I am sure you already know, I have spoken with a messenger from Catania. He came at the bidding of Governor Brynnell. The news is not entirely unexpected. After two winters of famine, some unrest must be anticipated. I had hoped the situation would remain stable long enough for this year's harvest to relieve some of the fears for the coming winter." Gaelen stopped to look at each of them in turn, his gaze resting last on Liannis. "You are aware that governing three demesnes is a great challenge, both for me personally, and for the council. Catania has been loyal for twenty years, ever since Bargia conquered it before Marja and I were joined."

He referred to the treachery of Lord Cataniast, Marja's father, and resulting battle of reprisal during which he and Gaelen's father were killed. Bargia came to rule Catania and Gealen had taken Marja to wife to strenghten the tenuous truce.

Everyone remained silent, waiting for the rest.

"But for almost two years now we find ourselves governing Lieth, as well, a demesne in utter chaos and great need." He turned to Lionn. "Lionn, I had intended to send you to Catania by mid-summer to determine the situation in more detail. Messages received over the winter tell us that Brynnell fears the unrest caused by the famine will erupt into treason and violence. This message today informs me Brynnell has not the necessary numbers of trusted men to be confident of countering such plots and there are rumours that cause him to believe support may be required."

Lionn's chin rose. He stood and squared his shoulders, drawing himself up to his full height, a mirror of his father. "I am ready, now, Father. We have been preparing for this. Am I to understand that I will be needed sooner than was thought?"

Marja's brow creased as she waited for Gaelen's answer, one hand moving to her throat. While Gaelen considered Lionn ready, Liannis knew Marja wanted to keep her son safe at home a while longer, though she tried to keep those thoughts from her son.

"Yes, Lionn, you will leave in two days. I will send five soldiers and two elite guards with you. We will all meet in council tomorrow. But I wanted to tell all of you what I have been planning before I bring it to the full council." Gaelen turned to Marja, giving her a fond look. "Marja knows of this already. It has been the subject of much discussion in the privacy of our chambers this winter."

Marja's eyebrows rose for an instant then her face cleared and she nodded comprehension. "Yes, I think the time has come."

Merrist and Lionn looked frankly puzzled. Liannis expected her own face must have shown a similar reaction as Gaelen tilted his head at her with an apologetic smile.

He took a deep breath, meeting each of their eyes in turn for a moment before continuing. Liannis recognized the habit. Something important and difficult needed all of their attention. They were to hold their responses until Gaelen had explained himself fully.

"I have come to a decision that will affect all of the One Isle. Catania has prospered under our rule ever since we conquered it after Lord Cataniast's treachery there."

Gaelen sent a warm look Marja's way. Her return gaze told him she understood that their union would never have happened if Marja's father, Lord Cataniast, had not betrayed Gaelen's father.

"But" Gaelen continued, "the situation has changed and now we face challenges there, again, as well as in Lieth."

Marja nodded but Liannis noted that the rest of them seemed to hold their breath, expecting more to come.

Gaelen reached up to pinch the bridge of his nose, the familiar gesture telling Liannis how difficult this was for him.

"I am but one man – one with good men behind me, it is true, but our resources are stretched to their limits. Had there been no famine this might have been delayed for a time, though I always intended it to happen."

Liannis had never known Gaelen to hesitate before. That he did so now told her that he felt uncertain about what he planned to tell them. He sighed deeply and straightened. "Friends, it is time that Catania once again ruled herself."

Lionn's eyes grew round in surprise, Merrist's jaw dropped open and Liannis felt a frisson of fear raise the hair on the

18

nape of her neck. This news came as a surprise even to her. She had thought that they would go to Catania to stabilize the situation, not to release Catania from Bargia's rule.

Marja, having been prepared for this, moved to stand beside Gaelen and placed a steadying hand on his forearm.

Lionn gathered himself first. "But how will this be done? Who will rule Catania? They have no ruling family from which to choose a lord."

Merrist had clearly been thinking along the same lines as he nodded vigorously.

Gaelen gave Lionn a grim smile. "That is what your mission to Catania will help us determine. You will speak to Governor Brynnell and his Council to find out who has the knowledge, the following, and the wisdom to be named Lord. You will gather information throughout Catania, with the assistance of your men, and get a sense of the mood of the people. To whom do they look, who do they trust? We need to know how close the threat of rebellion is, what is needed to restore stability. "

Liannis watched Lionn's face lose some of its confidence as the import of Gaelen's announcement sank in.

Gaelen and Marja saw it, too. Marja's brow creased again and Gaelen sent Lionn a small, tired nod of understanding. "I see you comprehend the gravity of your task. Good." He drew himself up, took a final deep breath, and let it out. "We will discuss the details at council tomorrow." He gave a rueful shake of his head. "I doubt any of us will get much sleep tonight." Signalling the end of the discussion by sitting and leaning back into his favourite chair, he looked at Marja. "Is dinner ready, do you think?"

It struck Liannis that Gaelen had not asked her and Merrist to go to Catania. Nor had Earth shown her. Yet she had sensed that she would not remain here and wondered what that meant.

MOTHER

Liannis woke in the middle of the night, the old, recurring dream vivid in her mind.

She and Merrist sat by the hearth in their cabin watching a small child at play by their feet. This time the girl held up her toy, a doll she had cradled. "Look Mama, Maya is asleep now, see?"
Liannis nodded, filled with warmth.
Merrist reached down and stroked the girl's hair. "Indeed, you have done well. What a good mother you are."
The child beamed back at him.

***

Liannis woke with a start but before she could shake the dream off another vision overtook her.

***

"Daughter."
Liannis recognized Earth's voice but did not see her.
"Mother, I hear you."
"Daughter, why do you deny what you see?"
"I do not understand. Mother, what does this mean?"
"Watch."
She saw the scene again. This time she saw Merrist reach over and take her hand, a contented look on his face.
Earth spoke. "Liannis, see your destiny."
"But I am a seer. This is forbidden."
"Daughter, the world does not remain constant. When the One Isle requires change to maintain the Balance, I do what is needed."
Liannis's mind roiled in confusion. "Am I not to be a seer, then?"
"You will still be my maidservant, but the burden has become too much for one. It must be shared. Merrist has proven himself loyal. You know that he loves you." A hint of amusement

20

crept into her tone. *"And I believe you love him, though you have done your best to deny it."*

Liannis heard the warmth in Earth's voice and sensed approval there. It gave her a small measure of calm, enough so that she could listen without terror. Earth was not angry with her.

Earth read her thoughts. *"The child is yours – yours and Merrist's. Together you will raise another who will serve me."*

"Mother, I have so many questions. How? Why?"

"It is time for a story from a time before memories, before history, a time when other changes became necessary to restore the Balance. Listen and see."

***

VISIONS

"Watch, Daughter."

Scenes flashed by in rapid succession. Liannis could barely register what she saw, much of it so fantastical she did not understand.

Earth showed Liannis cities much grander than she had ever imagined. Streets ran straight and true, wide, with smoothed stones over which drove wondrous carriages, shining with bright colours, decorated with gold and silver, pulled by teams of four or even six horses at once. Buildings rose taller than she dreamed possible. Lights on poles lined the streets, and shone brilliantly, tended by men who filled them with oil and lit them as darkness fell.

The people dressed in fine fabrics, ornately embellished with jewels, and gold and silver embroidery, or ribbons that shone when light fell on them.

Liannis beheld aparatuses that did amazing things, things that seemed impossible. One looked like a strange tangle of pulleys and wide leather belts upon which men threw bundles of straw. The thing took the bundles to a door high above where more men waited to take them and pile them in a great loft. Beneath the loft stood huge stables where cattle waited in stalls to be milked or sows nursed litters of piglets. Others held great numbers of beautiful horses. The size and scope of these buildings overwhelmed her.

The streets in the last city were devoid of children, but men and women hurried from shop to home, checking over their shoulders before entering, as if fearful of being followed or discovered.

Liannis wondered what they feared.

Earth showed Liannis another scene and she understood. She saw men in crimson robes and women in gold ones and knew them to be seers.

The men, the seers in crimson, walked the streets accompanied by armed guards in livery of the same colour. These guards carried strange weapons made of wood and metal, long and straight. Liannis saw one of these seers point at a woman

22

entering a shop. He gesticulated to the guard with him and Liannis heard him shout. "You! Take her." The soldier nodded, marched into the shop, and grabbed the woman. The seer followed and touched the woman's forehead, her struggles in vain.

He gave a triumphant, cruel smile. "You plot treason against us. Your life is forfeit." He gestured to the guards. "Shoot her." One guard held the woman while the other pointed his stick at her chest. Flame spat from it, blood bloomed on her bodice, and she slumped over, dead. They dropped her where she stood. Then, at another barked order from the seer, they killed the shop owner cowering behind the counter. He had not even been touched or spoken to.

Liannis shook with fear and awe. "Mother, what is this? Who are these seers in red?"

"Watch."

Liannis stared, frozen, as these seers ordered the guards to kill the rulers of the city and their entire families, then took over the castle.

These men used their abilities without hesitation, truth-reading anyone they chose, reading minds at will.

Liannis then saw the crimson ones attack the women in gold, the female seers. These seers had no soldiers with them, but many of these, too, read minds at will. Liannis watched them call flocks of birds down from the sky to assail the crimson men and fall upon them with wings, claws and beaks. The women summoned animals out of the forests to attack the crimson seers and their guards, to tear them apart.

The scenes passed before Liannis's eyes in rapid succession, showing the passage of time. All the while, the citizens' fear grew. The streets became almost deserted. Peolple emerged only when necessary.

The male seers had the guards hunt down and kill as many of the women seers as they could find. Those few who remained went into hiding. The guards, with their sticks of lethal fire, also hunted and killed the animals that had come to the women's aid. No order could be seen in the city, no laws, no trust. No one came to the aid of the women seers.

Liannis watched in horror as buildings were burned with people still inside, many of them children - the work of soldiers under the command of the crimson ones.

Time passed in a blur - many, many years. Then came the scorching sun. No rain to save forests, no rain to nourish the crops or fill the rivers. Wells went dry, granaries stood empty and crumbled, as did most of the buildings, even those made of stone.

The people, those few who had not died from starvation or at the hands of the soldiers and seers, formed ragged bands. They fought and killed the remaining seers and guards, crimson and gold alike, using stealth and whatever weapons they could find; pitchforks, cudgels, even the stones on the ground, until not one seer remained.

"Mother, enough! I can watch no more."

"Yet, we are not finished. See."

Time passed, more years than Liannis could imagine.

Earth showed Liannis what remained of the cities, the great stone buildings crumbled, covered in dirt and dust. Here and there, handfuls of people, thin and dirty, huddled in cave-like holes where doorways had once opened onto beautiful chambers. They now held only dark, hollow spaces, where the few families who remained could find some shelter from the burning sun. She saw no green, no animals, no birds ... no seers.

"You see, daughter, what happens when the Balance is not respected? When power is misused? I had not the strength to keep the One Isle from dying. I could barely keep myself from dying and disappearing."

Earth led Liannis's vision outside the cities. The entire landscape lay scorched and barren. Only the occasional stunted tree marred the featureless landscape. The sun still blazed, unrelenting, in a cloudless sky, with no hint at rain to come, only total desolation.

Liannis sensed great periods of time pass. The cities gradually disappeared under layers of soil, no longer visible. Here and there, widely scattered, small bands of people, handfuls of three, sometimes as many as ten, roamed the land in search of food. Over long ages the forests returned, and grass grew again. With them came the animals, first the small ones, rabbits, crows, small fish in the new streams and rivers, then larger ones, deer, boar, wolves. The rains brought life back to the land.

24

In time, the bands of people grew larger, villages sprang up, fields filled once more with crops, sheep and orchards. Cities returned, very small at first. The people organized, chose leaders, whose children eventually became lords.

"But they were still lost, Liannis," Earth said. "I could not guide them in what is needed for Balance." Earth had made herself visible to Liannis at the last, in her wise woman form and regarded her sadly as she spoke. "Look."

Liannis observed a lone woman, dressed all in white, speaking to the lords and the people. She gave them Earth's messages. As time continued, new seers - always women, emerged, gaining more abilities, serving Earth. This was the world that Liannis knew, the one told in the histories and stories she had been taught.

"She was the first new seer. You understand, Daughter, I could not survive such discord again. Yet, all things must be renewed. I chose women as my servants because they are the givers of life, and so less inclined to take it. It was they, not I, who decided that seers must not join, must not take a mate and bear children. It has served me to let that belief go unchallenged ... until now."

"The first seers after the desolation chose to remain unbound so they could serve me. The earliest of them understood that joining would restrict them. They needed to be free to move about unencumbered by the care of children or a mate. They taught those beliefs to the new seers who apprenticed to them. That custom came to be understood as law."

"It still seems a wise path, Mother."

"So it would be if things had remained as they were. But we once again approach times where cities grow large, where new inventions and discoveries create greater opportunities for both good and evil. That is why I have given the latest seers, like you, new and stronger abilities. The people need greater guidance than before."

Doubt gnawed at Liannis's mind. "Mother, have I failed you? Can I not still serve you best as I am? Why must things change? They have worked well until now have they not? Have I not served you well?"

"Indeed, Daughter. You have served me with the greatest dedication and obedience. And, yes, the Balance is returning ... for

25

now. But look back on the past three years. You do see that you have been given abilities that Liethis did not have. She could not touch another in order to send them calm in the midst of fear. Your ability to mind-speak animals is greater than hers. You are not aware of it, but your other abilities are also stronger than hers were."

The sadness in her face grew and she took Liannis's hand. "Liannis, your greater abilities have also caused you greater suffering. The burden you carry as my maidservant is too great to be borne alone. You will go mad if this continues. Indeed, you almost did. You need a helpmeet. And I have decided it must be a man, not another woman, who will share your burden, who will lift some of it from you. The needs of the people will continue to grow. So, too, will the abilities of my servants. But no one person can bear it all. You will be the first to break with the old way. And Merrist will be the first man to share this servitude." Her smile brightened. "I think you agree that he has proven his dedication to both of us. And his loyalty to you is unquestionable." Earth studied Liannis for a moment. "Perhaps you do not completely understand what he has sacrificed for you."

Earth touched Liannis's forehead with one finger. "Remember."

***

It was winter. Liannis and Merrist lay cocooned in a makeshift lean-to of pine branches covered with a layer of fresh snow. Their horses lay to either side, providing extra warmth. They had fled the turmoil and destruction in Lieth. Liannis was exhausted, unable to care for herself. Merrist had done everything. Now she slept with her back to him. He had wrapped himself around her from behind to keep her warm. She twitched and jerked in her sleep, crying out and muttering, as nightmares claimed her.

Liannis watched the dream. As Merrist drew her closer she heard him whisper into her hair, "Shhh, my love. Shhh. It will be all right. Shhh, dearest. Shhh."

***

26

Now Liannis understood what Earth wanted her to see. Merrist loved her, not just as her servant and companion, but as a man loves a woman. He had denied himself the expression of that love, even any hint of it. The strain caused him anguish. Only when he thought she slept could he allow himself to show his feelings. He had sacrificed so much.

And she had ignored it, refused to see it, pushed it from her. They had continued together without acknowledging what had occurred that morning, the moment lost, the incident soon buried and forgotten.

Liannis felt herself pulled back to that memory. She wished she could turn around and wrap her arms around Merrist, tell him she understood. She did remember. She had almost done that, then, when she woke to hear those hoarse, tender whispers. But when she had stirred he had withdrawn in haste, embarrassed, and in a ragged voice told her he would make tea and porridge, pretending nothing had happened. She had known, even then, that he hoped she had not noticed what he had done.

But she had noticed, and had pushed the thought away, just as she had the recurring dream.

***

WHAT NOW?

Liannis felt Earth must have taken pity on her. Unlike other times, when after a vision she would waken drained and needing immediate drink and food, this time she woke refreshed and alert. Brensa stirred beside her, also waking, so she knew it must be morning.

"Good morrow, Mama."

"You look well this morning, Liannis. Did you sleep well?"

Liannis could not share her vision, not until she could take the time to think about what she had seen, not until she had a better understanding and could begin to explain. So she simply smiled and nodded. "And you, Mama? Did you sleep well? How do you feel this morning?"

"I am happy that you are here with me. That is enough for now. Shall we join the others to break our fast?"

"Yes, I am hungry." Liannis rose and took Brensa's hand to help her up, reminded once again how frail she had become.

No one noticed that Liannis did not take part in the banter as they broke their fast in the lord's chambers with Lady Marja, Gaelen and Lionn. No one, that is except Merrist. Liannis noticed his inquiring glances from time to time but he held his peace. Liannis knew that Merrist ought to be the first one to learn what she had been shown, but she had no idea how to begin. Their beliefs of how they must behave together were about to turn upside down. Seeing him here kept the memory of what Earth had shown her so acute that she could think of nothing else. She had to get away to think.

Liannis gulped the last of her tea. "Since I will need to be present at the council meeting soon I need to return to my chamber to prepare." She hurried out and closed the door behind her before her friends could question her.

No sooner had she sat in a chair in her chamber than Earth spoke to her again.

***

"Daughter."
"Yes, Mother."
"Go to Gharn. You are not needed in Catania. Take
Merrist with you. All will be well."

***

Gharn? Why had Earth asked her to go to Gharn? But she
felt relieved that she would not be included in the party going to
Catania. That journey would have required all her attention. Her
opinions would be sought about everything that happened. A
journey to Gharn, alone with Merrist, appealed to her. She looked
forward to seeing Lord Dugal and Lionn's sister, Lady Sennia
again. Her initial pleasure faded as she wondered if trouble might
be brewing in Gharn. But, no, Earth had said all would be well.
Trusting that, she packed her small bundle, and leaving it ready for
later, went to join the council.

TO GHARN

Gaelen readily acquiesced to Liannis's wish to travel to Gharn after she assured him that Earth had told her she would not be needed in Catania. The mission to Catania could manage without her.

The next morning found Liannis and Merrist passing through the city gates, panniers packed. Cloud welcomed the exercise and Kira flew overhead in happy circles, glad to see Liannis again. The sun shone bright in a sky studded with pillow clouds buffeted by a warm spring breeze.

Normally, under such conditions, they would have ridden in companionable silence, each content in their own thoughts. Today, however, the silence held a good deal of tension. Liannis rode wrapped in concern over how she might approach Merrist with Earth's message. No openings presented themselves. She had no idea how to begin.

For his part, Merrist, too, seemed troubled and brooding. She dared not ask what was on his mind. And so they rode, silent, but far from comfortable. Neither spoke more than two words until they stopped to rest and eat their midday meal. Merrist avoided looking at her. He sat fidgeting until they had finished and both rested with mugs of tea, the small fire reduced to ashes. Finally, he glanced at her sideways. "Liannis, I had a dream ... actually I have had the same dream three times now." He looked back at his hands, silent again.

She waited for him to continue.

"Liannis, I do not understand why I should dream the same dream three times. It is ... well ... awkward, but I think I ought to tell you ... because I have a sense it is important." He sent her another furtive, sideways glance and returned his gaze to his hands. "It is ... a dream about us ... in the future, I think." He cleared his throat, and as if gathering new courage from somewhere, looked up and held her eyes. "Liannis, I know it means something. I think Earth wants me to understand something." His tone sounded almost defiant, as if he dared her to disagree with him. "I know men do not get messages from Earth, but I think I have."

Liannis's mouth had gone dry and she tried to find some saliva before she answered. "I am listening." Not the best response, perhaps, but all she could muster.

"We are in the cabin, the one you grew up in sitting in front of the fire." He looked away and cleared his throat again. "There is a girl child playing on the rug in front of us. She calls me Papa." It came out in a rush. When he had finished Merrist once more studied his hands as if they were the most interesting objects in the world, head bent and turned slightly away from her so she could not see the expression on his face.

She swallowed, took a deep breath and let it out again before she could speak. Even then, she managed only a whisper. "I have had the same dream."

His head jerked up. "You have?"

The astonishment on his face almost made her laugh, lightening the mood and helping her find her voice. "Yes, it is a sending from Earth. I believe you are right."

"But," he sputtered, "I am no seer. How do you accept this so easily?"

The situation struck her funny. Perhaps it was relief. A nervous laugh escaped her. But now Merrist had given her the opening she needed. "It seems that, as I would not listen, Earth had to choose another way to get my attention."

He gaped at her, mouth slightly open, eyes round, at a loss for words.

"Merrist," Liannis laughed again, "close your mouth before a bug flies in." Serious once more, she added, "We have a lot to talk about; things Earth has shown me and told me, things that will be hard to understand." She studied the dying embers. "Perhaps we should remain here for the night. I will build up the fire and make more tea." Now that the egg had cracked she knew she would be able to continue, though she still needed some moments to organise her thoughts.

Merrist seemed of the same mind. "I will see to the horses then, and bring our blankets. We will be fine under this tree, I think. Shall I set a snare?"

Liannis nodded as she poked the fire back into life and added more wood - the broken branches Merrist had dragged out from between the trees earlier. They were both stalling, she knew, but would soon run out of things to distract themselves.

31

When they resumed their seats around the fire, mugs of fresh tea warming their hands, Merrist broke the silence. "You have something to tell me?"

Braver than I, she thought and nodded, her mind made up. "But before I do, I must ask something of you." She watched his eyebrows rise slightly, expectant. "Merrist, may I read your thoughts?"

His eyes widened, but when she did not look away he calmed. "You may. I know you would not ask were it not important."

"Thank you." She held out her hand. He hesitated for only an instant and offered his own. "Show me what you felt, seeing that dream."

Peace. Rightness. Love, both for her and the child. Things as they ought to be. Their child – theirs, not fostered – theirs, his and hers.

Merrist knew that she saw. His face grew earnest and soft, all confusion and fear gone. "If this is from Earth, Liannis, if you have seen it, too, then this is meant to be."

He reached out with his free hand, took her other one then folded both hers in his. In that moment he became her equal. She sensed the change deep in her core. Here was a new Merrist, a stronger Merrist, a man ready to greet his destiny.

"Liannis, know that I love you. I have always loved you, from that first day when we rescued you from the snow."

She could only nod, too full to speak as he continued.

"If Earth sent this to both of us, it must be her wish, it must be our destiny." Liannis sensed some uncertainty creep back, not about what he said, but about her. "Liannis, do you believe this, too?" He hesitated before asking the question behind that one, the real question, the one that needed to be spoken out loud. "Liannis, do you love me?"

All the times she had pushed aside her feelings for Merrist, believing them forbidden, flashed by. Why had she resisted so strongly, when Earth had tried to show her she ought to accept them? A calm settled over her. "Yes, I need deny it no longer."

She sensed him fill with new confidence and earnestness. He reached up with one hand, still holding hers in his other, and stroked her face, a feather touch, full of meaning. "Will you join with me, Liannis?"

32

A great weight lifted from her and she felt freer and lighter than she had since childhood. "Gladly."

JOINED

Even with the fire built up and their small camp sheltered from the wind at the edge of the forest, the air still held a definite chill, especially when the sun sank low. And neither of them had any experience with the joining of bodies. They knew what was supposed to happen, of course, but both lacked familiarity with the finer points.

Keeping the cold at bay competed with their need to complete their union. This resulted in nervous laughter as they fumbled with clothing under the blankets. It helped them overcome their initial shyness until they each found themselves relaxing into the other, forgetting awkwardness, sharing the joy of new-found freedom to love without holding back.

Liannis felt no pain, nor did she bleed as many women do their first time. It is said that riding horses often has the effect of breaking the virgin's veil. Perhaps that is what had happened. Nor did she shed the tears that are said to often accompany a woman's first joining. She only felt a profound peace.

She sensed that the exact nature of the transformation in Merrist would not manifest all at once, that his changes would be revealed slowly as he faced new challenges, but Liannis sensed its importance. She knew that he would no longer merely follow, that from here on they would face the future as equals. She no longer had a servant; she had a partner.

Long after Merrist had fallen asleep, snoring softly into her hair, Liannis pondered what this meant, how their relationship would shift. She received no answers from Earth, but then, did not truly expect to. Soon, content to let it be for now, she snuggled deeper into Merrist's shoulder and fell asleep.

She woke to the sound of the fire crackling and the smell of fresh rabbit on a spit.

"So, sleepy head, you have decided to join me," Merrist teased as he poured a mug of her favourite white pine needle tea and handed it to her. "The rabbit is almost ready, and I have reheated the porridge from last night."

She stretched and threw off the blankets as she took the mug from him. "How did you manage to do all this without waking me?"

"I think a wild boar could have run right by your head and you would not have wakened. Not losing your touch, are you? Or are you becoming lazy?" The words belied the love behind them.

She returned his grin. "I have you to keep me safe. Why should I not sleep with such a one to protect me? Or do you plan on forgetting you duties."

"Duties," he shot back. "I think those are about to change." He handed her the bowl of porridge and a leg of rabbit. "I do not think it is fitting for the mate of a seer to cook while his wife lies abed."

Mate of a seer. The phrase sounded so strange to her ears. He must have realised it, too, because he sobered, the grin disappearing.

"Liannis, things will be different now, very different. I was joking, but I think I may have spoken more true than I intended."

"Yes, I think we have much to learn together."

"Hmmm. Perhaps this is why Earth told us to go to Gharn instead of Catania ... so that we would have some time to talk about this. We will need to decide what to tell people."

"Yes, that is a big worry. I think people will not accept these changes readily."

"Indeed, I have been thinking the same thing. And Liannis, I have been changed, somehow. I do not understand it all, but I feel different." His voice conveyed both awe and uncertainty. "I see things more clearly, somehow. And I feel a deeper awareness of our connection to Earth. Everything seems more alive."

MERRIST

He expected they would say it was arrogance, that he overstepped his place. He knew different. He had sensed its importance when the dream had come the third time, stronger than the last. Earth had a message for him, a man. Why, he did not know. The first two times he had thought it was just wishing. The third time, he had accepted there was more behind it, though still had not understood its true significance.

These last three years, he had learned that destiny never follows a clear path. Unexpected events change its course. That all began with the loss of his leg in the battle to regain Gharn for Lord Dugal. But he never imagined that his part would unfold in this way. He had made his peace with his role as Liannis's servant. It was honest work, likely the best that a man with a wooden peg for a leg could expect.

And that event allowed him to be near the woman he loved. He understood better, now, where his loyalty to Liannis came from. It never wavered. He never had eyes for any other woman, in spite of Liannis's occasional encouragement. Believing that he could never have her made no difference.

These years were a test. He knew it now, a test to see if he was strong enough for what Earth needed from him. No one knew if or when he may falter. He had seen the most stalwart waver in the face of great adversity. But he knew that this was where he belonged and it would take much for him to turn his back on what Earth destined for him. His legs may not have served him well but his mind and heart had. He now dedicated them to whatever Earth needed of him and trusted that what Earth asked would never require him to betray Liannis. That might ask too much of him. He had faith he would not be challenged that far. He knew it. He believed it. He was ready and was not afraid and he found strength in that knowing.

It surprised him that Liannis did not wake when he left their blankets. She had always been a fitful sleeper who woke at the slightest noise or movement. It was something she learned from Klast, perhaps, or was simply part of her nature as seer. But this morning the evenness of her breathing did not change as he moved away. Even the noise of stoking the fire and setting up the spit to roast the rabbit did not disturb her. Might this be what he would give her? Is this how he would help her cope with what Earth required of her? And what of the promise of the child? That was an even greater wonder.

He watched as she slept and vowed to protect her. She would have more such peace if he had anything to say about it. If that was the role Earth had chosen for him, he welcomed it. Her father, Klast, had been her rock before. Now the torch had been passed to him. The thought reminded him that Klast had said that very thing as he lay dying. Had he known?

They took their time going to Gharn. Where in the past he had not asked too much about Liannis's relationship to Earth, thinking it unfitting, now he pressed her. He needed to know as much as he could to prepare for what they would face once they reached the gates of the city.

Since he had nothing in his appearance to distinguish him as a servant of Earth he suggested it might be best to let his new status become apparent only as needed. It would be better to show, gradually, rather than declare. People believe their eyes better than words. Liannis agreed with that part at least. It helped that, unlike most women, Liannis had studied strategy, both in her training as seer and from her father. It made discussing plans easier, though they did not agree on all points.

"Liannis, I will continue to defer to you in front of Gharn's citizens. It is important that Lord Dugal and Lady Sennia understand and accept the changes first."

"But, Merrist, it is also important that we stay together, especially at night, so we can discuss what happened in the day and adjust our plans. I am not convinced that you ought to continue to act as only my servant. If you do you will not be able to stay with me at night," Liannis argued. "Besides, I no longer want the people to think of you as a servant. We must act as equals, or they will never believe things have changed. If you act the same as before, how will they accept you as you are now?"

And so it went. They still had not agreed when the gates of Gharn came into sight. Only then did the other reason for Liannis's insistence come to light.

"Merrist, I do not want to sleep alone any more. I fear I will not sleep at all if you are not with me. And not only because I

37

want to sleep next to you. " She looked at him shyly. "I have learned that I am able to sleep much better when you are beside me."

He reached across the small space between their horses to take her hand. Since he could not grip the saddle well with his wooden leg he slid sideways and came very near to falling off Warrior's back. That broke the tension between them as they both laughed at his near pratfall. "Show me."

He had discovered that being in actual contact enhanced their ability to understand each other. When she opened her thoughts he sensed fear, far more than she had let on. Only now, since Earth had made her his partner, was he able to understand the depth of her suffering when things were out of balance. Now he understood her fear that she would not be able to perform her duties, the pain when too many unhappy people surrounded her with their unspoken feelings, the deep fatigue after a vision, the energy needed to search auras or to truth-read. As an ordinary citizen none of that had been apparent to him other than seeing the visible effects on her. Now she let him see it all.

What he understood, too, was how much in these few days she had begun to rely on his energy and calm to balance her and to offer her some peace. With this new great challenge facing them, she feared she would not be able to do what was necessary if he did not remain by her side.

"Liannis, surely you know that Earth will give you the strength you need. She always has."

When she dropped her eyes and gave a reluctant nod, he let go her hand. He still believed he was right not to move things forward too quickly. "You know that I would prefer to be with you. But this time I still think it ill-advised. Humour me. I will stay as close as I can without giving things away."

"All right. But if something happens that you are needed for I will have to say something. And I refuse to treat you as my servant."

He snorted, almost laughing. "Liannis, you have never treated me as a servant. You have always shown me respect and seen to my comfort."

Her response was a wan smile. They had reached the city gate.

LIANNIS

A guard Liannis had met on a previous visit recognised her as they approached and by the time they entered the gate two grooms appeared to look after the horses.

Cloud, please allow the groom to look after you. We are not at home now.

Cloud huffed her displeasure. *Want apples. Tell him.*

That made Liannis laugh. Cloud was ever the vain and somewhat taciturn creature, letting her know that she served Liannis out of choice, not because she had to.

"Oh, groomsman," Liannis called out as he turned to lead Cloud away.

He turned with an inquiring look.

"Please see to it that both mounts receive a few apples and a nosebag of oats. They have not had anything other than grass for several days."

"I will see if we have any left, Lady. It is late in the season and they may all be gone."

When Cloud made her displeasure plain by mind-speak, Liannis said to the groom.

"If you have no apples then carrots will do."

"As you wish."

She and Merrist continued to the castle gate. Before they reached it, Liannis spotted Sennia hurrying to meet them. She noticed right away that Sennia was with child, her belly a soft mound under her gown. She wondered that Gaelen and Marja had not known. Perhaps the winter had kept them from sending the news. Or perhaps, knowing Sennia, she wanted to surprise them. Sennia always did have a rebellious and independent streak.

"Liannis, Merrist, what a wonderful surprise!" They gave each other a huge hug before Sennia turned to Merrist to give him one as well. Liannis wondered what the people would make of such familiarity with a 'servant'.

"What brings you to Gharn? All is well here," Sennia spread her gown smoother over her belly, beaming, "as you can see."

"Indeed, I do see," Liannis laughed. "And why have we not heard? Your mother will be furious that you have kept this from her. You know how much she wants a grandchild."

"I do not want her to worry. And even more, I do not want her here fussing about every step I take."

"Oh, Sennia," Liannis chided chuckling a little to take out the sting. "You know she will not fuss. She gave herself no rest at all, even during the Red Plague when she was expecting Lionn - or when you were on the way. I think she would be the same with you. She would not expect you to coddle yourself. This is all normal. And she knows you are no weakling."

"Perhaps, but I want to do this on my own." She lifted her chin in the defiant stubbornness Liannis had come to love about her. "Now come and eat. You must be famished after nothing but travel fare."

As they followed her to the lord's chambers Liannis had a moment to wonder why Earth had chosen to send them here. They did not appear to be needed. Nor had she been given any dreams about Gharn. All seemed peaceful. Perhaps they were only meant to tell Dugal and Sennia of the changes in Earth's plans and their status. But why them? It remained a puzzle.

Sennia looked surprised when Liannis requested that the four of them meet privately over dinner and that they must not be disturbed, but acquiesced when she told her the reason would become clear at that time.

Sennia, doing her best to allow them to eat in peace but practically dancing with impatience, watched Merrist take his last bite and wasted no time getting to the point.

"So what is it you two need to discuss that is so private? You have already said there is no trouble in Bargia, or anywhere else. Tell us. I cannot wait a moment longer." She made a face followed by an exaggerated sigh. "Being a lady can be so very stifling."

Merrist looked astonished at her outburst but it put Liannis at ease. This was the Sennia she knew and loved; impulsive, headstrong and direct. She saw Dugal cover his mouth with his hand to hide his amusement and knew that this was the Sennia he had fallen in love with less than two years ago.

Fighting a laugh, Liannis put on her meekest face and said. "Of course, my lady. Please forgive me for the delay and the

41

distress it causes you." When Sennia stuck out her tongue Liannis could maintain the façade no longer and joined the others in a shared laugh.

As she and Merrist explained what Earth had told them, and the changes in their status and relationship, it felt as though the air went out of the chamber. Dugal and Sennia grew silent and sat motionless, seemingly stunned and unable to respond.

"So," Liannis ended, "You are the first to be told of this. We still do not know what all the changes will mean."

In the long silence that followed Liannis studied their faces.

Merrist broke the silence. "So, what do you think? We will need your support to bring the people on side. Can we count on you?"

The question surprised Liannis. Merrist had not always been so direct. She had not had the courage to ask the question so bluntly.

Sennia responded first. "I hardly know what to think. But Liannis, I have known and trusted you since I was born. And I believe you are Earth's true seer. Indeed, I have seen the proof myself. If you tell us this it must be so, I do not understand it all but you may rely on my support."

Dugal, always more thoughtful and slower to react than Sennia, looked troubled but nodded gravely. "I, too, know you to be a true seer. So, yes, I will support your claims. But I think we are all aware how difficult this may prove. We must proceed with caution." He fell silent a moment, then repeated, "This changes our whole world. It will not be accepted easily. We must think carefully about how to handle this … very carefully, or all could go terribly wrong."

He had the right of that. Liannis doubted any of them slept well that night, Merrist and she in separate chambers, and Dugal and Sennia still trying to understand the news.

14

CRISIS

After the four broke their fast together, Dugal accompanied them to the stables to check on Cloud and Warrior. The stable-master had managed to find some shrivelled apples. They had just fed the horses the last of them and turned to leave the stable when Liannis fell, grabbing her abdomen with both hands.

She gasped, "Sennia! Quickly! She needs us." Merrist pulled Liannis up. She and Dugal left at a run for the castle, Merrist hobbling behind as fast as he could manage, leaving the stable-master gaping after them.

They were about halfway to the castle gate when a guard came running toward them, panic on his face. "My Lord," he gasped, out of breath. "Come quickly. Lady Sennia has fallen. She is in great pain and bleeds."

Dugal's pace did not slow. "Has the midwife been summoned?"

"Yes, my lord." The guard now ran at their side back toward the castle.

On entering the great hall Dugal could see that the news had already spread. Anxious faces peered at them as they rushed up the great stairs to the lord's chambers where he knew they would find Sennia. All eyes followed their progress.

The guard at the door opened it as soon as he saw them and moved aside for Liannis to pass but stepped back in front of Dugal to prevent him from following her in. "Please, my lord, this is women's work."

The door closed with Dugal still outside. Even as he opened his mouth to protest he knew he could not enter until granted permission by the midwife. That was the custom. If he broke it his people would judge it harshly. He might still have insisted on entering but the revelations of the previous evening came to mind. He ran his hands roughly through his hair and looked at the wary guard.

At that moment Merrist reached the stair. Dugal saw a strange look on his face.

"My lord, I must go in."

The guard's stance became more alert. Another from the floor below now followed Merrist up the steps, his hand on the hilt of his sword.

"We cannot, even I cannot." Dugal wrung his hands and then ran one hand over his face. "You know men are not allowed in the birthing chamber." Dugal felt his own resolve waver. He wanted so desperately to enter. But he was the lord. He had to uphold the law.

"My lord, you must let me enter. It is Earth's wish."

Dugal stared at Merrist, frozen with indecision as Merrist turned to push the guard aside. Soon Merrist struggled in the grip of both guards.

The first of Sennia's wails of anguish and pain broke Dugal's inertia.

"Open the door." Custom no longer seemed important. Sennia needed him ... and Merrist.

The guards hesitated only until Dugal roared, "Open the door or I will have you flayed," and shoved one guard to the side. It caused all three to stumble but the guards managed to keep their grip on a flailing Merrist. The door closed behind Dugal with Merrist still outside.

It did not take a healer's knowledge to see that Sennia would lose the child. The blankets were red with blood and her face twisted in pain. Though she tried valiantly not to cry out, each new wave caused her to double forward.

The midwife, after a glance at Dugal, went back to her work without a word of protest. She looked again between Sennia's thighs. "It comes now, my lady. It will be over soon."

Moments later Dugal watched the tiny, lifeless body of a baby slip into in the palm of the midwife's hand. Tears streamed down the woman's face as she shook her head in silent negation.

"Too small, my lady. She does not breathe."

"She?" Sennia asked, her own tears sliding silently into her hair and onto the pillow.

The midwife nodded. "Yes, a daughter."

Sennia reached out and the midwife laid the still, little body onto her open palms. Sennia looked at the babe for a long moment, then cradled her daughter to her breast and shut her eyes against the world. She had not even looked at Dugal. He stood by, helpless.

44

The midwife returned to her work. When the afterbirth slipped out Dugal watched the midwife massage Sennia's abdomen to slow the bleeding. But by the increasing depth of the frown between her brows and then the frantic expression on her face Dugal could tell that all was not well.

"Melinna, what is it? What is wrong?"

"The bleeding ... I cannot slow it. There is damage inside the womb."

The bleak despair in her eyes told Dugal how serious this was. Sennia would die if the bleeding could not be stopped.

Until then he had given no thought to anything outside this chamber. Now the commotion in the hallway came to his attention: Shouting and the sounds of a struggle. He could make out Merrist's voice, breathless with the fighting. "Let me in! I can help her. I must go in. She will die. Let me in!"

And the guard's, "It is forbidden."

Dugal looked at Sennia, at the midwife, and lastly, at Liannis. He heard Merrist shout again, "I can heal her." Merrist's voice had become more pleading. "Please, my lord, I can heal her. I swear it." The sounds of scuffling stopped.

"He says he can heal her." Dugal sent Liannis a questioning look. At her silent nod he looked back at Sennia again and decided. He opened the door.

"Let him in."

The guards stepped back and Merrist rushed to Sennia's side.

"My lady, I can heal you. May I touch you?"

She nodded sadly, her head turned away.

The midwife protested. "No, my lady. It is forbidden. No man may enter here. I still may be able to save you."

Merrist ignored her. "My lady, you trust me, do you not?"

Sennia gave a weak nod. Dugal could see her strength fading even as the moments passed. "Yes, let him come."

"No, my lady." The midwife wrung her hands in consternation. "Your reputation...!"

"Stand aside and let him work." Dugal placed himself between the midwife and the bed. "Merrist...?"

"This is the will of Earth. Else Lady Sennia will die."

That decided Dugal. He nodded and stood back as Merrist took Sennia's hand, closed his eyes and fell still.

45

The midwife stood back, hands over her mouth in confusion, silent now at the invasion of her place.

Merrist, eyes still closed, moved one hand to Sennia's belly. Then he looked up at Dugal.

"My lord, you must trust me. I need to touch her womb – on the inside. Lady Sennia is torn and the tear must be closed or she will continue to bleed. If she loses much more blood she will die."

Dugal began to shake his head but Merrist continued. "My Lord, I may be able to stop the bleeding from the outside but I will not be able to heal the tear. She will never bear more children if I do not heal her completely."

Dugal still hesitated but then saw Liannis take on the familiar look that told him she was in trance.

***

Earth showed Liannis two different scenes. In one Sennia grew old and wrinkled. A grey sadness hung on her like a pall. She had not produced an heir. The future of the demesne lay in jeopardy.

In the second she saw Sennia laughing with three children gathered about her, a set of twins and a younger child.

***

Liannis came back to awareness and turned to Dugal.

"My lord, it is so. Earth has shown me this. Please allow this."

Dugal looked from Liannis to Merrist and back to Sennia. When Sennia nodded he turned back to Merrist. "Do what you must. I will bear the blame."

Merrist did not even take time to breathe a sigh of relief. He carefully lifted the hem of Sennia's gown and began to probe between her thighs until his hand disappeared entirely into her womb.

Not a sound broke the silence while Dugal watched and waited, breathing only when his held breath forced him to. Spans passed. Merrist did not move. After some time Dugal could see that he was losing strength. Not knowing how Liannis knew this would

46

help, he saw her move to stand behind Merrist and place a hand on his shoulder. Dugal could almost sense strength passing from Liannis to Merrist as he continued to work, silent, eyes closed.

The afternoon shadows already darkened the chamber when Merrist finally withdrew his hand and opened his eyes.

"She will live and her womb will bear children again." He tried to rise, reaching for a cloth to wipe the blood from his arm, but stumbled and fell back to the floor. "It seems I must rest."

That broke the tension. Sennia lay asleep so Dugal rose and went to the door.

"Guards. Help this man to a bed. He has saved my lady's life this day. Earth be thanked."

Liannis spoke up. "Take him to my chamber. I will care for him there."

WHO AM I?

It did not surprise Merrist that no one argued with Liannis when she ordered he be brought to her chamber. People naturally followed the orders of a seer and she had a powerful reputation and presence. It was only reasonable that she would look after his needs when everyone knew he had served her for so long.

Her chamber lay close by so the two guards had no trouble dragging Merrist there, each taking an arm over a shoulder, and placing him, at Liannis's direction, on her bed. She ordered food and drink and made sure he stayed awake long enough to get some into him.

Liannis looked in almost as bad a state as Merrist. He could tell that the strength she had sent through him while he worked had sapped hers, as Earth's work always did. Once they had both eaten and drunk they slept for several spans.

The chamber had no windows, something Liannis requested whenever she visited the city. Having four thick stone walls around her helped to dull the pressure of emotions and activities of the people so that she could let her barriers down and relax enough to sleep. And so, when Merrist woke he could not tell what time of day it was.

"About time you woke up." Liannis, fully dressed, handed him a mug of water and held out the platter with the left-over food from the previous afternoon. "I will order fresh tea and more food."

So this is what it feels like after doing Earth's work. Merrist felt as if he could eat a whole goose and drink a whole pitcher of ale. "Ask for some ale, too."

"After the tea. Ale will not clear your head and we need to talk."

"I will drink the tea first, but I do want some ale."

Liannis opened the door to summon a maid as she answered. "Certainly, just drink the tea first. Else you will find you cannot think clearly."

She had the right of it, he knew, but he did not like having her tell him what to do now, as she had when he was still her servant. He had almost begun to say something to her when she must have noticed his expression.

"Merrist, when I first wake after a vision or after some other task that requires my abilities I have learned that I need certain things. The most important one is water or tea. Then food. And until I have these I do not wake fully or think clearly."

A rap on the door announced the maid and interrupted the conversation. It would wait until he had eaten.

They said little as they fell to. Even with the left-over food from before Merrist still felt ravenous. When they had sated their hunger and thirst Liannis poured ale for both of them, sending him a sly sideways smile as she handed him the goblet. "Is your mood improved?"

"Hm," he hedged, not yet willing to admit she had been right. But he could not help but return hers with a smirk of his own. He took a long drink of the ale and wiped his mouth on his sleeve. "Liannis...."

She waited, now serious.

He chose his words with care, clearing his throat. "Liannis, I do not know how I knew what to do for Sennia. I just knew. Is that how it was for you ... in the beginning?"

"No, I learned as a child. I sensed things but I grew into my abilities slowly. And later, I had Liethis to teach me - especially how to control my barriers so that I could be among people when I needed to. I did not receive my abilities full blown."

She studied him silently for a while. Merrist could tell she had more to say so he held his tongue.

"Merrist, I cannot explain this. It is as new to me as it is for you. It appears you have the ability to heal. But healers have always been women. It seems nothing is as it has always been." She shrugged, her brow creased. "Do you remember when I came to stand behind you and somehow my strength passed to you?"

"Yes, I did not think I could finish the work, and then I had the strength. Will that continue, do you think? And what am I now? A healer? A seer ... I knew what to do but I had no vision or dream? It just came to me."

"I have no more answers than you, Merrist. But when I slept I had a dream where you also lent me your strength when I needed it. It seems we will do that for each other."

"Liannis, I want to know. What am I? What more will I learn? I do not know myself as I am now. I am a stranger to my own self." He downed the rest of the ale, too frustrated to say anything more.

"I, too, am changing, Merrist. But I think one thing has become certain. We will be called to assist each other. So I think I was right. It is time for us to stay together. We do not know when we will both be needed again. And everyone will know what you have done, now. There seems no point in hiding the change any more."

He thought that over.

"It does seem so. There may be danger to each of us if people do not think these things come from Earth. If they believe we deceive them they could try to harm us, or even to kill us. For that reason alone, it makes sense for us to stay together as much as possible." He tried to lighten the mood. "It means you will have your wish after all. We will not be separated at night. You will sleep well."

She sent him a wry look. "Not if I have to worry about our safety." After a moment she added, "I think we need to see how Sennia fares, and to speak with her and Dugal. I want to know how they understand what happened. We will need their support even more now that people know what you did."

"Perhaps we ought to speak with Dugal first. We will need his presence I think, if we are to be allowed to see Sennia." Merrist strapped on his wooden leg as they spoke, and pulled on his shirt and boot. "I am ready."

Neither spoke as they left the chamber in search of Dugal. Merrist felt the furtive stares of servants and guards as they passed but no one said anything to them. The news had spread, and it seemed everyone waited to see what would happen next.

16

CONSULTATION

Liannis discovered that they had slept much of the day. That often happened after a vision or after using her abilities so Liannis was not surprised. But it made it more urgent that they speak with Dugal and see if they could meet with him and Sennia.

They found Dugal at weapons practice. Judging by the vigor with which he attacked his sparring partner Liannis guessed he needed to work off the stress from the events of the past day. His partner would not get away without fresh bruises and a renewed respect for his lord's skill. Their moves looked like a practiced dance, each motion smooth and controlled. Liannis knew this to be the result of their matched skill and not from holding back.

Dugal did not see them right away, so they stood at the edge of the training grounds and watched for a few moments. He caught sight of them when his swordplay caused him to trade positions with his partner so that he faced in their direction. It triggered an instant of inattention, which allowed his partner to get a solid blow in before the arms master called a halt. Dugal honoured the man's small grin of satisfaction with a salute and a rueful shake of his head. He had been caught out.

Dugal handed the weapons master his sword and strode over to meet Merrist and Liannis, pulling off his padded tunic as he did so.

"So, you are awake. I did not wish to disturb you as I knew you would need to recover." Without even looking behind him he held out the tunic behind his back, where the weapons master took it from him. "Let us talk while we walk. There is much to discuss."

"How fares Sennia?" Liannis needed to confirm this first.

"She mourns the loss of our child, as do I, but she has slept and eaten and the bleeding has not resumed." He turned to Merrist. "Merrist, I ought not to have tried to prevent you from entering the chamber. Forgive my lack of trust. It will not happen again. You saved Sennia's life. You have my gratitude."

Merrist shrugged. "My lord, even I did not know that this was what I must do. I can hardly blame you for not understanding. I still do not understand what I am becoming."

"Nevertheless, we owe Sennia's life to you."

"May we speak with you both in your chambers, my lord?" Liannis asked. "I think it important that we all have the same information."

"Yes," Merrist added, "and I would like to confirm that all is well with Sennia, if you will both permit."

"Certainly. Let us go there directly."

Along the way Liannis could sense the questions from the people as they stared at their backs. It felt as though tens of bees stung her at once. She took a moment to pull her barriers more firmly about herself. A glance at Merrist told her he had no such difficulties. He looked calm and at ease.

They found Sennia sitting in her favourite chair in her chamber, propped up with pillows, a blanket around her legs, sipping a mug of strengthening raspberry leaf tea. The pot sat within reach on a brazier beside her.Though wan and tired looking, otherwise she seemed well enough.

Dugal entered first. "My love, I have brought our friends to see you." He went to her chair and planted a kiss on her forehead before sitting down in his own.

Merrist held back.

Liannis went to Sennia's side and took her hand. "Sennia, we came to see how you fare."

"It seems I am to live." Her lips trembled. "Though a part of me wishes I would not … my child is gone, my dear babe." A silent tear made a slow path down her left cheek and into the neck of her gown.

"I know this is a great loss to you, Sennia. It is meet that you mourn. We mourn with you."

Merrist nodded sadly in agreement. "My lady, I wish to determine that you are truly healed, but to do that I must touch you." Merrist opened his hands in supplication, requesting permission.

"And will you be able to tell me if I will have more children, if I will produce an heir?"

Liannis spoke up. "Sennia, I can answer that. Yesterday, when Merrist wanted to place his hand inside your womb as you

52

lay bleeding, I had a vision from Earth. I saw you with three children, twins, a boy and a girl, and later another son. There was no doubt."

Sennia looked at Liannis, new hope in her eyes. "Then I am not to be barren?"

"No, when Merrist was allowed to heal you that door closed. You will be a mother and you will bear an heir."

Dugal came to kneel by her other side, taking her other hand. "Then all is not lost, my love. Do not despair."

Liannis let go, knowing that Dugal's touch would mean more to Sennia.

It seemed to loosen what Sennia had been trying to hold in. The tears flowed freely now, though she made no sound. After a long silence, she whispered, "It was my fault. I was in too much of a hurry. I did not watch where I trod."

Dugal squeezed her hand tighter. "No, my love. It was an accident. There is no blame. Such things happen." When she did not answer he asked, "Will you allow Merrist to examine you, in case there is more he can do?"

When Sennia looked away with a silent nod Dugal, moved back so Merrist could approach. "There is no need to get up, my lady. I can learn what I need from here. May I reach under your robe?"

"Yes." Her whisper was almost inaudible. She shut her eyes and turned her head as far away as she could.

It felt natural to Liannis that she should place her hand on Merrist's shoulder to share her strength with him as he worked. She could tell, when she touched him, that he did not even notice, so deep was his concentration. Was this to be their life, then, Liannis wondered; that he would lend her peace as she slept and she give it back again as he worked? The thought was comforting.

In only a few moments Merrist withdrew and stood up. "My lady, your womb is completely healed. I have also sent more strength into you so that you will gain back your own quickly."

Sennia raised her head to meet his eyes. "I do feel somewhat better already."

Some colour had returned to her cheeks. She managed a brighter look as she addressed Merrist. "Merrist, I owe you my life and my health. I do not know what I can do to show my gratitude."

"There is no thanks required, my lady. I did what Earth bid me, no more," Merrist demurred.

"But there is something important that you can both do," Liannis broke in.

All eyes turned to her.

"Merrist and I need to have the people know of the changes Earth has brought ... indeed is still bringing. What has occurred here must be told and the people must hear from you both that there is nothing to fear and that only good will come of it. Please speak of this as much as possible. I understand that you may wish to keep this private. But the people must be told that this was not just a usual miscarriage, that Merrist truly healed Sennia and saved her life. I know it will be painful to speak of it but you must. It is of the utmost importance."

Liannis watched Dugal and Sennia exchange glances. Dugal answered for both of them. "You may be assured that this will be done. I swear it."

Liannis felt a weight fall from her. "Thank you, my lord. Merrist and I will face many tests. Your words will help the people believe." At Dugal's understanding nod she added, "But you may also face challenges when you speak of this."

"Then we will meet them." Dugal squared his shoulders, his voice resolute, "Right, my love?"

"Yes, we will." Sennia sounded stronger, more like the woman Liannis remembered. She knew then that Sennia would be all right soon.

They left the couple alone soon after, assuring them that they would have dinner with them in the chamber later. Though they had only done a little work, both agreed they needed food and drink, which they went in search of in the kitchen. They took the food back to their chamber to rest and talk.

"I think Sennia will gain her strength back quickly, now."

"Yes," Merrist agreed. "She just needs rest, food and a little time to get over the loss of the babe. Her body is whole."

Later, when they left the chamber, each time they came within sight of two or more people together Liannis sensed they had been talking about what had happened. As soon as people spotted them they fell silent and split up to go about their individual duties. Those who worked together sent each other knowing looks as the couple passed. Liannis could sense the

54

suspicion, like a prickling sensation on her head and back. Some thoughts were so strong that she could 'hear' them. Most were hostile, though aimed more at themselves than at Dugal, for which Liannis was grateful.

"Merrist, I think we need to return home to Bargia after breaking fast with Dugal and Sennia tomorrow. I wish to see if there is news from Catania. It does not feel urgent but I feel drawn back and that is a feeling I have learned to heed."

"Yes, I also feel a need to withdraw from Gharn, to let Dugal deal with his people without our presence. I am ready to return to Bargia. I see no need to remain here."

"Merrist, I have a question."

"Hmmm?"

"Do you feel the press of emotions and needs of the people when we are among them?"

"No, thankfully I am not plagued by that as you are."

"I thought so. So we are still quite different, then."

"So it seems."

17

CLOUD'S VANITY

After breaking their fast with Dugal and Sennia next morning they saddled Warrior and Cloud and left Gharn for Bargia. Liannis called it home. For Merrist, Gharn was as much home as Bargia, as that was where he grew up. His early fealty to Dugal and losing his leg defending Dugal's right to rule made it easier, he knew, for Dugal to trust him with Sennia. Perhaps that is why Earth had sent them to Gharn first.

On the second day out Cloud caught her foot in a rabbit hole and sprained her foreleg. She apparently told Liannis she did not want Merrist to touch it even though Liannis explained that he could heal it.

"Merrist, you know how she is with others. She is in pain, which makes her even more testy."

It made Merrist angry that Cloud would not trust him. "Then tell her we will expect her to keep up whether she is in pain or not. Or you can deal with her yourself. Horses are supposed to serve us, not the other way around. And if you cannot convince her to let me heal her, you both deserve whatever happens."

Liannis looked shocked. Then her face clouded over and she glared at him. "I shall inform Cloud that is how you feel."

He was about to apologise when Cloud turned and nipped his shoulder, giving him a painful pinch with her teeth, which made him yelp.

Liannis saw it and burst out laughing. "Serves you right. I told her what you said." When she finally caught her breath again she said, "Merrist, you know Cloud is a proud creature. And now she is in pain as well. I think you ought to apologise to her. I am sure she will settle down and let you heal her if you offer politely."

"Politely!? I must ask politely, of a horse no less, for permission to heal her pain?"

Cloud must have sensed his indignation because she turned her rear to him and snorted loudly. Before Merrist could say anything more he felt a warm weight settle onto his boot. That sent Liannis off into paroxisms again, laughing so hard tears rolled down her cheeks and she had to bend over and hold her stomach.

"So, you side with a horse against me!?" His humiliation made him shout in rage. He spun around, and grabbing Warriors reins to take him with him, strode away.

When he returned, calmer, a span or so later, he saw Liannis with fresh tea in her hand, sitting beside a small fire. Cloud stood next to her holding her injured leg off the ground. If Liannis saw him she did not let on. The peaceful scene helped him release the last of the anger he still felt, enough to wonder why he had reacted so strongly.

He realised that he felt jealous of Liannis's ability to mind-speak some animals; that she could converse with Cloud and Kira as though they were friends. He had no such ability and it looked likely that he never would. He and Warrior would never have such a bond. The realisation humbled him and he felt ashamed of his outburst. When he looked back on what had happened he could see what had been funny to Liannis. By the time she turned to him as he approached the fire he could smile, picturing how being bested by a horse must have appeared to Liannis.

She handed him a mug as he sat by the fire, a questioning look on her face, but said nothing.

He cleared his throat. "So how does one apologise to a horse?"

Liannis's face cleared and she rewarded him with one of her brilliant smiles. "I will be happy to interpret for you." But Merrist saw that she could not suppress a mischievous grin.

Merrist raised his hands wide in mock surrender.

Liannis laughed. "I think she can wait until you have finished your tea. After all, Cloud was not exactly gracious with you, either." She sent him a sideways grin. "I did chide her. I told her she is lucky that we have you here to heal her else the journey home would be much slower and more painful. She is too proud sometimes. So now she is also ready to apologise, and to let you heal her."

When he had finished the mug of tea they both rose and Liannis put her hand on Cloud's neck, concentrating. Then without removing her hand she looked at Merrist and said, "Cloud, what have you to say to Merrist?"

Cloud lowered her head to nudge him with her forelock and gave a long, low whuffle. She left her nose just touching his

57

good leg. Merrist looked at Liannis in amazement. This was an apology even he could understand.

"Sometimes mind-speak is not needed." Liannis said. "Now it is your turn."

He turned back to Cloud and took both sides of her face in his hands to lift her head. When she did not protest he stroked her face until she shook her head and nudged him, lifting her sore leg higher to catch his attention.

In the corner of his eye Merrist saw Liannis's delighted expression before she stepped back out of his way.

It took only a few moments for him to wrap his hands around the swollen leg and take away the injury and the pain. "There, Cloud. Do you feel any pain now?"

Cloud whuffed and nuzzled his ear, setting her foot firmly on the ground. He needed no mind-speak to understand.

Liannis, watching from the side, clapped her hands in delight. "I think you will be friends, now. Cloud will not challenge you again."

Feigning anger, he said, "She had best not."

When they had got under way again Liannis offered, "Merrist, I am sorry I laughed at you. That was unkind."

He shook his head. "It *was* funny. I see that now."

"Yes, it was, but I still ought not to have laughed at you when you were so angry. What was it that affected you so?"

"At first I did not know myself, but now I see that I wanted to be able to mind-speak as you do. I wanted that ability. I was jealous ... not a noble sentiment."

"None of us are noble all the time Merrist. We all have our weaknesses."

"You, too?" he quipped.

"Oh yes, me too."

18

SUMMONS

"I am anxious to see Mama again and to tell everyone of the changes Earth has made." They were only a day's ride from Bargia. Liannis urged Cloud to go a little faster so they would be there by the next midday and be able to bathe before dinner.

"Yes," he said, as though reading her thoughts, "and a bath will be welcome. Cold streams are not pleasant this time of year."

Merrist had no sooner spoken than Liannis spotted a dark shape moving toward them. "Merrist, we have company."

Moments later she recognised the blue and yellow tunic of a Bargian guard. The man drew close but did not dismount; Liannis and Merrist also sat their mounts.

"What news from Bargia? Are we summoned to Catania?" Liannis asked.

When the guard shot her a surprised look she knew no one had prepared him. Liannis often sensed what to expect when Gaelen sent a messenger, or even when others came to her. Her old mentor, Liethis, had also had this ability.

"Indeed, Lady, Lord Gaelen sent me to seek you out and request you to delay your return and proceed to Catania immediately. I did not expect to find you already so close." He handed her a small roll of scraped leather, sealed with blue wax. "Your orders are inside."

"Thank, you."

"I am to accompany you. Lionn has already been sent a message to expect you."

The guard said this in such a dignified, formal tone Liannis almost laughed. She got that stiff reaction from those not familiar with her; those who thought seers must be shown great deference or were to be feared. The soldier's awkwardness exaggerated the common reaction, making it funny rather than annoying. She stifled her mirth.

"We will be glad of your company. And may we know your name?"

"Pardon, Lady. I am Strennock."

"You must call me Liannis. And my companion is Merrist. There is no need for formality." She had to halt his awkwardness before it began to annoy her.

Strennock inclined his head. "As you wish La ... Liannis." He blushed at his stumble, and then brightened. "Before I left, your mother, Brensa, loaded my panniers with some fresh travel fare. She was quite insistent that you eat this first." He reached behind, took a linen wrapped bundle from his left pannier and handed it to her with a smile.

The aroma reached her nose even before she had a chance to unwrap it, so she held her hands over the closed cloth and raised an eyebrow at Merrist. "Can you guess?"

"If it comes from Brensa, I wager it is honey cakes."

"Indeed." Liannis laughed. "Let us stop and make tea so we can enjoy them while they are fresh – and so I can read this scroll."

While she waited for her tea to cool, she broke the seal and read the scroll.

"Liannis, please proceed to Catania immediately. Lionn has identified three men who now vie to rule there. He is unable to determine a clear best choice. He suspects that one may not be trustworthy, although he has no direct evidence. He will await you there. Your assistance is needed to help choose the best man. Brensa fares well and understands the delay in your return." Gaelen's seal concluded the message.

Liannis handed it to Merrist, which caused Strennock to look askance, as though she ought not to show such an important document to a servant. She decided to challenge that. "Strennock, you will find that Merrist is aware of all that passes. I withhold nothing from him. I value his opinions."

Strennock mumbled something of agreement, but he avoided her eyes, and his face looked troubled. He would learn soon enough, Liannis thought, as must the rest of the One Isle. Since Strennock had nothing more to add to what the scroll revealed they made haste for Catania.

The next day Liannis could not shake a sense of urgency, although she had no message from Earth. Perhaps it was only the tone of the scroll, or that Strennock did not know more, or even the way Strennock scrutinized them with poorly disguised suspicion as they travelled.

Strennock's air of distrust made it impossible for Liannis and Merrist to discuss what they might face in Catania openly. They spent the three days journey in an uncomfortable silence, speaking only as much as necessary. Strennock kept as far apart as he could without leaving them altogether, his bearing sullen and dark. As they approached the city Liannis's sense of foreboding grew. Something felt sorely amiss.

"Merrist, we must contact Lionn as soon as we arrive. All is not well, though I cannot say what the trouble is. I hope he can tell us more."

When they approached the city gate, Merrist said, "I will see to our mounts. Go with Strennock to find Lionn. I will come as soon as the horses are settled. Perhaps I will glean some information at the stables. They will often say things to strangers without thinking it may be important."

They dismounted and Merrist followed a guard to the stables. When Liannis looked for Strennock to thank him and dismiss him she spotted him striding away into the city, his haste furtive. She sensed they had not heard the last of him.

Liannis always carried a small, plain, copper ring with her which served as introduction. It was a custom that had begun between her father and Lord Gaelen before she was born. At the castle gate she handed it to one of the guards and asked him to deliver it immediately to Lionn.

The guard took in her white seer's robes, eyebrows raised in curiosity, but asked no questions. "Please wait here." He hailed another passing guard and ordered him to watch the gate until he returned.

Lionn himself came to greet her, grinning with pleasure. "Liannis, how wonderful to see you. I did not expect you for another two days." He looked about to envelop her in one of his customary great hugs but caught himself and only grasped her forearm. Such a display would be inappropriate. Liannis smiled to herself. Lionn had learned discretion.

Her grin matched his. "Yes, Strennock caught us part way so we wasted no time." She decided not to concern Lionn with her misgivings about Strennock until she had something more substantial.

Lionn peered behind her. "Where is our friend Merrist?"

"Seeing to our mounts. He will join us shortly."

61

Lionn turned to the guard. "Have Merrist brought to us as soon as he gets here."

The guard gave a short bow. "As you wish."

As Lionn led her into the castle, she said in a low, teasing voice, "Such respect they show you, Lionn. Perhaps I ought to tell them a few things."

Lionn laughed. "You would! But you see, they have seen enough of me now they would not believe you. They see only their lord's heir."

" Ha! If they only knew!"

As they passed a castle maid Lionn called out, "Nessa, we will need food and drink for three in my chambers." The maid dropped a quick curtsey, nodded and hurried away, blushing.

"A conquest?"

"Only in her imagination. I have grown too wise for such dalliances."

"I am glad to hear it."

Lionn caught the half-tease in her tone and gave his head a rueful shake. "There will be no more Vernias."

They had no sooner seated themselves when the maid arrived and set down a tray laden with ripe sheep's cheese, fragrant, dark bread, cold fowl, sage tea and a jug of ale.

Liannis did not even feel the mug of tea Lionn handed her. It dropped from senseless fingers as she fell back into the chair.

"No!"

***

Merrist had his sword in his right hand and stood over an older, well garbed man who lay on the ground bleeding. Facing him, a soldier wearing the uniform tunic of Catania, waved a sword red with blood.

Liannis knew Merrist could not possibly hold against a trained soldier. Not with only one good leg. The man he protected, seemingly aware of his peril, dragged himself out from under and behind Merrist, as the two swordsmen sized each other up.

Liannis could only see, not hear, but the snarl on the guard's face spoke plainly enough. He would kill them both. Liannis could discern no one else in the stable. And even if there were another, whose side would he take?

Time slowed for her and she watched each shift of weight, each movement, as though the two moved through water, slow and graceful, like a sensuous dance. Movements that would have been chaotic and wild if seen at their real pace now appeared planned and purposeful.

She watched the guard thrust. At the same instant Merrist's wooden peg slipped on some straw and he fell sideways.

The force of the soldier's lunge, when it met with no resistance, caused him to lose his balance and fall on top of Merrist.

Both men threw aside their blades and began to fight with bare hands. On the ground Merrist had the advantage, being stocky and very powerful. He managed to roll on top of his assailant, and with one free hand, grope blindly for the dagger in the man's belt. Liannis feared Merrist would lose the advantage as the attacker almost rolled back on top of him, but another push had Merrist with his knee on the man's chest and the fellow's own dagger to his throat. Merrist's shouts brought two more guards running.

Time resumed its normal flow.

Liannis watched the injured man point and wave an arm, the other hand pressed into his side where a red patch of blood bloomed. The two new guards grabbed Merrist's attacker and dragged him away.

As Merrist rose Liannis saw blood on his right shoulder. Merrist ignored it, knelt by the injured man and placed his hands on the bleeding wound in his side. His eyes closed in concentration as he worked.

***

19

LIONN

"Liannis, what is it? What do you see?" Lionn shook her back into wakefulness.

"Tea."

At her croaked whisper he turned, grasped his own mug and held it to her lips, cradling the back of her head so she could drink. He knew, from past experience, she would need this before she could speak.

When she caught her breath she rasped, "The stables. Merrist is in danger. Another man has been wounded. Hurry!"

Lionn leapt to the door. "Guards!"

Two appeared immediately.

"To the stables. Hurry. Assist the man with the wooden leg. And the wounded man with him. Bring them both here."

"No, Lionn." Liannis raised a weak hand to stop Lionn. "First Merrist must finish what he is doing before you move them. Until he is done all they must do is protect him. Bring them here only when Merrist has finished."

He turned to Liannis, puzzled. "What?"

"He must not be interrupted before he has completed what he is doing."

The guards hesitated, waiting for clarification of their orders. Lionn looked from them, to Liannis, and back again, his mind made up. "The seer Liannis has seen. You must not interfere until the one with the wooden leg agrees. Then bring them both here." The guards strode away. "And fetch a healer," Lionn called after them.

He closed the door and handed her another mug of tea, laced this time with honey.

"Can you eat?"

"Some bread and honey."

"Butter?"

Liannis nodded. Lion noted that her strength was returning as she could hold her own mug.

While they waited for the men to arrive she told him briefly about the changes Earth had destined for her and Merrist.

64

When she paused, Lionn remained silent for a long moment and studied her face as if hoping for some elusive answer he might find there. When he spoke at last, his question was soft, hardly more than a murmur. "How can this be?"

"I do not know either, Lionn, only that Earth has deemed it so. We are in the midst of great changes, ones I am certain will prove challenging for all of us."

A rap on the door interrupted them. Lionn opened to four guards, two carrying the wounded man on a plank, the other two supporting Merrist. He was upright only because the guards had each taken one of his arms over their shoulders so they could drag him between them. He looked unconscious.

Lionn looked at Liannis. "Is he all right?"

She nodded. "I can sense no injury in him."

Lionn directed the men to lay Merrist on his own bed and turned his attention to the wounded man.

He appeared to be a person of consequence, as he wore fine clothing and new boots. He had no grime under his fingernails so Lionn knew he did not labour with his hands. A closer look brought back recognition of who this must be. He had met the man only two days earlier. Lionn directed the guards to lay the man on the bed in an adjacent chamber. When the guards had gone he looked at Liannis.

"How bad is it?"

He watched as she probed the man with her senses.

"His bleeding has stopped. I believe he will recover. I think Merrist may have happened upon him only just in time."

Lionn let out a sigh of relief. "His name is Brynnell, one of the three candidates for lordship of Catania. I like him. The other two are younger but Brynnell has proven a steady influence, a man with the ability to bring those with differing opinions to a common agreement."

A knock on the still open door announced the arrival of the healer woman.

Before she could approach the bed Liannis stopped her. "Healer, what is your name?"

Lionn sent Liannis a questioning look from behind the woman but said nothing.

"Mieran, Lady." Though her voice held some awe, she spoke firmly.

65

"Thank you Mieran. Before you touch this man I must ask you to permit me to truth-read you. This man is important. I need to know that you will not bring him to further harm."

Lionn understood. Since he had told her how important this man might be truth-reading made sense. He ought to have thought of the possible danger himself.

Mieran blanched, but quickly recovered. "I have nothing to hide. You may read me," and held out her hand.

"I need not touch you," Liannis reassured her.

Mieran dropped her hand to her side with undisguised relief, tucking it into the folds of her skirt, out of sight.

"Mieran, will you use your skills to the best of your ability to heal this man?"

Mieran drew herself to her full height, head high. "I am a healer. It is what I am pledged to do."

"You may tend him now."

Mieran wasted no time opening the bloody tunic and shirt, her eyes rounding in amazement. She turned to Lionn. "He does not bleed. How can this be? His clothing is bloody and I see the hole a weapon made in his tunic. But he bears no mark on his body."

Liannis broke in. "That means Merrist has succeeded in closing the wound. What further healing does he need?"

Mieran's gaze went to Liannis, then back to the inert form on the bed. Lionn heard her mutter again, "How can this be?" as she examined Brynnell more closely. When she finished she looked back at them. "There is nothing wrong with him. I think he has lost a great deal of blood but can find no evidence of it except on his clothing. He needs broth, sage tea, watered wine and rest. As soon as he sits on his own he must begin to eat - porridge with honey at first, then stews and meat to recover his strength."

She turned once more to stare at Brynnell then gave a small shrug of her shoulders. When she looked back at them again she slowly shook her head. "I have seen a wonder this day." She picked up her healer's basket, put it over her arm and headed for the door. "I am not needed here." She left still shaking her head, more to herself than to them.

Liannis followed her out the door. "I need to see to Merrist," she said to Lionn over her shoulder.

20

MERRIST'S ATTACK

Merrist came to with an urgent sense of danger. *The man – where was he? Where am I? My sword...*

"Merrist, you are all right. I am here. Drink this."

An arm that seemed familiar lifted his head and he felt a mug of cool water at his lips. *Liannis.* He drank greedily. "More." His eyes opened and he watched her pour another draught as he struggled to sit. His strength began to return but he still could not manage the mug without Liannis's assistance.

"The man?"

"He is well. You healed him. You have both been brought here to Lionn's chambers and are safe."

"He is important. I know it, though I do not know how I know." Memory returned. "Liannis, he is the one – the one who must become leader of Catania."

Liannis thrust a mug of sage tea into his shaking hands. He smelled honey in it and drank it down in two draughts, then took the bread and cheese Liannis held out. Chewing helped him think. Liannis watched him, looking puzzled, but, he thought, not disbelieving.

"Merrist," Liannis asked quietly, her voice earnest, "How did you come to this? What happened to make you think this? Have you been given a vision?"

A knock at the door and the appearance of Lionn interrupted them. "Merrist, you are awake. Can you tell us what happened?"

"Lionn, where is the man who attacked us? Has he escaped? I think I know why he tried to kill that man. The one I healed must become the next leader of Catania. Our attacker wanted to eliminate him."

Lionn frowned. "He is in a cell in the dungeon. We will deal with him. But Merrist, what are you saying? How do you know this, if indeed, you do know it?"

"Let me think a moment."

Two pairs of keen eyes waited, expectant, as he tried to remember the moments before the attack.

"I took the horses to the stables and handed them over to the young hand there. But instead of leaving the way I came, I found myself walking in the other direction, to the far end of the stables. I did not question it; I felt compelled to go there. Then I heard the sound a sword makes when it is drawn out of a scabbard. I began to run toward it – well, as much as I am able – drawing my own sword as I went. By the time I reached the place the sound came from, I saw one man on the ground, already bleeding. The other had his weapon raised for another blow which I intercepted with my sword. The noise of fighting and my shouting must have alerted the guards because they arrived right after I pinned the attacker."

He stopped and thought before he continued. "I do not know why they did not arrest me as well. They did not even question me when I knelt by the wounded man and tended to him. Very strange, now that I remember it. As I touched the man, I knew, instantly, that he is the one who must lead Catania and that I must heal him or all would be lost."

Liannis broke the silence first, her voice low and thoughtful. "Merrist, this is unlike the visions Earth gives me, but I think you did have a vision of a sort."

Lionn gaped. "He can heal and now he has visions, too? What more do I need to know before I leave this chamber?" He sounded angry, as though he suspected them of withholding information.

"Lionn, even I do not know who I am any more." Merrist shook his head. "Earth has changed me, and I fear those changes are not yet complete."

"I do not understand it all either, Lionn." Liannis added. "But I think we need to confer carefully before taking any action. May I suggest a meal be brought? Merrist and I are both weary and Merrist is still weak from his healing work. I hope things will be clearer before we sleep tonight."

Lionn looked about to protest but caught himself and took a deep breath.

"Since I do not have enough information to make any decisions, that does appear to be my only option." His tone still sounded frustrated but his shoulders came down and he had unclenched his hands.

After another breath he regarded them both. More calm now, he said, "I have never had reason to doubt either of you. I must trust you now or I will be a blind man with no direction ... and I need direction." He sent them a wry look and went to the door where he called a maid and ordered hot food and more drink to be brought.

Over a meal that revived them, Merrist and Liannis told Lionn all that had happened since they had last seen him – the visions, the changes in him, the news that he and Liannis would have a child.

Lionn said very little as they spoke; merely narrowed his eyes now and then, or gave his head a shake as if to rid himself of disbelief. A few times he pinched the bridge of his nose in the gesture he had taken on from his father.

Merrist studied him as they spoke. Lionn had filled out over the winter and Merrist could see, now, how much he resembled Lord Gaelen. He had not yet reached his full height and would surpass his father before he stopped growing. He already stood almost a head taller than most men. The only nods to his mother's looks were the russet tones in his hair and his vibrant green eyes.

While Liannis rose to replenish their mugs of ale, Lionn broke his silence. "My friends, you do understand how hard this is for even me to accept. If I did not know you as I do I would dismiss your tale out of hand. I fear for what the people will think. More, I fear what they may do."

Liannis nodded as she handed him the mug and sat down again, but neither she nor Merrist answered.

"And now you say you will have a child as well. And that this child will also be a have a seer's abilities, perhaps ones we have not yet seen." Then he voiced what he and Liannis had refused to speak of even to each other. "How can we keep you and that child safe?"

"I do not know," Merrist said, "but I hope we may rely on you to do what you can. Dugal has already pledged us his support, but he does not yet know about the child. Even he may find this too much."

"Liannis, you know you were asked to come to Catania because we need to choose a new leader here. We will need his support as well. This makes it even more important that we choose wisely. Although, if what you say is so, we already have an idea of who that must be."

Lionn looked tired, more worn than Merrist had ever seen him. He could not have bargained for all this when he came to Catania in search of a new ruler.

"Several people have already seen that I have the ability to heal; Lord Dugal, Lady Sennia, the midwife and her helper, now the healer woman here." Merrist did not feel nearly as confident as his words suggested. "I hope that their tales of what they have seen will lend some truth to what we claim."

~ 21 ~

BRYNNELL SPEAKS

A furtive knock came to the door. Lionn sent Liannis a questioning look.

She nodded. "I sense no danger."

Lionn rose and opened the door. A nervous guard blocked the way preventing a man behind him from entering. "Sir, he insists on seeing you."

"I need to speak with you, sir. I have information you need to hear."

Liannis saw Brynnell peer around the back of the guard, ghostly pale but standing without assistance.

"Let him enter."

The guard stood aside, a doubtful look on his face, and let Brynnell pass.

Lionn took an elbow to steady Brynnell as he led him to a chair.

Liannis closed the door and reached for a mug of strengthening sage tea that already sat keeping warm on a brazier. "Here, Brynnell, rest a moment and drink this. Then tell us what you have."

Brynnell's hands shook with the effort to hold the heavy mug but he managed without assistance.

Liannis prepared a small platter of cold venison, and rye bread on which she spread butter and honey, and set it on the stool beside Brynnell's chair. He needed to eat and stew was not available at the moment.

Brynnell took in her whites for the first time and his eyes widened a fraction before he collected himself. "Thank you, Lady."

"I am Liannis and that is what you may call me, Brynnell. I do not like formality." She smiled and tried to send calming sensations toward him. "Eat, Brynnell. You need to recover your strength. We have time to hear what you have to say."

Brynnell sent Lionn a questioning look. "Sir, I have much to tell you ..."

"Then speak freely, Brynnell. Liannis and Merrist both have my full trust. I wish them to hear what you have to say."

Brynnell looked at Merrist. "So that is the name of the man to whom I owe my life. If you had not come when you did …"

"Indeed. It seems my timing was guided."

"Guided, sir?"

"Yes, I was about to leave the stable in the other direction but felt compelled to come to where I found you. I believe Earth sent me."

Brynnell gaped then he caught himself and snapped his mouth shut. He swallowed the bite he had taken before speaking again. "Sir, I think I was stabbed – a mortal wound, or very near. Yet there is none I can find on my body. Did I dream this?" He shook his head. "No, my clothing is bloody. And I am weak from loss of blood. My injury was real." He straightened and his voice took on a steely tone. "Please explain, sir, what did you do to me? How is it that I am whole?"

"I healed you, sir. Earth has given me the ability to heal."

Lionn intervened before Brynnell could question Merrist further. "Brynnell, you came here to tell me something. I need to know what that is. But I will ask Liannis to truth-read you as you speak. I must know if you can be trusted before we answer any more of your questions."

Brynnell hesitated only a moment. "As you wish. I have nothing to hide."

22

LIANNIS

Liannis knew from their earlier conversation that Lionn favoured Brynnell as the best choice for ruler of Catania so she was pleased that he had no objection to being truth-read. It also agreed with Merrist's stunning revelation earlier. She had time only to determine that Brynnell could be trusted to be open with them when she heard a woman's voice in the hall crying out along with a rapid knocking at the door.

Brynnell reacted even before Lionn or Merrist. "That is my daughter." He began to rise to go to the door but Lionn held his hand up to stop him and raised an eyebrow to Liannis in question.

"It is all right. I sense no danger."

Lionn opened the door to the guard who stood blocking a distraught young woman from entering. "Let the woman in, Gerrant, thank you."

"Papa, they said you had been killed!" They stood back as Brynnell's daughter rushed to kneel beside the chair where Brynnell sat.

Brynnell patted her hand. "It appears they are mistaken, as you see." Brynnell addressed Lionn. "Sir, may I introduce my daughter, Joranna, the joy of my life."

Joranna's eyes roamed the room and, when she realised who was there, looked embarrassed and rose hastily to dip a blushing curtsey. "Forgive my rudeness."

"There is no need to apologise, Joranna. As you see, your father is very much alive." Lionn turned. "Liannis, is there more tea?"

She had already poured some of the now cooled tea into her own mug, as she no longer needed it and there was no extra one, stirred in some honey, and handed it to Joranna, who once more knelt beside Brynnell.

"But, Papa, were you not attacked and wounded? What has happened? How is it that you live, or that you do not lie abed with injuries?"

Merrist answered first. "Joranna, your father was indeed mortally wounded. But he has been healed and will make a full recovery. All he needs now is rest and good food."

Liannis wondered at the wisdom of Merrist's declaration, but had no time to think of the consequences just then, as Brynnell confirmed this, adding, "I know not how, my dear, but it seems this young man has the power to heal."

Knowing that it would do no good, Liannis felt she had to say it anyway. "Joranna, please keep this to yourself. Do not speak of it outside this chamber. We wish to keep it quiet, at least for now."

Joranna looked dazed. Liannis realised that she was in a state of confusion and that her words had passed over the young woman un-comprehended. If it had not done so already, this news would soon spread like a contagion. Their time to agree on a strategy for letting the people know of the changes Earth wrought had been taken out of their control.

They learned nothing new from Joranna or Brynnell to enlighten them as to where the attack had come from, or why, although they all suspected it had to do with the contest for leadership of Catania.

With the night almost giving way to dawn, Brynnell was helped back to his bed, Joranna by his side to keep watch.

Sleep was out of the question for Liannis, Lionn, and Merrist. They had too many urgent things to discuss. So they remained in Lionn's chambers until time to break their fast.

"Lionn, I understand that Charest has chosen not to bid for the position of Lord of Catania. He has governed here for twelve years. Why has he declined?"

"That is so, Liannis. He gave me two reasons. First, he has no children, so will not be able to guarantee succession. Secondly, he feels he is too old. His health has begun to decline so he says he has not enough years left to see that Catania remains stable and to train a successor of his choosing."

"I see." That made sense to her, though she knew many men would want that kind of power in spite of such hindrances. "And you say Charest also favours Brynnell. But Brynnell is also no longer a young man. Does he have an heir that is qualified to succeed him?"

Merrist broke in. "Brynnell is in robust good health. He will regain his lost strength and will bear no lasting effects from his injury. I expect he will live many years yet."

74

"That is good to hear. No, Liannis, he has no male heir. Joranna is his only child. That is a concern." Lionn's worry showed plainly as did his fatigue.

"What of the other two candidates?" she asked.

"We will not know until he is questioned but I suspect Grund sent the assassin against Brynnell. Grund has a large following but I do not trust him. There are rumours of plots and he has made enemies among the tradesmen and shopkeepers. There have been accusations of dishonesty and fraud, though none have been proven." The furrow between Lionn's brow deepened as he spoke. He ran a hand roughly over his face. "Frellick is the third candidate. I have spoken with him. He is young and ambitious, but I have not seen or heard anything that suggests he cannot be trusted. Yet, I do not believe he has the maturity or wisdom to handle the challenges that will arise from such a change in governance. He lacks the depth of experience that will temper his impulsiveness."

That made Liannis laugh. "Lionn, you sound like an old man. What is his age?"

Lionn blushed. "Twenty-one."

"And you are twenty."

Lionn feigned his haughtiest expression and huffed, "What are you implying?"

Their shared laughter broke the tension. Knowing they would make no further progress they agreed to eat in the common dining room and then try to catch a few spans of sleep before calling a meeting with Charest after midday. They needed his insights on the three candidates as well as on the attack on Brynnell.

23

VISITATION

Though they had had no sleep for a day and a half, still sleep eluded them. So Merrist and Liannis found comfort in the sharing of their bodies, after which they fell into a light slumber in each other's arms. And, to Merrist's great amazement, shared the most wonderful dream.

***

Earth, in her woman's guise, just as Liannis had described her. She came to them, smiling, almost gliding over the grass as she walked, her long, dark hair flowing gently behind her.

Their bed, on which they still lay, had been transported into an open meadow, or so it appeared. They sat up together, hands still entwined.

Then, without knowing how, they found themselves standing in front of her. Earth took the hands they still held together between her own, flooding them both with a warmth he could not describe, except to say it was the most loving sensation he had ever felt.

"My children, it is time." Earth released their hands and turned them to face each other. "See what you have begun." With one hand on Liannis's shoulder Earth took his in her other and placed it on Liannis's belly. "Behold your daughter."

A light grew within Liannis's womb, like a globe of sun. Within it the form of a babe appeared, tiny but clear. She smiled at them with such knowing, such wisdom and such love. Then she faded back into the globe of light and it, too ebbed slowly back into nothingness.

Earth released her touch on them and stepped back a pace. "She will remember nothing of this when she is born. But she has chosen you, and will be called to serve me when she has grown. She will have a seer's abilities, powerful ones, but they will not all be the same as yours, daughter. And she, too, will one day take a mate."

"How will we keep her safe?"

76

"She will come to no harm, though the way will not be easy. Even I cannot see all, but this I know. She will live to choose if she will fulfill her destiny. That choice will be hers when the time comes. That promise must sustain you."

***

They woke refreshed, though Merrist knew they had slept less than three spans. Too full to speak, their eyes met for a long moment, then looked away. They rose and dressed hurriedly. A knock on the door called them to the midday meal, from whence they would go to meet Charest. The impact of the dream faded into the back of his mind as his attention focused on the business at hand.

24

BRYNNELL

Charest had had the foresight to call the two remaining candidates to meet with them. Before the first one arrived they had a span to discuss each one's merits privately. He confirmed what they had already found out. Brynnell seemed the clear forerunner but he expressed concern that Brynnell might not recover his strength and so not live long enough to build a stable foundation for the new dynasty.

Merrist assured him he need not worry. "Brynnell is well on the way to recovery. He will sustain no ill effects from the attack and is in robust good health."

Liannis decided the time had come to tell Charest about the changes Earth had wrought, though she said nothing about the coming child. That must remain secret, at least until she and Merrist had come to a clear understanding about how to disclose it, or until she could no longer hide her condition.

"Liannis, are you all right? You have that faraway look and did not answer Charest." Lionn leaned toward her. "Do you need anything?"

She shook herself back to the present. "Forgive me. My mind wandered for a moment. I am well. Charest, please repeat your question."

"I see that I must believe that Earth has given a man the power to heal, else Brynnell would lie dead. I find that alone stretches credulity. How am I to believe the rest? And what am I to say to the people when they question it – as question it they will, without a doubt? No, the people will not like this."

Merrist answered before Liannis could. "Charest, no doubt news of my healing gift has already spread. It can no longer be kept secret. But for now, perhaps that is all that need be confirmed."

Liannis agreed. "Yes, that cannot be kept from them, nor should it. But Merrist, they will also see that we are more than seer and servant. I expect that is what will be the greatest challenge – that I as a seer can still see true, guided by Earth, when, in their eyes, I have flouted Earth's law."

She turned to Charest. "There will be difficult challenges. We need your support if Catania, indeed the entire One Isle, is to weather these changes. All we can offer you is our word that this is Earth's decree. Other than seeing that Brynnell is healed we have no proof to offer."

"Charest," Lionn broke in, "may we rely on you? Will you back us, at least until you have seen more?"

"It seems I have no choice. If I do not, Catania will surely fall into complete chaos."

Lionn and Merrist both showed the relief Liannis felt. One hurdle had been overcome, for now.

"Are we ready to speak to Frellick?" Lionn took charge again.

Liannis admired how he was handling this challenge and could see that he had learned much over the last year. Gaelen need have no concern over his ability to become Lord of Bargia. Her childhood playmate had grown into a strong man. Liannis wondered for a moment if he saw the same level of maturity in her. Or Merrist, for that matter.

Charest nodded and rose to open the door. "Frellick, please come in."

Frellick had not quite lost the gangliness of youth, though he had reached twenty-one years. Perhaps he would always have that lanky look, tall and spare. A thick shock of black curls kept falling into his eyes, which he raked back regularly without seeming to notice. That habit, as well as his quick movements and almost breathless eagerness gave him the appearance of a young horse with too much energy that had not quite been tamed into steadiness. Liannis liked him immediately. His enthusiasm was infectious, as was his smile. She could see why people were drawn to him. His willingness to be truth-read also spoke well for him.

"And I have already chosen the woman who will join with me. Floraina shares my views and will be a great support to me. She comes from a good family. And," he added, suddenly shy, "I am confident we will have heirs. We have many years together ahead of us."

Had he not been so serious Liannis might have laughed. "I wish you a long and happy life together Frellick."

"Do you see anything in our future, Lady?"

"No, Frellick, Earth chooses what she wishes me to see."

Charest rescued her. "Do we have any further questions?"

She, Lionn, and Merrist all indicated they had none.

As Frellick rose to leave he turned to Merrist. "So it is true that you heal? That Brynnell owes you his life?"

None of them had spoken of the events of yesterday. It appeared Frellick had already heard and could no longer hold in his curiosity.

"It is true. Earth has given me the ability to heal."

A look of awe came over Frellick's face and he could find nothing to say. Since no one came to his rescue he gave his head an embarrassed shake and opened the door to leave.

"He believes," Liannis said when the door had closed. "I think we can count on an ally there. But I see what you mean regarding his youth. One day he may make a good leader, but that time is not yet. " She grinned at Lionn. "Next to him, you are an old man."

Lionn did not rise to the bait. "So you agree that he is not ready."

All three nodded.

Charest rose and headed for the door. "Shall I have Grund come in? I expect he will prove a greater challenge."

The light mood disappeared with his prediction. "Yes, ask him in." Liannis expected he would already have grown impatient at being kept waiting.

GRUND

Grund strode in with an impatient swagger and challenged them before he even sat down.

"Bah, I see no reason for this. What need have we of a seer? And what business is it of a seer's servant to be included in this meeting? I will not submit to scrutiny by a servant. Send him away." He leaned way back into the chair he had just sat in, slid his pelvis and legs forward and crossed his arms across his chest, glowering at Merrist.

Liannis could sense his fear, in spite of his bravado, and could tell that he was avoiding meeting her eyes. But Lionn and Charest had charge here so she waited to see the game played out.

"Grund," Charest began, "you are here at the express invitation of both myself and Lord Gaelen's heir, Lionn. Need I remind you that Lord Gaelen still rules here and that it is he who has decreed this process?"

Grund squirmed a little but did not change his posture. "Of course I yield to Lord Gaelen's command, but I will not submit to that servant." He thrust a belligerent finger at Merrist and quickly returned his arm back to his defiant pose, now staring at the table, avoiding acknowledging anyone.

Lionn caught Liannis's eye and raised one questioning eyebrow. She gave him a tiny nod to show she had seen. He turned back to Grund and asked, "Grund, I must ask you to agree to be truth-read by Liannis. Will you agree?"

Liannis sensed the fear in Grund grow as he raised his head to Lionn. "That ...," he sputtered, "that ... man ... has corrupted the seer. I no longer trust her and will not agree to be truth-read in his presence. Have you not heard? He is privy to all her secrets. He controls her. I have this from a reliable source, a man who travelled with them. He must be arrested, must be kept from her, and from everyone. He is a monster."

Until now Merrist had remained calm but this made him bristle. When he leaned forward Liannis broke in before he could speak.

"Merrist is a servant of Earth, as am I. He is here at Earth's behest and will remain. If you are unwilling to be truth-read we must conclude that you cannot be trusted."

Merrist sank back into his chair, his face a dark scowl. He, too, crossed his arms. Then, as if he knew he looked just like Grund, carefully placed his hands in his lap.

Charest now leaned toward Grund. "Sir, you do yourself no service by refusing to submit. It is we who will choose the next ruler, nay, Lord, of Catania. If you believe you are the most worthy candidate surely you will wish us to see that as well."

"But do you not see?" Grund almost jumped out of his seat in Charest's direction. "The seer is corrupted. She no longer sees true. I cannot allow myself to be tainted by her or her corrupter. She no longer serves Earth. If she were a true seer I would gladly submit. But she is not, and so I do not." A triumphant smirk curled about his lips and he relaxed back into his seat, now with an air of superior arrogance.

Before anyone could stop him, Merrist leaned forward again. "Grund, I have it from a reliable source that you were behind the attack on Brynnell. Is this what you are hiding? Is this why you refuse to be truth-read?"

Liannis thought Grund might take the challenge when he began to rise up but he caught himself and took time to think before answering. Now a sly look came into his eyes. "What attack? I have heard that he is well and has come to no harm. If I had sent someone to eliminate him, he would surely be dead. Perhaps this is a ruse to discredit me and have me eliminated from the competition. Perhaps he is the one who cannot be trusted. Perhaps you are his accomplice." The last emerged as a snarl. Grund sat back, with a satisfied sneer.

Charest slapped both hands down on the table. "This has gone far enough. Liannis, truth-read him. I am governor here still, and I command it."

Grund paled but remained defiant. "She will say what she wishes. Her words cannot be trusted."

Liannis held up a hand. "I think it is time. Grund," She pierced him with a glare. "Brynnell lives only because Merrist, Earth's chosen servant, has healed him."

When Grund began to rise and sputter protest Lionn barked at him to sit and listen, or be expelled.

Liannis continued. "Earth has given him that ability, among others. And, in case you wish to challenge Charest on that, we can call on witnesses to other healings he has performed. Brynnell was not the first. Furthermore, as Earth has chosen Merrist, he is here rightfully at her behest and will never be excluded from any negotiation where she wishes him to be present." She let the words sink in, and then added, "Now, I will truth-read you, willing or no, as Charest has commanded. You have forfeited the right to refuse."

As she spoke she could feel Earth's presence welling inside her, adding power to her words. She could tell by Grund's expression that he saw it, too, though he said nothing. All his aggressive posturing leaked out of him and he shrank slightly, his arms loosening their defiant hold on each other, though he still glowered at her from under lowered brows.

"Grund, I have some questions, to which you will answer yes, or no. Nothing further is required. I will know if you speak true."

His eyes flickered and resumed their glare.

"Did you send someone to assassinate Brynnell?"

Grund lunged out of his chair, causing it to topple behind him as he roared, "I will not answer," and made haste for the door.

Lionn beat him there, sword out, and barred his way, shouting for guards.

Grund had his dagger out by the time he reached the door. Before he could thrust it at Lionn the alert guards burst in, pushed Lionn aside and had Grund on the floor, disarmed, hands behind his back.

"Take him to the dungeon." Charest had come to stand between Lionn and Grund, dagger ready to defend his lord's heir. "He has shown himself to be a traitor this day." Though obviously shaken, Charest's voice remained strong.

Grund struggled as the guards lifted him to his feet and pushed him out the door.

"False seer! You debase the station to which you lay claim. And you, you are no healer. You do not serve Earth. False! Both of you. False!" His voice rang down the corridor into the main hall as they took him away. The shouting continued as they bore him out.

26

REGROUP

They all resumed their seats at the table but no one spoke for a time. It seemed none of them knew what to say about what they had just witnessed; it was so far from what they had expected.

Lionn collected himself first. "Well, the hare has certainly escaped the snare now. I expect his accusations will already have flown across half of Catania by the time they reach the dungeons. We will not be able to contain it."

"I suspect the rumours about Liannis and I have spread even before this," Merrist said. "From what Grund said, Strennock, who accompanied us here, has been making his suspicions known from the moment he entered the city. He disappeared so quickly I did not even have help with the horses."

"Yes, if we ever had any wish to slow the spread of our new status that has been taken from us." Liannis looked worried but resigned. "I expect Earth may actually be pleased."

Charest's eyebrows came up in surprise. "Truly? Do you think Earth approves of such events?"

"No, not approve, certainly, but I have been reluctant to allow news of this to spread. I have been resisting it. Now, I suspect Earth is pleased that we no longer have that option, though she would not approve of the means by which this came about."

"I see."

"Charest." Lionn brought them back to the purpose of the meeting. "It is clear we now have only two candidates left. And I think we all agree that, while Frellick wishes to be a good ruler, he is not ready to take on such a responsibility."

The other two nodded.

"I wish we had more time for this decision. While we agree on the best choice the people may not see it as we do. They may think we ought to have more candidates. So, I must ask you, Charest, how is it that you have not put forward your candidacy? What prevents you? We have heard from Lionn what you have told him, but we would like to hear more."

Charest grew sombre. After a long pause he leaned forward and placed his hands in front of himself on the table, fingers loosely together. "I am no longer a young man. I have not spoken of it, but my strength has begun to fail. I fear I may have an illness which will rob me of the years necessary to establish a lasting stability. Even were I not ill, I think I have not enough years left to settle Catania. Nor do I have an heir, and, were I to join and conceive one I have not the years to see to his training." He sat back again. "No, Lord Gaelen asked this of me some moons ago. My decision is firm. It would not be in the best interests of Catania for me to become its lord."

Merrist leaned toward him. "I can see about your health if you wish. I cannot say if I can heal you but I offer you the attempt." When Charest began to shake his head, Merrist added, "Even so, your other reasons suffice. I think we must accept your decision." When the others all nodded, sadly, it seemed, he said, "The offer of healing is still open, Charest."

Lionn, surprised at the news of illness, spoke up. "Indeed. Avail yourself of Merrist's offer. If he is successful I think the extra years you gain may make your services valuable to whoever does become lord. I expect that man, likely Brynnell, will need a strong advisor."

Charest glanced at Lionn, then quickly away, seeming to take great interest in his hands. Then, as if he had suddenly made a decision, he looked at Merrist." I am an old man. Forgive me if I find these grave changes Earth has wrought difficult. But I know you all to be in Lord Gaelen's trust, and that Liannis has been a true seer. So I must show my trust, as well. I will submit to your care, Merrist, with gratitude. Perhaps, if you are successful, mine will be another voice of support against the crisis that must a surely come."

Lionn looked around the group and saw that all of them relaxed. The tension went out of the chamber. The air became lighter, along with the mood.

"Bravely spoken, Charest." Lionn made no attempt to disguise his relief. "You honor Lord Gaelen, and indeed, Catania, with your loyalty. We are in your debt."

Charest made a small dismissive gesture. "It has been my honour to serve."

"Shall we get back to business?" Liannis smiled at Charest. "I believe, since we have no other suitable candidate we must speak again with Brynnell. I would like to question him further."

85

Merrist rose to follow. "I think he will be strong enough now to see us in his chamber. I would not advise him to come here. In a day or two he will be mostly recovered, but now he must rest."

"Charest, will you accompany us there?"

"As you wish, sir." Charest looked relieved.

Merrist suspected he was still anxious about the offer of healing and welcomed the reprieve.

On the way back to the castle Merrist could not ignore the curious stares and frightened looks of many of the people they passed. He caught Liannis's eye and knew she had noted it, too. He thought of the coming babe. How was he to keep Liannis and their child safe? Oh Earth, how?

27

BRYNNELL

They found Brynnell sitting at the small table in his bed-chamber sharing a light meal with Joranna. She had answered their knock and stood nervously aside.

Charest took no notice of her and went straight to Brynnell, giving him a thorough looking over. "You look well, Brynnell. It is hard to believe that a day ago you lay near death."

"Yes, indeed. Yet it is so. Yon Merrist healed me." Brynnell sent Merrist a grateful look, still with some awe in it. "Earth shows us new wonders, Charest … Joranna, please take the tray away to the kitchen. We have finished and I must speak with these good people."

As Joranna hurried to obey after dipping a brief curtsey, Lionn came forward and began to help her place the remains of the repast on the tray, most un-lordly behaviour. Liannis could not help but see the look that passed between them. The attraction could not be missed. Where would this lead, she wondered?

"Brynnell," she asked, "are you well enough for a meeting, here in your chamber?"

"I am, and welcome." Brynnell's face broke into a broad smile. "I feel almost myself again."

Lionn called out to a maid to have more chairs brought and ordered tea, ale, bread and cheese.

Merrist asked if he might examine Brynnell, to which he gladly acquiesced.

"I agree, Brynnell." Merrist stood up with a smile. "Tomorrow you will be well enough to return to your own home, where I am certain Joranna will look after you well."

"She is a good girl," Brynnell beamed, "though with so many suitors I fear she will be lost to me soon."

"Does she favour anyone?" Lionn's tone seemed a touch too interested, Liannis thought, though the others did not appear to notice.

Brynnell laughed. "No, she rebuffs them all, which makes them even more eager. Joranna has a strong will and knows her mind. She will not be easily swayed by flattery."

A brief flash of relief crossed Lionn's face before he came back to the matter at hand.

"Brynnell, my friend," Charest began. As he told Brynnell of the events of the past spans his brows knit closer together and colour drained from his face.

"So, you understand the great challenges you will face." Lionn made it a statement, knowing it could not be argued. "Do you still wish to stand as candidate? This will be more difficult than you anticipated."

When Brynnell began to nod Liannis held up a hand to stop him. "Brynnell, we need to know that you will support our claims … that you will be able to stand against those who will not believe in the changes Earth has decreed. That will be a greater challenge to your position than any other. Already the people have begun to take sides. Many others are fearful. What is more, we need to be confident that those who currently support you will not fall away."

Brynnell spoke up. "Charest, you will have my full support."

"But," Liannis interrupted, "will your men, the guards and the soldiers remain behind you if they need to deal with unrest from this? Do you believe that the people have enough trust in you? Can you quell the opposition long enough to establish some stability in the new regime?"

Brynnell and Charest regarded each other for a long moment. Brynnell broke the silence first, speaking with care. "I see the gravity of what we face. Forgive me for speaking frankly." He addressed Liannis and Merrist directly. "If the two of you leave Catania quickly and quietly, so that no further incidents bring attention to yourselves, I believe we can control this." He held up both hands. "I mean no disrespect, but if you remain, I fear the problem will become greater than can be managed."

"I am afraid I must agree," Charest added quietly.

Lionn looked about to protest, then seemed to change his mind and remained silent.

"Liannis?" Merrist held out his hand to her. "Shall we share our thoughts before we speak?"

Liannis shook her head. "I think we need to be open here. These men will have to deal with what we decide today. Perhaps if we speak our thoughts freely we will all learn more together."

Merrist raised an eyebrow, but hesitated only an instant. "Very well, here are my thoughts. I agree with Charest and Brynnell." His tone held a note of defiance at first then lost its edge. "Our purpose here has been fulfilled. The candidate has been chosen. To remain beyond that purpose will merely invite more incidents and conflict. We must now trust these men to fulfill their charge."

Lionn disagreed. "Do you not think we need you here to warn us of dangers? Liannis, do you not think you ought to remain, that Earth will give you messages? You have been here only two days. Will it not seem that you are fleeing if you leave again so soon?"

All eyes fixed on Liannis. When no vision or message came from Earth she knew the final decision would be left to her. Would it be the right one? And for the right reasons?

Her hand went, of its own accord to her belly. She wanted to be away from here, away from the danger to her child. Did that affect her answer? She stilled her mind and breathed deeply. What would be the reasons to stay? Since Earth had not shown her what to do, what reason did she have to believe that she had further work for her here? They had uncovered a traitor. They had chosen the man who would be lord of Catania. He had strong support in Charest and the followers of both men.

She blinked and realised that she had not spoken, that everyone still waited for her to answer. She took a deep breath. "I, too, agree with Brynnell and Charest. Lionn, if Earth wished me to remain I think she would have sent me a sign or vision. We have accomplished what we came for. Now, I think we must trust these worthy men to lead as we have chosen them to do."

Charest relaxed. "Liannis, I thank you for your confidence."

Brynnell nodded. "I am grateful that you did not take our request remiss. I swear that we will remain loyal to Lord Gaelen. And that we will do our best to win the people over to the changes Earth has made."

Lionn still looked uncomfortable but did not press further. "So be it, then."

***

89

"Daughter."

"Mother?"

"Lionn must return to Bargia with you."

"As you wish, Mother."

"You have done well, Liannis. Remember I am with you."

"Thank you, Mother."

***

Liannis woke to four faces regarding her, two astonished and awed, the other two knowing and concerned.

Merrist handed her a mug of tea, already laced with honey.

"A message from Earth?" Lionn asked.

She nodded as she downed the tea. "It seems all three of us are called back to Bargia."

"Well, that answers my next question." Lionn sounded relieved. "But does this mean there is a problem there, or that we must leave these gentlemen to make their own decisions?"

"She did not say, though I sensed no urgency."

"Then, since we are no longer needed, perhaps we ought to leave these two men to themselves." He rose and headed for the door, looking back at Merrist and Liannis to follow.

"Good advice."

Lionn stopped and addressed Brynnell again before opening the door. "Brynnell, if you have not thought of this already, may I suggest that you enlist Frellick to your side? I do not think he will hold a grudge against you for winning the contest and he will be an asset to your advisory committee."

"Indeed, Sir, I had already planned on asking him. It will strengthen my position to have him and his followers on side."

Brynnell began to rise but Lionn waved him back down. "Stay seated, Brynnell. Gather your strength for the coming challenges. There will be many."

Merrist went to stand beside Charest, who had remained seated. Liannis wondered why but his meaning became clear at once.

"Charest, will you allow me to examine you before we go? I may be able to heal you of the ailment that saps your strength."

Charest began to protest. "I am an old man. There is nothing you can do for me that cannot wait yet a while."

90

"Charest," Liannis broke in, before Merrist could respond, "there will be trying times ahead. Brynnell will need your counsel. If Merrist can give you more strength, if he can heal the ailment that robs you of it, I think you would be remiss to refuse. Catania needs you. Brynnell will most certainly need you."

"What if there is nothing to be done?" Charest looked nervous.

"I will not harm you, Charest. If I cannot help you, you will not be worse off."

The appeal succeeded. Charest sat back into his chair and looked at Merrist. "I can do no less than my duty."

Merrist knelt beside him and placed a hand on his chest, eyes closed in concentration. In only moments he withdrew his hand and opened his eyes. "There was a growth on your lung. It will not bother you again. You will find your strength returning. I expect you will live several more years in good health."

"But I felt nothing." The astonishment in Charest's face was almost comical. He stopped a moment, as if examining himself. "Yet the pressure is gone from my chest and I breathe freely again." He took a deep breath as if to demonstrate.

Merrist rose to his feet, a pleased look on his face, though his colour had drained and Liannis knew the effort had fatigued him. "Good."

28

TO BARGIA

Merrist suggested that they leave as quietly as possible in the morning and asked to have their mounts brought to the castle gates so that they need not draw attention to themselves in the stables.

Charest wished to see them before they left, so it was mid-morning before they rode free of the city.

"Brynnell wasted no time," Lionn observed.

"Yes, and with Frellick at his side he will have two strong allies."

"Hmmm." Liannis looked pensive. "But I wonder what they will do about Grund. He is powerful. I fear he will rally support."

"Why," Merrist protested, "will they not hang him for treason?"

Liannis shook her head. "That is not certain. They must try him first and I am not convinced that his actions will be deemed treasonous. Though he did try to attack Lionn, he did not succeed and has not harmed him. And he has already tried to discredit us as false and corrupt, which may offer him a defense."

Lionn agreed. "We must uphold the law if this transition of power is to succeed. He will be tried. I do not think they will release him. He did pull a dagger on me. But I do not think they will succeed in proving treason."

"And that will allow him to gather more support against Brynnell and against us."

Merrist could not tell if Liannis's pallor came from fatigue, worry, or the coming babe. She looked wan and drawn. He needed to get her to Bargia, to her mother and friends. She needed rest.

In the service of speed they stayed on the well-travelled way, making no attempt to hide. They had agreed that this would also lend an air of normalcy to any who saw them. Acting like fugitives would only serve to add to the rising suspicions. The first night they found shelter and hospitality with a sheep herder and his family.

When those good folk realised they had their lord's heir as guest they insisted the party take the cabin. The man and his mate slept under the stars. Merrist would rather have been outdoors, but Lionn told him that to refuse the offer would have insulted the herdsman.

Of the three only Liannis slept soundly. She had eaten little at supper, too fatigued to force the heavy mutton down.

They were roused just at dawn by the sound of shouting, of horses, and their host pounding at the door before bursting in. The hut had no means of locking the door against intruders.

"My lord, I cannot stop them." He had a pitchfork in his hands.

Past him, Merrist saw three rough looking men, two with daggers in their hands, the third with his sword drawn. The herdsman's wife lay inert on the ground, bleeding from a wound to her head. Merrist did not have time to see if she lived.

The man with the sword, the apparent leader, stopped at the open door. "Surrender, false cowards, or we will kill the heir of Bargia. Lord Gaelen will see what comes of being corrupted by those false to Earth."

The poor herdsman had been knocked aside by the leader and now sat, pitchfork still in hand, looking wildly from one to the other and back to his wife.

"See to your wife." Liannis said. "You cannot help us here."

The man shot Liannis a grateful look and scurried, crab-like on his rear, to his wife's side, leaving the pitchfork behind.

Lionn and Merrist remained in the doorway, swords in hand, ready to fight, but Liannis stepped out between them.

"Whom do you name false? Go home to Catania and witness to the people what you see." Liannis's voice was not her own. It held such power that the men stepped half a pace back, astonished. Her eyes blazed with an intensity such as Merrist had never seen in her. He stood rooted to the ground. Lionn appeared likewise unable to move.

Liannis took another step outside the door and stopped. "Behold."

At that instant, out of a cloudless sky, a great bolt of lightning struck the ground between Liannis and the three men. It hit so close to the leader that he fell back onto his rump and his sword clattered out of his grip. The other two jumped back, almost falling over their own feet, but managed to stay upright. Where the

93

lightning had struck stood a hole as wide as Merrist's arm-span, half as deep and black with soot.

As soon as Earth released them from their inertia, Lionn and Merrist jumped in to disarm the three men, and tie them to a nearby tree.

Liannis stood rigid, the power still flowing through her. With the same voice she spoke to Merrist. "The good wife needs a healer. Go to her."

Merrist scrambled to help the herder's wife. With his hands upon her, the wound on her head closed.

She opened her eyes. "What happened?" She sat up, bewildered, and looked about her. As memory returned she clutched her husband in fear and clung to him.

"You men of Catania, return and bear witness to what you have seen." Liannis turned to Lionn. "Release them. They will not harass us further."

As soon as Lionn had untied their attackers they jumped on their horses and raced back the way they had come. Soon dust was all that remained to remind them they had been here.

Lionn caught Liannis just as she collapsed and carried her into the hut.

The healing had not taken all of Merrist's strength. He quickly assessed Liannis and roused her enough to take some water before laying her back down to sleep.

"You sleep, too, Merrist. I will keep watch. I do not think anyone will bother us now." Lionn went to the door. "Good sir, bring your wife in and lay her on the bed beside Liannis."

When the man shook his head violently and clung harder to his wife, Lionn took a blanket out to them and placed it around the woman's shoulders.

The herdsman pointed a shaking finger in Merrist's direction. "H-he healed my Mellia. He healed her."

"Yes," Lionn confirmed. "He did. Merrist is Earth's new healer and Liannis her seer. Remember this and bear witness to it, should anyone question you about it." He folded another blanket as he spoke and placed it on the ground. Then he gently pressed the two down so that they lay together where they had sat. This seemed to calm them and soon both slept.

Sleep eluded Merrist until Lionn hauled a fresh bucket of water from the well. He drank another large mug of it. Then Lionn

94

gave him a gentle shove, much as he had the herdsman and his wife.

"Merrist, you will be no use to anyone if you do not sleep."

He was right, of course. Merrist moved so that he lay next to Liannis, one arm over her, and let his eyes close. *Safe. Both of them still safe.* He slept.

29

HIATUS

They left the herdsman and his wife, now well again, at dawn the next morning. Liannis would have pressed to leave earlier but both she and Merrist needed to recover; she from having Earth speak through her, and Merrist from healing the shepherd's wife. Though grateful to Merrist, she thought the couple were glad to see the last of them.

This was the first healing Lionn had witnessed in person. When Merrist had helped Charest the results had not been visible to the outside observer. He had seen Brynnell only after they had brought him to the castle. While Lionn had believed what Merrist and Liannis told him, this made it more real for him.

"Now I will be able to say that I have seen Merrist heal with my own eyes, I will be able to bear witness to his ability." Lionn's excitement showed in his voice and the dancing of his eyes. "It ought to make it easier to convince the people, do you not think?"

Liannis did not share his enthusiasm. "It will help, I think, but not as much as it might."

"No," Merrist added, "people will resist it and it could even make them question you and cause distrust."

Much of their conversation on the remainder of the trek home to Bargia hashed this over and over. They came to the conclusion that they would have to wait and see, that they could not predict anything. "But I am certain that Earth will protect us as much as she is able. The future can change as a consequence of events but I believe that Earth would not bring us such troubling changes if she did not feel she could control some of the outcome." Liannis touched Merrist briefly on his arm so that he would understand that she meant that Earth would keep their child safe, as they had told no one yet of her condition. He gave her a doleful look, as if to say he did not feel so confident.

As Lionn rode a half a length ahead he did not notice the exchange.

Three uneventful days later the familiar hills surrounding Bargia city came into sight. "Race you to the gate." Lionn shouted as he spurred his mount into a full gallop.

Cloud welcomed the challenge and soon Liannis and Lionn found themselves neck-and-neck with the gate in sight. Merrist and his heavier warhorse, Warrior, lagged only a length behind.

The guards at the gate recognised them as they approached and had the gate open before they reached it. Liannis and Lionn passed through side by side, laughing, exhilarated, glad to be home.

Merrist entered right on their heels, looking much more sober. "Merrist, my friend, why the long face?" Lionn punched him in the arm as he dismounted.

Liannis caught Merrist's eye and gave a small shake of her head in warning. *Not yet.* "Merrist does not like to lose," she teased.

As Lionn helped her down, Merrist added, "Warrior is not built for speed."

Cloud snorted and Liannis caught her message. *Warrior has heart. Good horse.*

"Now, that is a first. Cloud just gave Warrior a compliment."

Cloud tossed her head in disdain. *Still stupid. Heart but no mind-speak.*

Merrist raised a brow in question but Liannis just shook her head with a laugh. She sensed a grumble of resentment when she handed a groom the bridle but Cloud followed the other two horses without audible complaint.

By the time they reached the castle and entered the great hall Marja strode across to meet them, having been informed by a guard of their arrival. Upon giving Lionn a welcoming hug she drew back and wrinkled her nose. "I see that a bath is in order before all else. You all reek of a sheep-cote."

"Indeed! We have slept two nights in the home of a shepherd and his wife. Not even three nights in the open can remove that from our clothing." Lionn's face split into his infectious grin. "But I am famished. Mutton and rabbit on the spit are not my most favoured fare."

Marja beckoned to a maid. "Sehla, see to three baths and have food brought to each chamber." The maid dipped a brief curtsey and hurried away, summoning another as she went.

"My lady, Merrist and I will have both our baths in my chamber." When Marja stopped and gave Liannis a questioning look she added. "We will explain everything later. We have much to tell you."

Marja had not been the wife of a lord all these years without learning to take a hint. She simply called to another maid. "Let Sehla know that two of those baths will be in the inner chamber that Liannis uses ... and food for two there as well."

The maid looked about to say something, then caught herself. "As you wish, my lady."

"Well, that will cause the gossip to fly." Marja sent Liannis a wry look. "I trust the explanation is a good one." When Liannis did not offer an answer Marja's smile became a little forced. "I have already received word that Gaelen will join us at supper. You have two spans to bathe and rest. We will meet in our chambers at that time." Her brisk tone told Liannis that it took an effort of will not to press for an explanation.

"My lady, I will go and greet Mama, first."

Marja became instantly contrite. "How thoughtless of me. Yes, you must go to her first. You will find her in our garden."

"How fares she, my lady?"

Marja's smile was more genuine now. "She has gained a little strength. Now that she knows you will return to her she seems more content, though she still says little and retreats into her thoughts. I think she dreams of Klast."

"I expect you are correct."

As Liannis and Marja entered the lord's chambers to see Brensa, Merrist carried on to their chamber to take his bath.

Liannis crossed the sitting chamber and went into the garden where she found Brensa seated on a sunny bench, needlework stilled on her lap, a faraway look on her face.

"Mama."

She looked up as Liannis approached. "Ah, Liannis." Brensa reached out her hand for Liannis to take as she sat beside her. "I see you have returned." A small smile played at the corners of her eyes and she gave the hand a quick squeeze. "You see? I told you I would wait, and here I am."

The gesture had a child-like quality. It confirmed for Liannis how much she had already slipped away, and that she remained only to please her.

"I am glad, Mama, for I have a great deal to tell you."

"Will it please me?"

"I think so, Mama, though it will surprise you as well."

Brensa grew serious then, as if remembering herself. "Is it for my ears only or ought we to wait so that Lord Gaelen and lady Marja may hear it, too. Perhaps I ought not to be the first to hear it."

Liannis leaned in to her ear, as though conspiring with her. "Part of it is for you first Mama. And I believe it will please you. You have earned that."

That brought Brensa's full attention. The child-like aspect fell away and she was Liannis's mother, in her full mind, once again.

"Mama, Earth sent me a great vision. One which changes everything." Liannis proceeded to tell her that Earth had made her and Merrist mates, joined together, and that they would have a child.

Brensa took the news as though she had expected it.

Her equanimity took Liannis aback only for a moment. She surmised Brensa had somehow known that Earth had sent Merrist to be with Liannis, if not as her mate, at least as her protector. Liannis suspected her mother had sensed it long before she, herself, would admit the message in the recurring dream. When Liannis finished, Brensa gave a great sigh, as if a weight had been lifted from her. "Good. You will not be alone, then, when I reunite with Klast."

"No, Mama, but I do not wish you to leave me yet. Can you remain a while longer?"

"You say there will be a child?" Liannis could hear the curiosity, and even hope in her voice.

"Yes, Mama, and I think it will not be long."

"Perhaps Klast will want me to stay until then, so I can tell him about it. He will want to know, I think." The far-away look had returned to her eyes.

"I think so, too, Mama." Liannis kissed her cheek. "I need a bath now, Mama. I will see you at supper, and then you can hear all the rest of our news."

Brensa responded with an absent nod.

Liannis let herself out through the garden door.

30

NAIRIN'S REQUEST

Lord Gaelen and Lady Marja took their news with much greater calm than Merrist expected. The announcement that he had the ability to heal did not even raise eyebrows.

"I am relieved to have the rumour cleared. The news of your healing Sennia had already reached us," Gaelen said, "But the story has grown so that we did not know what to believe."

"I am so sad that Sennia lost the babe. We had only recently heard of her pregnancy, and then only accidentally via a messenger with other news. I was looking forward to becoming a grandmother." Marja looked at Merrist, not at Liannis with her next question. "Will she truly be well and bear children?"

For the first time, Merrist felt accepted as an equal to Liannis. It helped to ease the doubts he still had about himself and his future role. "Yes, my lady. Sennia is completely healed and her body is ready to receive another child. I am certain of it. But the question of how many must be answered by Liannis. It is she who has seen."

If Liannis felt envious of the deference given him she did not show it. To his relief Merrist sensed only pride from her.

"My lady, Earth has shown me that Sennia will bear three children, a pair of twins and a third child. One twin and the later child will be sons. Dugal will have an heir." Liannis beamed at Merrist. "And for that we must thank Merrist and his new-found ability to heal."

"He has done more than that, Father." Lionn related what had happened in Catania. "So Brynnell lives to stand as candidate for Lord. He has Charest behind him and we expect Frellick has put his support behind Brynnell as well. Grund rests in the dungeons awaiting trial."

At the mention of Grund, Merrist saw Liannis stiffen and focus on something only she could see. They all grew silent and waited for the vision to pass. When Liannis sagged and came back to awareness Merrist had a mug of tea, laced with honey, ready at her side, knowing she would need it.

She took it with trembling hands but did not need assistance. No one urged her to speak. They knew she would tell them as soon as she was able. They were not kept waiting long.

"It is Grund. He has been sprung and is free. He has fled just north of Catania city and gathers his supporters. He will not let this rest and will do all he can to prevent Brynnell from taking power."

"Do you see what must be done?"

"No, my lord. As you know, Earth does not always know the future, and even when she sees she does not always show me."

"I will speak with the council tomorrow and arrange to send a contingent of soldiers to support Brynnell. I fear he will need our assistance."

No one had anything to add so Gaelen brought them to new matters. "There has been a change regarding Lieth, as well. I am pleased that you are all here to discuss it."

Liannis accepted a platter with bread and preserves and a slice of fresh goat cheese from Marja as Gaelen spoke.

Merrist watched Liannis's colour return as she ate.

Gaelen rose from his chair, as he always did when he had something difficult or important to say. His restless nature would not allow him to remain seated when he needed to think. It seemed he thought best on his feet. When he did not have room to pace he would shift from one foot to the other in mimicry of it.

"Marja knows of this already but I have not yet taken it to council. Lady Nairin requested a formal audience with me this morning." He stopped moving and looked around to make sure he had their full attention. "You will remember that she renounced all claim to lordship of Lieth, both for herself and her children. She did this at the time to protect her children and so I would have a free hand in putting down the rebellion there and could rule without opposition."

If there had been any doubt that Gaelen had their attention before, it vanished now.

"Nairin now wishes to set up a regency for her second son, Wartin. She says that she feels useless here in Bargia and that her children have no real future here. She wants Wartin to achieve his birthright."

When Lionn half rose out of his chair and looked about to protest, Gaelen waved him back down with one hand.

101

"Nairin says she has not forgotten her oath of allegiance to me. She asks our support in this and says that she will not press her petition if it means acting against us. But she is adamant that she wishes to return to Lieth and reinstate her son as Lord, with herself as regent. She recognises she cannot succeed in this without our support and asks me to present her request to council." Gaelen let them take this news in silence and, after a moment, resumed his seat.

Once again, Merrist admired his skill. He brought to mind how Gaelen had managed to control three demesnes and keep them all from bloodshed through almost twenty years, in spite of two years of famine.

Liannis was the first to speak. "My lord, has she said when she wishes a decision by?"

"No, but I think it best we decide soon. Lieth is still in disarray both from the rebellion and Earth's great cleansing by fire. The famine of the last two years has made survival their most immediate goal, but now that this harvest looks promising, I predict we will see factions forming that will compete for leadership there. I have seen no clear leader emerge, thus far, from among the people. Something must be decided soon, before challenges and competitions arise. I cannot be present there enough of the time to keep order indefinitely."

"Does her change of heart mean that Nairin can no longer be trusted?" Lionn asked. "That would certainly surprise me, but it must be considered."

"No, I do not think she will renege on her oath if I put her to the test. And young Wartin has shown himself to be an intelligent and thoughtful child. His character has proven much stronger than that of his older brother, Rellnost. I see good potential in him. He studies well and trains hard. It is as if he wishes to prove that he has not his brother's weaknesses. Perhaps this is what has caused his mother to pursue this path."

"Perhaps," Merrist offered, "a greater question is whether Lieth will welcome the family back. Their legacy has not been a strong one. Can this be achieved without bloodshed, do you think?"

When the conversation slowed after more discussion Merrist noticed that Liannis looked tired. "Liannis, shall I accompany you to our chamber? You look like you need to rest."

102

31

CODDLED

Liannis knew just what Merrist meant by his offer. His concerned expression said it all. "No, Merrist. I am fine." They had not disclosed the news of her pregnancy. She wondered if they ought to have.

"But you have had little sleep these past nights."

"I am enjoying the company, Merrist. Leave it."

Gaelen gave them both a searching look. "Is there something you are not telling us?"

Before Merrist could give things away Liannis said, "No, my lord. Merrist is just being overly solicitous. He still tries to do everything for me. He coddles me."

Merrist sent her a glare but kept silent.

Later, when they had finally gone to their chambers to sleep, he brought the incident up. "Liannis, you are expecting our child, a child who is important not only to us but to Earth. You need to take better care of yourself." His tone held barely suppressed anger.

"Merrist, I do not need to be coddled. Nor do I like being told what to do, no matter that your intentions are good. I am quite capable of deciding what is best for me ... and for my child."

"Our child! Perhaps you forget that." His hurt tone stung Liannis. "And you have never known when to give up. You always push yourself beyond your limits. When I was your servant I could not tell you to stop. But now I feel I must do what I can to protect you and *our* child. Earth has given me that responsibility."

Liannis took his hand so there would be no misunderstanding between them when she answered, so that he would feel that she understood but also needed to hold her ground. She kept her voice low.

"Merrist, it is true that Earth demands new things from you. And I love you for trying to protect me and our babe. But I cannot abide you hovering over me like a mother hen. I can decide for myself whether I need to sleep, to eat, or to do my duty. Earth guides me. And I am an adult, Merrist, not a child." She lowered her voice even more, still keeping his hand in hers so he would understand her true meaning. "We will both see many trials in our time ahead. It does no good for you to create more where there are none."

She could tell that Merrist still held some hurt, not yet ready to give in. What could she say that would reach him and close this distance between them? "Merrist, we will face dangers together. You will not always be able to protect me. We are no ordinary mates. Tradition will not serve us here. If you insist on being my constant champion you will keep yourself in such turmoil you will be unable to do anything well. We must both trust that Earth will see us through what we must do." She squeezed his hand to emphasise her next words. "My love, you must trust that I will know what I need. I need you strong for the tests ahead, not wasting your strength on such minor things. I know how much you love me and our babe. You do not need to be at my shoulder constantly for me to see that."

She could feel the last remnants of anger and hurt seep out of him.

"It is just that I fear for you, for us all. I am helpless to keep you safe with such unpredictable things happening. And as a man, I feel it is my duty to protect you. It is hard to stand back and do so little."

"So little? Merrist I think we will both be called upon to do a great deal ere we have finished. This is only the beginning."

"That is exactly it!" Merrist threw his hands up in frustration, letting go of hers. "And I can control none of it."

"I feel that sense of helplessness, too, Merrist. But I have had more time to become accustomed to it. We will weather it together. But we can only do that if we are united."

His only response was a weary, doubtful nod. She decided to say what she had decided.

"I think it is time to tell the others we will have a child. Mama already knows. Do you object to me telling them tomorrow when we break fast with them?"

He gave her a long look then sighed.

"Yes, there seems no reason not to tell them."

32

CONFERENCE

Gaelen called a meeting with his advisory council next morning. Janest had to be helped in. He looked very frail and shook with tremors. It saddened Liannis to see him like that. Janest was the last of Gaelen's original advisors, inherited from his father, and the eldest of the current roster.

Liannis looked at Merrist in question. He gave a small shrug as if to say he didn't know. She determined to speak to Janest later. Perhaps Merrist could heal him and give him some more time, or at least, make the time he had left more comfortable. But even as the thought came into her mind she felt a small sense of wrongness about it that she did not understand.

Gaelen rose to get their attention. "Friends, welcome. It is good to have Liannis and Merrist here to add their thoughts on the matter before us." He sat down again. After he apprised them all of the news from Catania, he went directly to Nairin's request. "Now, I have been checking on Wartin's progress. He is a serious lad, intelligent, and he applies himself well to both his arms training and his studies. He has shown a strong aptitude for strategy and history. I suspect his interest stems from the fall of Lieth and accompanying death of his lord father."

Gaelen looked around the table. "So, today, we must decide how to proceed. What are your thoughts?"

Liannis followed his gaze and saw a mix of curiosity and thoughtfulness, but no alarm or outrage. No one, it seemed, felt overly concerned that Nairin had changed her mind in wanting a regency set up for Wartin.

Merrist surprised her by being the first to speak. "My lord, am I correct in believing that Nairin has not seen Lieth since the great cleansing?" When Gaelen confirmed this he went on. "Then, I think she will find Lieth much changed since she fled it. I have no doubt that she has been informed of events, but nothing can possibly prepare her for the destruction there, or for the changes in its governance. The Lieth she knew no longer exists."

Merrist had, once more, impressed her. He had not had the life-long training in history and strategy that Lionn had, nor herself, for that matter. Even though she was a woman, her father

105

had taught her all he knew, and he had been the best. But Merrist showed a remarkable aptitude for it.

Janest fought to control a tremor before he spoke. "That is so, young Merrist." He addressed Gaelen. "My lord, may I suggest that Nairin be escorted to Lieth, to see the damage and the changes that have resulted. She may well change her mind again when she understands the severity of the challenges she and her son will face, should they wish to proceed with her request." He gripped the arms of his chair and eased himself back again, clasping them in his lap as he relaxed, and took a deep breath as if to draw in strength from the air. But clearly his mind was as sharp as ever, and he was as dedicated to his duty.

How old was he now, Liannis wondered? Seventy perhaps? Her poor friend ... and Gaelen's.

With everyone in agreement it did not take long for that decision to pass. Gaelen would visit Nairin, taking Liannis with him, and propose the journey to her. They decided that Wartin should not go this time. If Nairin decided not to pursue the regency it would be better that Wartin not know just how completely his home had been destroyed until he was older. He had not yet reached his tenth year day. If Nairin agreed with the plan she would be escorted by a full cadre of soldiers. Liannis and Merrist would also accompany her as well as one member of the advisory council.

33

NAIRIN

When they informed Nairin of the decision Liannis saw a new strength and resolve that had not been apparent in her before.

"Lord Gaelen, I am determined in this. I have a duty, not only to my son, but also to Lieth. The troubles my people find themselves in are, in part, due to my late husband's weakness. Let me go and see my home."

Gaelen gave her a short seated bow. "As you wish, my lady."

"And if, after seeing Lieth, I still wish to set up a regency for Wartin, will you support me?"

"You may rely on our co-operation and support as long as we deem it in the best interests of both Bargia and the rest of the One Isle. If it becomes apparent that it brings war, or greater destruction, I will protect Bargia and the One Isle. My first duty lies there."

When Nairin bristled he hastened to add, "For now, let Bargia and Lieth remain close allies. Lady Nairin, the peace we live in today has been hard won. I will not invite further chaos. You well know the toll the famines of the last two years have taken. I would be remiss in my duty to my people if I supported an endeavour that would plunge us, once more, into war."

Nairin drew herself together with effort. "I do understand, my lord. And I, too, have no wish to inflict further hardship on either of our peoples."

"Then let us prepare. You will leave in three days."

"Thank you, my lord."

When they left Nairin's apartments and walked back to the castle Gaelen asked, "Liannis, what did you sense from her. Can she be trusted?"

"She has changed, my lord. But I do not sense that the change is a threat to Bargia." She looked at him. "But this is my own impression only, not a message from Earth."

"I understand." The crease between his brows did not ease. Her answer had given him no comfort.

"My lord, you did not give the council any opportunity to address the changes Earth has made to myself and Merrist. Do you think that wise?"

"Perhaps not, but I believe it best to keep the two issues separate. I have learned that talking too much about something can often make a problem bigger if there is nothing that can be done to change it."

She had no answer to that so she kept silent.

As they neared the castle doors Gaelen said, "I wonder if the people would find the changes easier to believe if Merrist could heal someone here in Bargia." He looked at her, one eyebrow raised. "Janest, perhaps? I saw you exchange glances with Merrist after you watched Janest come in." He gave her a wry smile. "I admit to it being a selfish thought, as well. I fear he will not be with us much longer and I will miss his counsel."

"I will speak with Merrist about it, my lord, but I sensed a wrongness when it passed between Merrist and me. I cannot promise anything."

"Please do what you can."

They had reached the bottom of the great stair. A maid hurried to greet them. "My lord, shall I summon the others and have dinner brought to your chambers or do you wish to eat in the dining hall?"

"In my chambers please, Lannan, and have Merrist and Lionn join us."

Lannan dropped a curtsey. "Right away, my lord."

As they ascended the steps to Gaelen's apartments Liannis looked out over the great hall, the guards at their posts, alert but mostly relaxed, the maids scurrying about their work, free from fear. Almost without knowing she spoke aloud, she said, "This will not last – this peace." A frisson of foreboding chilled her for a moment.

Gaelen sent her a sharp, quizzical look. Then, as if he felt it, too, he murmured. "I fear you are right." At the top, he turned to her. "Perhaps Lionn ought to go with you to Lieth."

"No, he may be needed in Catania."

Brensa met them at the door before Gaelen could ask her to explain.

34

TO LIETH

When Merrist and Liannis met with Janest, to speak about healing him, Janest merely shook his head. He took Liannis's hand when she knelt by his chair. "My dear, I have had a long and rich life. Longer than most. I do not think that Earth wishes me to remain much longer. Sometimes I think I hear my dear wife telling me we will soon be reunited. I look forward to that." He raised a shaking hand to pat Liannis's cheek. "I know you will miss me. You have always been a favourite of mine."

Tears slid, unabashed, down Liannis's cheeks. She did not attempt to rub them away. "But Lord Gaelen still has need of you. Could Merrist not at least make you more comfortable?"

"Let me examine you, Janest. Perhaps that will help your decision." He knelt at Janest's other side.

"If you wish, young Merrist."

It surprised Merrist that Janest showed no disbelief or hesitation once he had been told of the changes Earth had made in him and Liannis. Janest took it all as natural, the only one so far who had. But when Merrist placed his hands on Janest's chest he could feel nothing. He soon had to admit that something was blocking him.

Janest patted his hand.

"So you see, Earth has deemed that I am not needed much longer, and will grant me my rest." He turned to Liannis. "Do not mourn, Liannis. This is as it should be. I am content with it."

"Will you still be here when we return from Lieth?"

"I expect you will have an opportunity to say farewell before winter. But I do not think I shall see another Spring Festival."

Three mornings later, Merrist watched Liannis carefully as their party left for Lieth. The journey lasted six days. The two of them could have done it in four, but with Nairin present they had to travel more slowly.

Nairin had grown unaccustomed to riding and had brought an attendant with her as well, to assist her with her hair and dressing, as well as to add to her status.

Against Merrist's advice, Liannis had let the group know that she had a kestrel as a familiar, though not that they mind-spoke, so Kira was able to come down and ride on her shoulder. In the past Liannis had told Kira to stay out of sight whenever they were with people who did not already know about her. However, no one seemed to think it strange. Merrist supposed, next to the other momentous changes, this was a small thing. It felt right, and Liannis certainly seemed to enjoy Kira's company. Merrist often wondered how much they communicated. Every now and then he would see a smile cross Liannis's face and knew she must have heard something from either Kira or Cloud.

He kept their small tent well away from the rest at night and made sure Liannis slept and ate well. That way he worried less for her health.

Gaelen had sent a scout ahead to advise the people in Lieth that Lady Nairin was on her way to visit. That was all the man had been told, so no one there knew the true purpose of the journey. Merrist wondered how many people would come to greet her when they heard, and how they would receive her.

The scout made good time, for he met them on his way back the third day out, where he joined their group. "Many people are anxious to see you, my lady. But some are still angry and will not welcome you. I cannot guarantee there will not be danger."

They had all been warned to expect this so it came as no surprise.

Nairin took it calmly. "I have been prepared for this. I am aware that things will not be as they were when I left."

But nothing could have prepared her, or even Merrist and Liannis, for what greeted them when they reached Lieth City.

The pair had not been back since the quaking and the great firing that had cleansed the city and left it in ruins two years ago. Gaelen had retained a cadre of soldiers there to keep order and had sent three trusted men to act as advisors and work with the citizens in their attempts to rebuild. These men also had to assist in forming a new government, though still under Bargia's rule. They had expected more progress. At least Merrist had.

As their party neared the city they had to cross the fields and berms that had been scorched by those fires. The grass now grew again in green profusion, though no living trees remained, only an occasional charred skeleton. On the flatter areas Merrist

110

saw new crops of spelt, beans, maize and vegetables beginning to grow. Where crops could not be grown he spotted small herds of sheep, goats and a few cattle grazing, though not nearly as many as he had expected. Yet, the signs of new growth gave him a feeling of optimism as they approached the walls of the city. That feeling proved short-lived.

No one spoke when the gate came in sight. The walls still bore soot from the fires; black, ugly and foreboding. The gates had been repaired with rough planks, and though closed, hung askew on fire-warped hinges, leaving an impression of disrepair and poverty. No guards stood watch to hail newcomers.

35

LIETH

Leaving little Leyla behind in Bargia while she went to Lieth was hard for Nairin. She knew her daughter was in good hands, but she had lost so much in the last two years that she felt a need to keep her children close. Wartin, at age nine, had already gone into training in the youth barracks. She saw him less frequently now, so separation from him did not cut as deep. But at the sight of Lieth City all thoughts of Leyla vanished.

The landscape looked much as Nairin remembered it until the party approached the city. While Nairin had been warned about the degree of destruction and devastation she should expect, words could never have prepared her for what she encountered. It hit her like a physical blow.

A swath, almost as wide as she could see, of treeless grasslands dotted with soot-blackened rocks and charred stumps began the assault on her senses. The orchards and copses that had not burned in the great purging had been cut for firewood. Nairin could tell that the grass, while new and green, would not grow high yet. If she looked carefully she could spot the occasional tiny sapling trying to find a foothold in the soil. A few sheep grazed on the low hillocks in the shadow of the city wall and on the outlying berms. Nairin clung to those sights to give her hope.

That wall, and its gate, dashed even the small hope Nairin had found to cling to. Soot from the great fire still blackened its surfaces. It would be several more years before the rains and snows would scour them free of their funereal pall. And the gate. Her heart lurched at the sight. She remembered it as beautifully carved, strong and straight, both a welcome beacon and a safe barrier. Now she saw doors of crude, thick wooden planks, undecorated, hanging crooked, no guards visible to prevent unwanted entry. Was there nothing left worth protecting, she wondered?

Liannis sidled her horse close. "My lady. This must be hard for you. Do you wish me to summon a guard from inside to escort us in? It will give you some time to brace yourself. I expect what you will see inside will be even more difficult to bear."

Nairin drew herself up. "No, that will only delay things. I have come to see what is left of my city and that is what I shall do."

Liannis inclined her head. "As you wish, my lady."

Nairin drew her horse to a halt several paces from the gate. She had grown pale and now sat with her hands in front of her mouth, her reins hanging, un-minded, on her horse's neck. She muttered into her hands, "Oh, Earth." Then she squared her shoulders, took the reins again and said, in a tight voice, "Hail the gates."

Nairin forced herself to look straight ahead and kneed her horse forward. Liannis and Merrist stayed close, one on each side. Two guards hurried to place themselves in front of her.

Nairin kept her voice steady as they reached the gatehouse, repeating her earlier command. "Hail to summon someone." She wondered if there would even be anyone there or if they would simply be able to open the gate themselves.

At the rap of a sword on one of the planks and the call, "Guards, open the gate," a muffled voice called out "Who goes there?"

"Lady Nairin and her party from Bargia."

One side swung open.

"Welcome, Lady Nairin. We have been expecting you." A worn tunic displaying the crest of Lieth covering his otherwise nondescript clothes was the only thing that identified the man as a guard. "Lord Gaelen's messenger arrived only four days ago. We have prepared a chamber for you." He stood back to allow them to pass.

One of Nairin's two guards went through the gate side by side with Liannis, who had positioned herself in front of Nairin.

Liannis turned back. "I sense no immediate danger my lady. It is safe to enter."

"Forward. I must see."

Nairin went ashen on entering the gates, her lips a tight, thin line and the knuckles of her hand showed bone-white where she clenched the reins. She barely registered the two guards who had approached to greet her. She stared straight ahead, past them, down the main street. A dark slash beginning fifty paces away, that ran in a long diagonal across the street, before disappearing

113

between some rubble that had once been two imposing stone buildings, gripped her attention.

The rift. When Earth had brought the cleansing fires, to rid the city of the rats and vermin that had made it uninhabitable, a great shaking had taken the entire city. It created this rift which crossed much of city centre, making it perilous to traverse.

Many of the buildings that had remained standing until that moment had fallen into ruin. The fires had devoured all that were wood. Earth had ordered that anything that could be burned must be. That had left only the remaining stone structures, many of them damaged by the quaking as well. But Earth had still been merciful. On Gaelen's command all the people and the animals, those that had not already starved or died from disease, had been evacuated well outside the city wall before the quaking and fire.

One of the guards addressed Nairin. "May we help you down, my lady?"

At the question Nairin gave her head a small shake, as if waking from a trance, looked at the guard who had spoken and whispered, "Yes," She let herself slide into his grip to stand beside her horse. She said nothing more but walked straight to the beginning of the rift. There she fell to her knees, touched its edge with both hands, knelt back and wept.

One of the guards must have thought her about to throw herself into the crevasse, for he sprang forward and made to catch her, but drew back again.

Though Nairin's shoulders heaved with weeping, she uttered no sound. Great tears slid in profusion down her cheeks and watered the scorched rock, leaving dark, wet blotches where they fell.

After some time Nairin collected herself, rose, and looked behind her at the crowd that had begun to gather; thin, mostly ragged, and silent. They showed no outward emotion, just a quiet curiosity. She wondered if many of the children even knew who she was. No one spoke. It felt like the whole city waited, hushed, though they knew not for what.

At one back edge of the crowd she spotted a smaller, different group, this one more agitated, appearing angry. So, she thought, not everyone would welcome her. She would consult Liannis about this. She would need to be on her mettle, though she had been warned to expect no less. It was well that no one had been

114

told the reason behind her visit else her reception might be more openly divided.

When Nairin swayed as if to fall Merrist made his way between the guards to her side and placed the fingers of one hand on her sleeve. "My lady, let me help you. Your people await. Will you speak with them?"

Nairin felt the healing strength Merrist poured into her and found hers returning. She met his eyes, making no effort to hide her grief, and nodded. Merrist took her elbow and kept contact as she faced the crowd. New tears coursed down her face as she stretched out her free hand as if reaching for the people. Though she spoke in only a whisper, somehow all there heard her plainly.

"Oh Earth, my poor people, my poor city."

Three men, better dressed that the rest, stepped forward and went to one knee at Nairin's feet. "My lady, welcome. We are at your service."

That familiar gesture roused Nairin. "Thank you gentlemen. Please rise."

As they rose to their feet the one who had spoken said, "We were told of your pending arrival, my lady, and have done what we can to prepare lodgings for you. I fear they will not be what you are accustomed to, but it is the best we have."

"I thank you...?"

"Prell, my lady, forgive me. And these are Morins and Karel, your loyal servants."

Nairin nodded acknowledgement, then lifted her head and, once more in control of herself, addressed the crowd in a steady voice. "My people, I weep for your suffering. But now my strength leaves me and I can bear to see no more. I must rest. Tomorrow, I will walk the rest of our poor, blighted city."

That seemed to break the spell. A low wave of murmurs began among those who had come to see. When Nairin turned back to her guides to follow them to her chambers the crowd behind her began to disperse. She knew they, and many more, would return tomorrow.

INSIDE LIETH

Liannis noted that while the lodgings that had been prepared for Nairin were in the castle, they were not her old apartments. Those housed one of the families that had risen to power after Lieth had been razed. Three more families, all led by men who held places of power among the current leadership, also occupied apartments in the castle.

Nairin had to make do with one chamber which contained only a plain but clean bed, a chair and a small table holding a wash basin and pitcher of fresh water. Even this furniture looked newly made, as did all the rest Liannis had seen. While this room's furnishings appeared well crafted, it was clear that, even in the castle, utility had taken precedence over decoration.

Unlike the finely woven and embroidered bed linens Nairin was accustomed to, the bed wore plain sheets like those usually found in much more modest homes. She showed no reaction to her straitened circumstances. Instead, she graciously thanked the maid who showed her in for the care she had taken to see to her needs.

"Is it possible to have a tray brought to my room? I do not have the energy left to eat with the others in the hall." Nairin's tone was almost diffident.

The maid dipped a curtsey. "Certainly, my lady. I will see to it right away. Is there anything else you require? I can have a bath brought, if you wish."

"Perhaps in the morning, when I have slept."

"As you wish, my lady." The maid hurried away.

Nairin turned to her attendant. "You will share my bed, tonight. It appears there is no separate one for you."

The maid's look of relief was almost comical. Perhaps she had expected to sleep on the floor.

Liannis could tell that the poor condition of the castle added another blow to Nairin's already battered senses. Liannis shared her sorrow. Nothing of what she remembered, from when she had acted as nursemaid to Nairin's children, remained, since everything that could be burned had been. No tapestries decorated the walls. The wooden sconces filled with candles that had lined the walls were gone, leaving only black soot marks from the fire.

Nairin could see that attempts had been made to scour the walls, but the blackness had entered the very pores of the stone, and could not be scrubbed away. The great hall looked cavernous without its chairs, benches and huge banquet tables. The only furniture now was one long trestle table at the far end, flanked by two benches and one armchair. Even the ornate doors that had been the main entrance had been replaced by heavy planks, well crafted, but without any ornamentation.

No great candelabras hung from the ceiling. The only light came from torches in the old iron brackets set at regular distances in the walls, and two portable candle stands at either end of the table.

"Where will those people who accompanied me be housed?" Nairin asked.

"We have arranged for the seer across the hall. The others will sleep in the smaller chambers at the other end of the great hall, my lady. It is the best we can do," a guard in the yellow and blue tunic of Bargia, told her.

"I understand. There is no need to apologise. You have done well to find lodgings for everyone. I also saw no signs of people living in the open when we came through. That pleases me."

The guard squared his shoulders, no longer apologetic. "That is so, lady, and all homes have the tools needed to cook, and blankets and clothing to keep warm. We have worked very hard. But two years of famine have hampered our efforts."

"Yes, I am sure that is so. I expect we will have a better understanding when we see the rest of the city tomorrow."

The guard shuffled his feet, looking uncomfortable before speaking. "I feel I ought to warn you that not everyone welcomes you back, my lady. Some still blame Lord Merlost for what has befallen Lieth. They say he was weak and unable to hold back the coup that led to Garneth's tyranny. They want none of his family here."

Liannis expected Nairin to bridle at the man's audacity but she showed no reaction.

"Thank you. I think I saw a group of them earlier. We are prepared for some opposition to my presence. You may inform

117

people that at this time I have only come to visit. I wish only to see my home and how my people fare."

"Then you do not plan to recover your family's position and rule again?"

The man had overstepped his bounds this time.

"That is an impertinent question." Nairin bristled. "All I will say is that I will be returning to Bargia in the next several days. And do not forget that Lord Gaelen still rules here."

"Forgive me, my lady." He gave a short bow. "I am, and remain, Lord Gaelen's loyal man."

They all still stood outside the chamber assigned to Lady Nairin. Liannis turned to look at movement that caught her eye below in the great hall.

There stood Merrist, at the far end of the great hall, his hands on the arm of a guard wearing the colours of Lieth, his eyes closed in deep concentration. A small crowd stood watching, many with looks of either astonishment or suspicion. Merrist opened his eyes and let go the man's arm.

The man raised his hand, flexed it, opened and closed his fist, his eyes growing wider. His voice reached even where they stood. "He has done it! Look, I can use it again! I will wield a sword again!"

By the reactions in the group Liannis knew that by morning much of Lieth would have heard that Merrist had healing powers. There would be no rest for them now. But then, she had not really expected any. And now she would not bother to have Merrist sleep apart from her either.

The look Merrist gave her when he saw her watching was almost apologetic. When they were able to move away and depart for their chamber he said, "I had no choice. Something moved me to do it. I think it was a message from Earth." He gave his head an exasperated shake. "I truly wish these messages were clearer. They are just feelings. Sometimes I wonder whether to trust them."

Liannis thought about that a moment before answering. "That puzzles me as well, but I think that if you were not meant to do the healing something would prevent you. As with Janest, remember?"

"Hm, true..."

"I think you must trust yourself ... and I must trust you more, as well." She took his hand as they reached the door and smiled at him.

37

MORNING

Liannis woke next morning with a dull ache in her head, though her stomach showed no signs of rebelling. When she went to the window slit to look outside the day that greeted her held grey skies filled with dark clouds. While Earth had not sent her any message or vision, she had a feeling the events of the day would match the weather.

Merrist came to join her, putting his arm around her waist. "I think we will need to be on our mettle today. We were fortunate yesterday, but that group at the back of the crowd will not stay behind long. We will hear from them."

"Yes, I fear you are right." She sighed and stretched. "We had best go break our fast and make ourselves ready."

When Merrist opened the door they were met by two guards. "We have orders to accompany you to the dining hall. Lady Nairin will meet you there."

"Has something happened?"

"Nothing to fear, yet, Lady, but there is a group waiting outside the castle doors demanding an audience with Lady Nairin. They do not look friendly. We do not know what they mean to do."

"Ah yes likely from the group at the back of the crowd yesterday. I expected them."

"Liannis, do you sense danger?" Merrist gave her an inquiring look.

She thought a moment before answering. "No, not danger, exactly, but Nairin will be challenged today. I hope she is ready."

"We have prepared her," Merrist said.

"Hmmm," she acknowledged.

Nairin soon joined them, also escorted by two guards, for a hasty meal of sage tea, porridge, bread, and boiled eggs. The bread had been baked the day before but they had honey for it and the tea was hot.

As soon as they finished Nairin stood.

"I am ready. I wish to see the rest of the city today."

When Merrist began to open his mouth to protest Nairin shook her head and held up her hand to stop him. "I will tell the mob at the castle doors they may have audience with me after I have toured the city. I will not be deterred. My people expect me."

"My lady," Liannis ventured, "I think it may be wise to let those at the doors know that you are here on a visit only, and that no decision has been made about a permanent return. I fear they will prevent your progress through the city without that assurance."

Nairin studied her a moment, then squared her shoulders. "If I do not, will they prevent me, will they lay hands on me?"

"Earth has not shown me such, my lady, but I do know that today will not be pleasant."

Nairin looked grim. "I suspect you are correct." She turned and stode down the corridor, the guards scrambling to gather around her.

Liannis managed to stay beside her. Merrist took up the rear. Liannis had a fleeting thought that he ought to be beside her but pushed it aside. Now was not the time to lose courage.

As they approached the doors they could hear insistent voices from the other side. Four guards, swords held ready, two of them shifting from foot to foot, stood facing the barred doors, their backs to the approaching group. They said nothing in response to the demands outside. While the thick wooden planks of the doors did not permit them to see beyond, the repeated refrain soon became clear. "We demand to see Lady Nairin. Open the gate. Let us in." Each time the guards remained silent, those outside pounded on the door and began again.

Liannis turned to Nairin, speaking quietly for her ears only. "My lady, have you any plans for what you will tell them? They will not be satisfied with glib or angry answers."

"You have convinced me that I will be well advised to tell them that I have no firm plans to return to Lieth. That I am only here to see my old home." Nairin lowered her voice more. "Since that is, thus far, the truth, as I do not have any pledge of support for a regency in my son's name, there is nothing more to tell."

From her tone, Liannis could tell that Nairin had become firm in her decision to return as regent and resume the rule of Lieth. It seemed that what Nairin witnessed the afternoon before, and the angry demands of the men outside, had cemented her resolve. While she acquiesced to Liannis's suggestions of what to say, she obviously did not like it. Liannis decided not to press her

121

on that now. Their situation was delicate and she hoped Nairin would keep her word, if pressed.

"That is well, my lady. I will stand behind you if I am questioned."

Nairin turned to the guards. "Open the doors. I will speak with these men."

Two of them stepped back, adding their presence to the cordon around Nairin as the other two pulled the bar and swung the doors outward, pushing the waiting men back before they pressed into the opening.

38

CONFRONTATION

Momentarily frightened, Nairin almost took a step back, but collected herself just in time. She would not show these bullies weakness. That would only embolden them. She squared her shoulders, kept her head erect and waited.

"We do not want you here!"

"Merlost brought this all on us. Leave here."

"We will govern ourselves."

"You are not welcome here. Leave."

It was well that Nairin had not prepared a speech, as the men at the doors gave her no opportunity to address them. So she remained still and waited for them to run out of things to shout at her. While her late husband, Lord Merlost, may have lacked the talent to govern, Nairin possessed some skills of her own. She had not needed to deal with rabble since fleeing Lieth, but now she gathered her knowledge around her like armour, steeling herself to be ready when the shouting died down, as she knew it would. She did not have to wait long.

When quiet came, and they stared at her with stolid and some puzzled expressions, she stepped forward.

"My people."

That brought a rumble of dissent but when she waited to say more it died down again.

"Two years ago I was forced to flee Lieth, my beloved home. Lord Merlost stayed to face Garneth and his plotters, traitors who rose against your lord. My children and I were fortunate to escape with our lives and have been living in asylum in Bargia. The traitor Garneth had your lord murdered. Not long after, my eldest son, Wernost, heir to Lieth, lost his life in a tragic accident."

A shout came from the rear. "Why have you returned? Go back to Bargia."

Nairin stopped and searched until she found the man who had challenged her. Facing him directly, she said, "I am coming to that. Do me the courtesy of hearing me out." She shifted her gaze back to the man she thought to be the leader of the group. "I have faced many losses, as have you all. Until now, I had only tales and stories from others to tell me what state my beloved home was in. I needed to see it for myself – to see the destruction Garneth and his followers caused. I have much more to see and will not shirk until I have witnessed it all."

When the leader moved as if to speak she gave a short chop with her hand to stop him. That she succeeded confirmed for her she had full control. Good.

"I have come to learn how my people fare, what is left of my city, how recovery is going forward. I wish to see all of it with my own eyes." She paused and looked around, letting her words penetrate. "So far, while I am dismayed by the damage I see, I am proud of the strength you, my people, have all shown. I see new building. I see people in warm homes, with enough to eat, albeit not abundance. I see hope, industry and cooperation among you. My breast swells with pride. *This* was Lord Merlost's legacy. You say he was weak. Perhaps. But it was not he who brought this upon you. While he ruled you had plenty, peace, and bright futures. That blame belongs on the shoulders of the traitor Garneth. Think, my people. What would our dear city look like now if Garneth had not overthrown your lord?"

Nairin let that sink in before continuing. She could see doubt cross the faces of some of the men. She saw them glance at each other, waver in their resolve.

She pressed on.

"My people, I have come with no plan other than to see my home and my people. Now, I would like to complete that journey and to speak with the rest of my people. Nothing is decided beyond that. But, remember, I am also a mother, with a son who has lost his birthright. Wartin is a fine, strong lad, who is training well in Bargia. I want what is best for him."

There, she had planted the seed. She left it at that, not elaborating, and deliberately changed directions. "In a few days I will return to Bargia. But now, good men, I would like to walk the city, to speak with my people and to see what wonders you have accomplished since the great destruction."

She stepped boldly forward and began to walk. The gamble paid off. The group divided to let her pass. She allowed herself an inward smile of satisfaction. Good. She had won this confrontation. They would soon know that *she* was not weak. Let them chew on what she had said for a while.

124

When she had passed the group, and could move freely into the street, she allowed herself to look about, noting that Liannis and Merrist kept close by but did not seem alarmed. The guards, too, did not crowd her as protectively.

Her small victory boosted her strength to face what had become of her home. She had promised to see the entire city and wanted the people to see her as strong and confident. So she halted her progress only long enough to eat at one of the few inns that had resumed business.

As she made to leave the inn to resume her exploration she called the innkeeper to her. He had gone to great lengths to make her welcome and comfortable but had only rough fare to serve. The man went to one knee before her. "My lady."

"Rise, my good man. I wish to commend you on a clean and well run establishment. And the stew was well cooked and seasoned. Thank you for your hospitality and for the good food we have enjoyed. May you prosper in the years to come."

The man was so flustered by the praise that all he could do was stutter, "Thank you, my lady."

During her progress Nairin made sure she spoke to, or acknowledged, as many people as she could. The crowd that followed her grew as the day wore on. Only when the sun cast long shadows beside the walls did she relent and return to the castle. At the gates where the journey had begun that morning she turned once more to the crowd.

"My good people. When I arrived yesterday the destruction I witnessed was more than I could bear. My heart ached for you, my city and my people. But today I have witnessed a wonder that has erased my grief and transformed it into pride. You have shown such courage, such determination and industry in the face of difficulties no one who has not witnessed them could imagine. I know that Lieth will again be a city envied by its neighbours and allies." She paused and stretched out her hands open toward them in what could be seen as either a plea or a benediction, a gesture she calculated carefully for its effect. "Thank you, my people, for the kindness and acceptance you have shown me today. It shall not be forgotten." She turned and strode into the castle without looking back and went straight to her chamber without a word.

The gates closed behind her.

When Nairin entered the chamber she turned to her maid. "Have a tray brought – food, tea and wine. I will speak to no one else this day."

The maid hurried to obey.

39

MERRIST

In their chamber, as they shared a cold supper, Merrist grew increasingly still.

"Merrist, what is it?" Liannis asked him.

"I feel a strong urge to return to Catania. The reason is not clear to me. Do you sense anything? Has Earth sent you a message?"

"No, nothing. I wonder why?"

Merrist reached out and took Liannis's hand to see if touch would clarify things, as it often did.

"Anything?"

He watched the blood drain from Liannis's face. "What?"

"You are called back, as you say, but I am not to go with you. You must return alone." Her face took on an almost panicked expression. "Merrist, how will I be able to warn you of danger? How will I know if you are safe? ... And how will I sleep without you to keep the voices away?"

Merrist had anticipated some of this. "Liannis, you know you can search my aura to know if I am safe. And if there is danger, I believe that Earth will do something. I do not think we are meant to be separated for long, and certainly not by my death." He squeezed her hand. "As for sleeping, that I have no answer for, my love."

"But why has Earth not warned me, explained it to me? I do not want you to leave me alone. Why am I not to go with you?" Liannis's pitch rose with each question.

"Perhaps Earth will speak to you tonight in a dream. I do not wish to go but I feel this pull that I cannot resist. I must be gone as soon as we have broken our fast in the morning. It is almost a pain that grows with each span that I delay. But I will remain with you until then."

"I did not think Earth would separate us. Merrist, I am afraid."

"Perhaps that is a result of your condition. They say women do get more emotional. It is unlike you to react this way."

When she did not answer but only looked away, he lowered his voice. "Perhaps we ought to try to sleep. You have had

127

a long day with little rest. Come." He rose from his chair, still holding her hand and helped her up. He wondered if either of them would be able to sleep but it was the only thing he could think of to suggest.

The urge to leave immediately kept him awake much of the night, but he was gratified to see that Liannis finally drifted off in his arms, her body relaxing, limp and boneless, against his. These were moments he cherished. A span or two before dawn he, too, fell asleep, only to be awakened as the first soft light stole in through the window slit.

He looked at Liannis. She lay rigid, eyes wide. He recognised it as her vision trance and hoped it meant that she was getting the explanation she sought. He shared her concern, though he had not voiced it aloud. He did not wish to leave her alone. He feared she would not look after herself and their child. And if she could not sleep she would soon exhaust herself. And, he had to admit, he had come to rely on her visions to give him a sense of safety. He would not have that when they went their separate ways.

Watching Liannis taken by her vision he shook himself fully awake and looked about the chamber. She would need drink and food when she woke from her trance. There was fresh water in the pitcher so he filled a mug in readiness. The tray from their evening meal had only one chunk of bread and a small slice of cheese left, both of which had gone dry overnight.

He went to the door and slipped quietly into the hall where he summoned a maid to bring fresh food and white pine needle tea, Liannis's favourite. Then he slipped back into the chamber and began to prepare his pack for travelling. It felt suddenly very lonely to be packing for only himself.

By the time he finished, a light rap at the door announced the maid with the tray. It pleased him to see boiled eggs and a small cup of strawberry preserves alongside the porridge, as well as fresh dark bread and the usual cheese, butter and honey.

Liannis came to just as he set the tray down on the small table beside their bed. Merrist quickly handed her the first mug with water, which she gulped down while he poured the tea. Not until she had taken several bites from the platter he arranged for her did he ask what she had seen.

"Earth says you must not fear. Your road will be difficult and dangerous but it is necessary for you to go to Catania. Trouble brews there that Earth says will need your talents to turn." She sent him an unhappy frown remembering the other part of the message. "Earth says it will not be safe for me to return to Catania with you. I must accompany Nairin back to Bargia. Gaelen will need my opinion on the situation in Lieth and Mama needs me. It seems we are each needed in different directions."

"I knew much of that from the feeling I have. Is there no more?"

"No, Merrist, Earth does not always tell me everything, and even she sometimes does not know what lies ahead. That is what makes our work so frightening. But Earth says she will guide us and we will know what to do. Still, it does not make my worry go away. And you must stay strong and not sway from the tasks you encounter. That is the most important. We both must. Oh, I wish we did not have to separate."

Merrist thought that over, not very encouraged. He wanted to know more. Finally, he looked back at Liannis. "Yes, I see that this is how it has been for you all along. Did Earth have anything more for you?"

"Only that I must accompany Nairin back to Bargia and see Mama on my return. She did not say what that meant. But she did tell me that Mama is no worse than when we left Bargia; that she waits for me."

"I see." Merrist swallowed another hunk of bread, wrapped the rest of the food in the linen it was served on, gulped a mug of tea, wiped his mouth on his sleeve and came to stand by the bed. "Liannis, I must leave … now. I can delay no longer. The urge is becoming painful."

Liannis rose and allowed herself be enveloped in his firm embrace, trying to let it calm her, with little success. "I know."

"Do you also know how hard it is to leave you?"

"Yes, but we have no choice. Be strong, Merrist, and please come back to me whole."

He gave her another squeeze and, grabbing the bundle, hurried out the door, afraid he would not be able to if he stayed any longer. He left the door open and glanced back to see Liannis hug herself, a worried look on her pale face. He gave her one last wave and turned the corner where he could no longer see her. Before full light he had already left the city gates.

40

BACK TO BARGIA

Nairin spent two more days in Lieth, allowing herself to be seen and spoken to. At no point, even when given positive encouragement, did she admit to her plans for a regency. And that was in spite of the lack of open opposition after that first encounter. The majority of the people had seemed mostly curious and showed no animosity. Rather, they had treated her with deference.

On the fourth day, after breaking fast in the great hall with a number of the citizens, she, and those with her, left Lieth for Bargia.

All, that is, except for Merrist. Liannis explained that Earth had called Merrist away and Nairin said no more about it.

Liannis checked each night on Merrist's aura and found no change. While she did not have the ability to 'see' others as a scene, she could seek out people she knew well, or loved, and know their state of mind or health by the colour of the aura they wore in her sight. So far she saw nothing had befallen Merrist that would affect his aura. She took some comfort in that. He was safe.

On the journey, Liannis had time to think about the changes in Nairin. She had no doubt that Nairin's resolve to return and set up a regency for Wartin had become stronger. She did not need her special abilities to see that. So she thought about what to say to Gaelen about it on her return. Would she recommend that Gaelen support her claim? What suggestions would she have for Gaelen as to what form that support should take?

Nairin said little after they left Lieth but she held her head high as she rode and kept her face impassive.

On the third day, when Liannis had sorted out her own feelings and observations, she approached Nairin where she rode a little apart, keeping her voice low so they would not be overheard.

"My lady, Lord Gaelen will ask me for my opinions on our return. Before I speak with him and his advisors I would like to hear from you. Have you made a decision about requesting a regency on Wartin's behalf?"

Nairin gave her a knowing smile. "Need you ask?"

"I think I know what you wish but I must have it directly from you, my lady."

Nairin gave her a curt nod. "Then, for your ears only, I will confirm that I believe Wartin must have his birthright. And not only because it is his right, but now that I have seen Lieth again with my own eyes I see that my people need it as well." She turned to hold Liannis with a direct gaze. "You saw how almost all of the people acted in my presence. They want me there. They accept it as what ought to be. They suffer from lack of clear government and look to me with hope that I will bring back an order they recognize."

Liannis did not feel quite so strongly about that but she did understand that something was missing in Lieth that was more than buildings and food. While Gaelen had provided men to keep order, and direct much of the reconstruction and recovery, no clear leaders had emerged. No one person had shown the strength and ability to rule. The task had been too great and the losses too numerous. Gaelen's men still gave direction to much that served as leadership in taking Lieth back from disaster. The people followed them out of what looked like habit. Liannis knew that Gaelen had hoped a more solid leadership would have arisen naturally by now. Since it had not, it did seem that Nairin might be able to accomplish a smooth transition back.

As if reading Liannis's thoughts Nairin spoke again. "The people long for strong leadership. I believe I can provide that. Wartin is only just turning ten years old. He cannot rule in his own right until he is nineteen. That gives me almost ten years to prepare Lieth, and to groom him into the kind of leader his father failed to be. Merlost was a good man, a good father and a good husband, but he lacked the traits of a ruler. Rellnost did not have those traits either, poor lad. Perhaps his death will have meaning if Wartin proves to be the lord that his father could not be. Wartin shows all the signs that he has what is necessary."

"All you say is so, my lady. Wartin is a fine lad who shows signs of being strong, steady and intelligent. He is well loved by the other students and has shown leadership in his studies."

"Then may I rely on your support when I tell Lord Gaelen?"

"There are many things to consider, my lady. The challenges of leading Lieth into a full recovery are still immense. They will not be met by the promise of Wartin's abilities alone."

131

Nairin drew herself up and her attitude cooled. "I see."

Liannis allowed Cloud to widen the space between their horses. For the moment nothing more could be said.

41

TROUBLE

Unlike Liannis, Merrist did not have the ability to check on auras to determine how others were faring. This left him preoccupied with worrying about her as he made his way to Catania. Yet, in spite of his impaired vigilance for his own safety the first four days of his journey remained uneventful.

Since he already knew from Liannis's prior vision that Grund had been sprung from prison and would likely be doing all he could to create distrust and dissent, Merrist took the precaution of entering Catania from the north gate, a lesser used one than the one they had left by. He planned to make his way secretly to the castle to seek out Brynnell and Lionn to find out what he could. He still had no idea why Earth had called him back to Catania but he did sense that he would not be welcomed by all, after the hasty departure they and Lionn had made only a short time ago.

Choosing a less important gate proved to be no help at all. A man with a wooden leg is an unusual sight, one that does not go unnoticed. Perhaps if he had entered by the main gate the guards there would have escorted him to the castle. It occurred to Merrist that he might have drawn less attention had he removed his leg and stored it in one of the panniers. Men who had lost a leg usually used crutches. But hindsight is useful only for self-recrimination, which is to say, not at all. That thought almost made him chuckle.

Merrist had not even reached the stables, located at the north end of the city, before he had a group of whispering children following him from a 'safe' distance. They remained outside as the stables were forbidden to them. A stable hand who came to greet him glowered wordlessly as he accepted Warrior's reins to lead him inside. The man's attitude made Merrist want to see that Warrior was well looked after so he followed him into the stables. Before his eyes could adjust to the dim light inside rough hands grabbed him from behind, pinning his arms behind his back. At the same time a third man relieved him of his sword belt and dagger. He had time to shout only once before he found a dirty rag stuffed into his mouth. No one came to his rescue.

The men carried him by the arms and legs, unseen by anyone, out the back of the stables to a shed close by. Struggling only served to make the men hold tighter. When his wooden leg twisted out of position and threatened to break, he ceased trying to escape. Soon they had him neatly trussed and gagged.

"Th' master 'as bin waitin' fer ye."

The speaker stood limned in the doorway by the afternoon light. Merrist knew he would not recognize him again, even if he saw him. He might know the voice, though. It held a tone of cruelty that raised the hair on the nape of his neck. But the man said no more, and Merrist was left in the dark when the door shut and blocked the light. He heard the bar slide into place.

Merrist spent the next spans listening to the rumbling of his stomach and wondering how badly his leg had been injured. It throbbed and every movement made him wince. But he determined that it was not broken and decided it would heal on its own.

A few spans later the door flew open and Merrist found himself blinded by the light from a torch. Before he recovered he felt a sack being shoved over his head and was hauled roughly to his feet. The same voice from before growled next to his ear, "Th' master be waitin' fer ye. Come nice 'n quiet, or I hev te conk' ye". He, and another man, half shoved, half carried him until they lifted him and threw him onto the bed of what must be a narrow wagon. Merrist could feel both sides when he rolled onto his back.

"Keep still … or not, an' gimme th' pleasure of shuttin' ye up".

Merrist could almost hear glee in the fellow's voice and decided it would not be in his best interest to try to attract attention. He needed his wits about him. While the sack prevented him from seeing where they went, he could tell by the sounds and the time it took that they left the city through the same gate through which he had entered and travelled down a side path that veered to the right soon after they left the gate behind.

The two men who had come for him spoke not a word, in spite of sitting thigh by thigh on the narrow bench Merrist knew would be at the front of the wagon.

Merrist thought it must have taken about a span before they reached their destination outside the city. He did not know where he was but had no trouble identifying the voice of the man who greeted his captors.

Strennock!

"Throw him in with the others. Let him learn what happens to traitors and false seers. Oh," Strennock's voice took on a cruel note, "and remove his wooden peg. Let him grow a new leg if he's so powerful a healer. Throw it in the hall outside the cells where he can call to it. Mayhap we will use it for firewood."

That brought a conspiratorial rumble of laughter from his companions. It also brought on the first real fear in Merrist. The thought of them burning his leg, rendering him unable to walk until he could fashion a new one, filled him with dread. Strennock had found the one thing he could effectively threaten Merrist with. It took all of his will not to try to cry out and beg them to reconsider. Instead, he dug his fingernails into the palms of his hands to distract himself with pain.

Merrist felt himself lifted again and dragged a short distance away, heard a heavy door open, and he was dragged into what must be the hallway Strennock mentioned. There he was shoved to the floor where someone relieved him of his leg. The man threw it against a wall where it landed with a sickening thud that made Merrist jerk as if shot. All his attention stayed focused on that sound. *Had he heard a crack? Was his leg still whole?* He could not tell.

Merrist heard another door unlock, was lifted again and thrown bodily through the door to fall face first onto the floor. The sack over his head prevented a broken nose, though he knew he had lost some skin from his left cheek. Before he could roll over he heard the door clang once more and a bar slide into place to lock it. Now he was bound, gagged, blind and legless.

He fought down the panic that threatened to rob him of his reason. He tried to recall the short period of training he had received as a soldier before he lost his leg. Breathe. Yes, that was the first thing to do. Merrist slowed his breathing and concentrated on the sounds in the room. There! A shuffle … and breathing that did not belong to him. He was not alone. He tried to make a sound around the gag that he hoped would be understood as a plea for help. That was, if the other person could help. He might be tied and hooded, too. He squirmed around until he could lever himself to sitting and listened again.

More shuffling and grunts of pain.

Then hands searching him. "Keep still."

135

The hands found the knot that held his hood in place and after some fumbling it lifted off his head and Merrist felt cooler air on his face. But he still could see nothing. The cell had no windows and no light had been left to see by. The darkness was complete. He felt his gag being removed before the hands felt for his wrists and began to untie them.

"Where are we?"

"Quiet. They may be lis'nin".

Merrist lowered his voice to a whisper. "Thank you." His hands felt a surge of fire as circulation returned. He tried to rub them together but could only make a clumsy effort for several moments. He repeated his question in a whisper. "Do you know where we are?"

"Old lord's summer house. This be 'is dungeon." The man's hoarse response did not hide his obvious pain. "Who be you?"

"I am Merrist. Who are you? Why are you here?"

"Whilsh. Worked the stables. Tried t' stop Grund from takin' th' place over."

"You are in pain. Did Strennock do that to you?"

"Hamstrung when I tried t' run." The man's low voice lost all feeling. "Laughed. Said I be never runnin' again. Shoulda killed me. Better off dead."

"Are there others here?"

"Three, nex' cell."

"We need a plan. Let me think."

The only response was a dull, disbelieving grunt.

136

42

OH, EARTH!

The day before the party was due to arrive back in Bargia Liannis grew uneasy. Not wanting to make conversation she held back behind the rest. She ignored Cloud's efforts to engage her by complaining. The apples had run out so she had no more for her. Kira rode on her shoulder, on the perch her father had made for that purpose, but Liannis seemed unaware of her presence as well.

Although Liannis usually reserved checking for Merrist's aura until she settled for the night and would not be observed, today she could not resist. She stopped Cloud and told her to stand still. No one turned back to see that she no longer followed them, so Liannis closed her eyes and sent out her senses to search for Merrist. What she saw shook her. Merrist's aura was normally a cool blue, calm and even. The last days it had been shot through with bits of red and orange, denoting anxiety, which she put down to worry over not being with her. Even so, Liannis had known he was still safe.

Not so this time. She had no problem locating Merrist but hardly recognized the change from the cool blue she expected. Not only did it show many more shots of orange and red, she also saw streaks of black, which told her that he faced fear and pain. A grey pall hung over his entire aura, telling Liannis that Merrist must be either ill or very fatigued.

"No!"

No one ahead turned back. She was too far behind for them to hear. Only Kira responded by nuzzling her ear and uttering a low 'chirrrr' as if to comfort her.

That brought Liannis back to awareness. When she saw how far behind she was she urged Cloud to catch up. The party had just stopped to make camp for the night and attend to cooking their evening meal. No one seemed to notice Liannis's distressed withdrawal. As soon as she could get a bowl of stew from the pot she removed herself as far away as she could and lay out her blankets to sit on.

Not until Cloud nipped her shoulder did she realise she had blocked out Cloud's mind-speak. *Hungry,* came the insistent prompt.

I am sorry, Cloud. Something has happened to Merrist. I am so worried. Go and forage.

Hmph, came the indignant retort before Cloud moved away to a nearby patch of grass.

Kira, little one, you may hunt, now.

Kira, seeming to sense that all was not well, fluttered about Liannis's head for a bit then finally flew off high into the sky to search for unsuspecting mice.

Liannis did not touch her stew, or the mug of tea that sat beside her. As soon as Cloud and Kira had gone she fell into a deep sleep, falling over onto her side.

***

Merrist lay on the floor of a windowless chamber in complete darkness. Yet Liannis could see clearly. The thin straw that served to cover the floor crawled with vermin. He was not wearing his wooden leg. Where was it? There, hanging from a peg in the wall outside what she now knew had to be a cell. The sight made Liannis's chest clench in fear. With neither his leg nor a weapon he would be helpless and unable to escape.

The man on the floor next to him looked near death. She could hear a moan of pain escape his lips. He appeared to be delirious. Not a man he would be able to call on for help.

Merrist, too, lay inert. Had he been injured? Or was he asleep? She could not see blood on him and his breathing appeared steady. He must be asleep, then. That gave her a small measure of comfort. Then he seemed to look straight at her. "Liannis." He must have been dreaming because he let out a great sigh and let his head fall to the side, eyes closed.

***

Cloud's wet nose, whuffling against her left cheek, brought Liannis to groggy wakefulness. Kira hopped from foot to foot in front of her face, emitting worried chirrups.

Liannis's mouth felt like dry linen. When she tried to say "Water" only a croak came out. She looked around dazedly for Merrist.

138

With a sickening lurch the memory of her dream surged back. Merrist was not with her. He was in danger.

When she tried to raise herself to sitting she almost lost consciousness again with the throbbing pain in her head that assaulted her. She squeezed her eyes shut and braced her hands on the ground to prevent falling over. When the spinning subsided she cracked her eyes open and looked around until she spotted the mug of tea she had set there before she fell into the vision. Taking great care not to move too quickly and increase the pain in her head, she slid over until she could reach it. Her hands shook with the effort of putting the mug to her lips. The tea had grown cold but it was wet and she needed to drink.

She lowered the empty mug to the ground and wrapped her arms around her knees, resting her head on them.

The dream. What did it tell her? … Merrist was alive, mostly unhurt. She tried to calm herself with that. She pushed the fear for him about not having his leg, away. It helped … a little. When the tea settled and her head stopped spinning she made herself reach for the bowl of cold, congealed stew and eat it, knowing that unless she did she would not be able to stand or even think properly. She barely tasted it.

By the time she set the bowl back down the first streaks of pink showed on the horizon. Soon Nairin's party would wake and begin heating the morning porridge. But Liannis need not be there to assist. She lay back down and fell into a fitful doze until she heard her name called.

Nairin's attendant approached with a bowl and a mug. "It is time to break your fast. Here. I have brought your tea and porridge." She handed them to Liannis with a doubtful, somewhat fearful expression, and hurried away again as soon as Liannis had taken them from her.

The hot food and tea helped Liannis regain some strength. Summoning Cloud with mind-speak, she rose, took her bowls and mugs to the campsite, and made ready to ride.

43

WHAT NOW?

When Merrist was wakened by the sound of a door opening and a pale light filtering into his cell, he knew he must have dozed off. The urgency of his situation brought his wits back instantly. He took advantage of the light to survey the cell, the door and his cell-mate. That poor man lay unresponsive. Merrist hoped he had not died as he slept.

"Grub." A rough fellow, with a grey speckled beard, unbarred the cell door and shoved a bowl and a bucket of what Merrist hoped was water into the cell, then pulled the door shut and barred it. When the man left the building he did not shut the outer door again, so some light filtered inside.

That was just enough for Merrist to see his leg, now hung by its straps from a peg in the wall out in the hallway. In the dim light coming through the small barred window of his cell door Merrist thought it looked intact. He allowed himself a sigh of relief and turned his attention to the bowl and bucket. He had not eaten or drunk anything for almost an entire day and felt weak from thirst and hunger. As he drank his fill of the water, which he was pleased to discover was fresh and cool, he eyed the man next to him. He was breathing, at least.

Merrist set aside the water and ate his half of the stale bread and hard cheese. At least it was filling. It seemed they did not mean to starve their prisoners. His hunger somewhat assuaged, Merrist sidled over to his cell-mate and began to examine the man's leg. It burned to the touch, full of festering. Merrist knew if he did not heal it soon the man would die of the fever that even now kept him from waking. He did not have much time. But Merrist also knew he had to keep his head or he would have no strength to defend himself, or even to eat and drink, after a healing.

Still, he was a healer and could not let the man die. And he might need the man's assistance later if he wanted to escape. By the time he had thought all this through he had already begun sending healing energy into the man's leg to remove the festering and the pain. When he sensed that the wound was clean, and the man pain-free, he forced himself to stop. But he knew that, given time and energy, he could heal the man completely and help him walk again. Just not yet. He needed to rest.

The man groaned and opened his eyes before Merrist finally removed his hands. "Wha?"

Merrist reached for the bucket and held it so the man could drink, which he did with great gulps until Merrist pulled the bucket away and took another long draught himself, noting when he stopped that there was not much left. "Can you eat?" Merrist pulled the bowl within the man's reach. "I'll help you." He broke off a chunk of bread and dipped it into the water to soften it. "Here."

The man managed three bites, then lowered his head to the floor and tuned away. "No more."

"Are you in pain?"

At that the man turned back to him, a slow look of surprise crossing his face. "Nah, it be gone."

"Good, I have healed the wound and removed the pain. You will regain your strength, now."

The look of surprise turned to awe, then puzzlement and lastly, disbelief. "Tha' be na' possible."

"Yet, it is so." Merrist waited for that to sink in then added, "I am a healer. I have examined your wound and I can restore your leg so you will walk again."

The man roused himself so that he could reach his wound and began to probe it with great care, sending Merrist suspicious glances several times as he did so. "Where be th' cut?"

"I healed it."

The man pulled up the blood crusted leg of his trousers so that he could examine his leg more closely. Finding no cut and not even a scab he lowered himself back down, his energy spent, and gave Merrist a long, probing look. "You ha' done this?"

"Yes."

"An' ye say ye c'n make me walk?"

"I can, though it will be difficult."

"Wha' sort o' magic be this? Be it ev'l?"

"No, it is a gift from Earth. She has made me a healer."

The man looked at Merrist again, as though trying to make up his mind. After several moments he said, "Then make me walk. If ye' be false I lose nought."

"I will, but I must ask something in return."

When the man did not answer, his face darkening again with suspicion, Merrist added. "When I heal it weakens me. I need food and drink. Will you make certain that I drink the rest of the water and eat some of that bread and cheese?"

The man looked at the bowl. "I c'n do tha'. I dinna wan' it."

Merrist wasted no more time, not knowing when their captors would return. He wrapped his hands around the man's leg and closed his eyes. First making certain no festering lingered, he explored the damage. There! He could feel the first severed tendon. He willed it to stretch until it met its counterpart and knit the ends together. Time lost all meaning. He found the second one, coaxing it back into position and mended it in the same way. Strengthening the attached muscles came last. It felt like a web of warmth flowed from his fingertips and wrapped itself around the injury, helping it resume its proper shape and function, coating it with strength.

Merrist realised he must have lost consciousness, for when he came to he found his head cradled in the man's hand and felt the bucket of water tipping to his lips. He greedily drank all of the water that remained. When he could speak he asked, "Your leg?"

"Look." The man held up his injured leg and bent it back and forth to show that he had control of it."

At that moment they heard footsteps crunching the gravel, approaching the building. "Shhhh, lie down. Don't let them know." Merrist grabbed a chunk of cheese and lay down, motioning the other man to do the same.

It took a moment for the man to understand but he lay down and went still just before the cell door opened again. It was a different fellow, this time, who said nothing, just reached in and retrieved the bowl and bucket, then left again, closing and barring the cell. On the way out, he uttered a cruel chuckle and swatted Merrist's leg to send it swinging and clacking against the stone wall. At the outer door he paused, seemed about to shut them in the dark, then gave another chuckle and left the door open. Merrist assumed it was to taunt him with the sight of his unreachable leg.

When their jailor was out of earshot Merrist whispered, "I am called Merrist. What is your name, sir?"

"Whilsh."

"Whilsh, try to stand. Let me see how strong your leg is."

After a moment's hesitation Whilsh rolled to his hands and knees and, with great care, levered himself to his feet, holding his hands out for balance. Once there, he put his weight onto his injured leg and found it held him up. With each movement the awe on his face grew. When he succeeded in taking two small steps he turned to Merrist. He opened his mouth as if to say something, then stopped and stared at Merrist, his lower jaw slack. He tried a few more steps, reaching the wall and placing one hand on it for support. When he turned back to Merrist a slow grin wreathed his face. "I be walkin'. Ye healed me."

Merrist had a piece of cheese in his mouth that he was doing his best to wet with saliva so he could chew it, so he merely smiled and nodded. When he could speak again he said in a low voice, "Whilsh, they must not find out. We must make a plan to escape. I will need your help. And I need my wooden leg to walk. We must get it back."

The wonder on Whilsh's face faded into resolve. "I be yer man."

"Good. Now I need to sleep or I will be useless. Wake me when you hear someone come back."

"They be bringin' more food and water jus' afore dark, then come back fer th' bowl an' bucket."

"Good, let me sleep until then. I will need more food and drink to regain my strength."

"Ye kin ha' mine."

"Thank you. Some perhaps, but you will need to eat to regain your strength, too. We will see."

With that Merrist turned onto his side and knew no more until he felt someone shake his shoulder.

44

HOME

The party from Lieth arrived home in Bargia on the sixth day with a few spans to spare before supper.

Despite her anxiety for Merrist, Liannis's first thought, after handing Cloud over to the groom, was for her mother, Brensa. She hurried up the grand stair to the lord's chambers where Marja had told her she would find her.

Lady Marja, already prepared for their arrival by the messenger sent ahead, had ordered a bath prepared in Liannis's inner chamber and food brought there. That could wait.

Brensa greeted her with a tentative smile. "Liannis, Marja told me you had returned safely." She patted the seat next to her. "Come, sit. Tell me all your news."

Liannis embraced her mother before sitting down. "Mama, it is good to see you looking better."

"Knowing you would return has helped." Brensa's eyes narrowed as they scanned Liannis with growing interest. Her hand reached out and came to rest on Liannis's belly. "What is this wonder?"

Liannis said nothing, allowing her mother to concentrate. Brensa had a small healing talent and so could sense the babe within her. She watched her mother's face transform until she looked up and gave Liannis the first genuine smile since she had returned from her winter-long absence.

"When you said Earth had made great changes and there would be a babe I did not dream she would make me a grandmother so soon."

"Yes, Mama, and she will be a seer."

Brensa's eyes grew soft with a far-away look. "I remember when you announced to Klast that you would belong with us. You told him your name. I shall never forget the wonder of the moment he shared that vision with me." She turned back to Liannis. "Has she told you her name?"

Liannis started the shake her head but stopped. Something told her to take her mother's hand and hold it to her belly again. "Close your eyes, Mama." She closed her own as well. A warm light bathed them both. Liannis sensed she shared this vision with

144

her mother. They looked deep into a cocoon of soft red. There, a perfect, tiny babe regarded them with ancient understanding.

Now, the new child spoke to them through their minds. "I am Ayliss." Her smile enveloped them both in perfect love. Long after the vision faded, Liannis could still feel the warmth of that look.

"Ayliss … Ayliss." Brensa breathed the name twice before collecting herself back to awareness. "Now I know I must stay until this child is born. Klast will want me to tell him all about it. I wonder if he knows he will have a grandchild."

A lump formed in Liannis's throat and she had to swallow before she could respond. "I do not know Mama, but I am glad you will not leave me yet."

Sitting straighter as though she had just remembered something important, Brensa asked, "Where is Merrist?"

"Earth called him to Catania, Mama."

"But surely he ought to be with you during this time?"

"He is needed there, Mama. He cannot always be beside me. He, too, has his duty to Earth. He is needed in Catania. But it is good to know you will still be with me when he cannot."

Liannis watched her mother think that over. She seemed to grow taller, her shoulders straightened, and her expression took on a new resolve. Liannis thought it best not to reveal the danger Merrist was in. There would be time for that when they shared their supper with Marja and Gaelen. Liannis knew Lionn would not be there, as he had also been sent back to Catania.

Brensa reached out and patted her hand. "We must go home."

When Brensa did not elaborate Liannis understood 'home' to mean the cabin she had grown up in. She did not agree that this would be an advisable thing to do, with Brensa so fragile, but felt it best not to press her. Instead they chatted over tea.

"Mama, I need a bath before supper." Liannis rose and kissed her mother's cheek. "I will share all my other news when everyone gathers back here to eat."

The bath and light meal refreshed Liannis, so that even after she had told her friends everything she knew she had no desire to return to her lonely chamber. They all talked into the evening, long after Liannis had urged her mother to go to bed and tucked her in. She had noticed Brensa nod off in her chair and

145

knew she needed rest. She also returned because she wanted some time to speak more frankly with Gaelen and Marja about Nairin's decision and Merrist's predicament. She wanted to protect her sensitive mother from her anxiety.

"So you have learned no more about Merrist since your vision almost two full days ago?" Gaelen's brow knit with concern. "Have you checked for Lionn? Is he safe?"

"He was safe two days ago. I can look for him now, if you wish."

"Oh, please do." Marja clenched her hands together and tucked them into the fold of her skirt. Liannis had seen them tremble before she hid them.

"Yes, if you can do so." Gaelen remained calmer, though Liannis could sense his deep concern s well.

Liannis made herself relax into the chair and closed her eyes, sending out her senses. She soon found Lionn's aura. It showed no signs of distress. Indeed, she saw sparks of excitement and ... was that arousal? Did he have a woman with him?

She pulled herself back to awareness in the chamber and gratefully accepted the mug of tea with honey Marja handed her. "He appears safe, my lord." She almost blurted out her suspicions but stopped herself just in time. There was no reason to alarm Gaelen and Marja with no evidence that Lionn acted inappropriately. She decided to trust that the lesson learned from his encounter with the traitor Vernia, two years ago would have made him cautious of liaisons with young maids. "Lionn is well."

Marja's shoulders relaxed.

"Do you have strength left to look for Merrist?" Gaelen asked. "I want to know if I must send troops to Catania. If Merrist is captured, can you tell by whom and if he has escaped?"

"I can see how he fares, but unless Earth offers me another dream that is all I will know. I fear to sleep lest I find he is in even more danger."

Gaelen nodded. "That will be better than nothing."

Liannis closed her eyes once more. When she found Merrist's aura he appeared no worse than the last time. If anything he seemed less fearful, though the grey pall still hung over his usual blue. There was nothing more she could glean.

Liannis opened her eyes and shook her head at Gaelen. "I am sorry, my lord. I see no change. He seems not to be moving and his aura looks weakened. I hope it is only from fatigue and not injury or illness. I hope he is merely asleep." She thought about that for a moment and added, "The last time, I sensed another with him. Perhaps the fatigue is from a healing he has done."

The thought did nothing to alleviate her concern. A look at Gaelen and Marja told her it had not eased theirs either.

"Liannis, we have taxed you too far. Go to your chamber and sleep. We will speak again in the morning." Gaelen rose and offered her a hand. "Do you need someone to accompany you, or have you enough strength left?"

Liannis stood. "I will manage." Her last thought as she left for her chamber was that she had not told them of the coming babe. Ah, well, time enough for that when they broke their fast in the morning. She placed a protective hand on her belly and sent a plea to Earth to keep all of them safe.

45

ESCAPE

For the next two days the two prisoners kept still while Merrist learned the rhythms of the day; when meals came, who brought them, when the door would be left open for light.

Whilsh's devotion to Merrist grew as the strength in his leg returned and he found himself able to walk with greater ease. Merrist could ask anything and the man would obey without question.

Whilsh's awe made Merrist uncomfortable but he did not try to discourage it, as he might need the man's loyalty at some point. His testimonials would support Merrist's claims and increase doubt about Merrist among their enemies.

By the third morning Merrist had devised a plan.

That evening, when the bar slid back from the outer door, Whilsh stood ready, waiting beside the door to their cell.

As usual, the unsuspecting guard did not bother to search the cell to determine if the two prisoners still lay inert on the floor. He shoved the wooden bucket of water in first before reaching back to pick up the bowl of bread and cheese. When his head and shoulders came back through the low doorway, along with the bowl of food, Whilsh made his move.

He had grabbed the bucket of water while the guard's back was turned and before the man could even look up the bucket came down full force against the side of his head, sending the water flying out onto the floor and wall as it emptied. The man uttered a soft "oof", and crumpled, inert, halfway into the cell.

Merrist gagged him with a rag he had torn from his shirt. The two dragged the man into the cell, tied him with the ropes from Merrist's earlier bindings, which their enemies had neglected to retrieve, and settled him against the wall. While Merrist bound the man, Whilsh unhooked Merrist's leg from the peg in the wall and handed it back.

Merrist wasted no time strapping it on. He did not bother to check to see if it was whole. They needed to get as far away as possible as quickly as possible. It would not be long before someone came to see why their jailor had not returned. While Merrist suspected that discipline was lax, he did not delude himself into thinking someone would not notice when the guard did not come back.

On the way out Merrist paused by the other cell only long enough to pull back the bar and unlock it. "Escape if you can," he told them in a loud whisper.

Neither of them had any weapons, but on the way out Merrist spotted a hammer and a pry bar on the floor, inside the door to the building. He handed the hammer to Whilsh and kept the iron bar for himself. The light had begun to wane but they would still be able to see for the next half span. That presented the greatest danger. If they were missed too soon they would be hard-pressed to find cover and hide. Merrist had no illusions about what their captors would do if they were retaken.

Merrist had learned the layout of the manor and outbuildings from Whilsh. The manor lay above the prison to their left, the stable below and to their right. A clear expanse lay between their prison and the stables. This clear space would present the greatest danger, at least until they made it to the stable, as the view from the manor had no obstructions and there was only one lone tree to hide behind. He decided their best chance for escape lay in making a dash for the stable and hiding there under the bedding for the horses. They could wait there until either darkness hid them, or their captors spread out in search of them so they could be dealt with one at a time. And they needed mounts if they were to put any distance between them and their enemies and those could only be found in the stable. As well, two fewer horses for their enemies meant less chance of recapture.

The raucous sounds coming from the manor house, of rough men enjoying too much ale, covered them as they hurried, unseen, to the stables, darting from a wagon, carelessly left there, to tree and behind a pile of manure.

It took a moment for Merrist's eyes to adjust to the dimness in the stable, now in almost total darkness. But his quick survey confirmed what Whilsh had told him. The horses still wore their bridles. Even their saddles had not been removed. Such cavalier care of animals made Merrist hiss in anger, though another part of him was grateful as he knew this would make their escape easier.

Merrist revised the plan of action. As soon as he saw the horses he abandoned the idea of hiding in the straw.

149

"Which ones?" Merrist whispered to Whilsh.

"Th' two at th' far end."

The plan was that as long as they did not hear sounds of pursuit, they would try to remove as many of the saddles as possible from the horses they did not plan to ride. This would increase their lead time. They managed to yank off five before they heard shouting. That left only the two they had chosen for themselves and one other.

"Get on your horse and keep as low as you can. Be ready to run." They had left the gates to the two stalls unlatched so their mounts could push them open with their chests. The other stalls remained latched, another deterrent to their pursuers. Merrist knew each moment counted.

"Shhh. Wait. When I say 'run' get out as fast as you can and head for the city. I will be right behind you."

A brief probing of the saddle had told Merrist that a dagger had been left stuck into a seam where the stitching had broken or been cut, another sign of sloth that turned into a stroke of luck. He sent a silent thank you to Earth. That was all he had time he had.

A glance at the stable doors showed two men limned in the waning light.

"Run!"

Whilsh sprang out of the stall and knocked over one of the men with his horse as he leapt past. Merrist caught the other on the head with his iron bar, wincing at the thought that he might have killed him, and followed Whilsh close behind.

The first man had regained his feet and ran out of the stable after them, shouting to alert the others.

To Merrist's great relief the gate to the property had not been closed, more evidence of laxity for which he felt grateful. By the time their pursuers had saddled and followed, full darkness covered them.

"Is there cover ahead?" Merrist called out to Whilsh.

"Copse on th' lef'. No' far."

"Make for it. We will need to hide or they will follow the sounds of our horses. We cannot stay on the main trail."

A grunt told him that Whilsh understood. A few moments later Merrist saw a swath of black just a shade darker than the open trail and knew it for the copse. He hoped it was large enough to provide cover.

They melted into the blackness amid the trees. "Keep still", Merrist whispered when they had moved deeper in.

Four horses thundered past. "Further in. Quick!" Merrist urged. "They will return soon when they do not catch us. They will know we are here."

As Whilsh followed him, Merrist asked, "Is there another way to the city? Can we stay hidden until we are closer?"

That elicited a low chuckle from Whilsh. "Dinna fear. I ken this land. There be ways."

The sounds of returning horses cut off further conversation. Merrist could hear men talking but they had gone far enough into the woods that he could not make out what they were saying. "Shhhh." He felt they ought to wait for dawn to move but Whilsh had other ideas.

"Foller me."

Whilsh did not wait for Merrist to respond but began to make his way with apparent confidence in the direction of Catania City, following some trail only he or his horse seemed able to see. Merrist began to protest, then thought the better of it and gave his mount its head. His horse seemed to know what to do.

46

DECISIONS

Liannis slept fitfully and woke early. Knowing that Gaelen always rose before the others she made her way to the small chamber he used when he did not want to disturb Marja and wanted to think. Marja often slept later than he did.

"My lord."

"Liannis, please, be seated."

"I thought I might find you already awake." She took the mug of tea he handed her as she sat opposite him. "We did not have time to discuss how you wish to proceed with Nairin's plan to request a regency for Wartin."

"Yes. Lieth needs to become separate from Bargia again. If not with a regency, then we must find another way. It is not possible to rule Lieth well when I also rule Bargia. I am not getting younger and while Lionn has learned a great deal, I do not think he is ready for the burden of two, possibly three demesnes, if we include Catania. That situation is far from settled as well."

"Indeed, I think the greater danger lies in Catania."

Gaelen pinched the bridge of his nose, sighing, and then looked back at Liannis. "It would seem so, from what you have told me. But what do you sense of the feeling in Lieth toward Nairin? Will they accept her as regent for Wartin? For that matter, will they accept Wartin, since his father lacked the strength to rule well?"

"Lieth is still far from recovered from the damage done by the great fire and rift. They have no thoughts of rebellion with so much work left to do to make their city prosper again. While there is a group of dissenters, I think the majority of the people want guidance and leadership. Your men have done much, but they are not 'of Lieth'. The people still see them as temporary, which is as it should be. Nairin made a strong impression on them. I think they will accept her. But I have some concern about her change in attitude. She is not the same woman we gave asylum to when her husband was ousted by the traitor, Garneth. I have not been able to determine if the change will make her a stronger, better ruler, or if she will use it for the wrong ends."

152

"That is a concern of mine, as well. I must be certain that she will remain loyal to her oath of alliance with Bargia, and that she will teach Wartin to do so as well."

"How does Wartin in his studies? He appears much different from his brother, Rellnost. Does that remain so?"

"Yes, he studies hard and shows promise as a strategist." Gaelen grew thoughtful. "I think I will propose to the council that we accept Nairin's decision on the condition that Wartin continue to study and train here until he reaches his majority. He must continue to return here for the winters until he is of age, spending only two moons each summer in Lieth."

"If Nairin agrees."

"Do you think she will refuse?"

"Perhaps. She is protective of her children after the loss of her eldest. It will depend on how it is presented to her."

Gaelen thought for a few moments again. "I think I will have her come to the council chambers and present her with the proposal there. Until now our meetings have been private. I hope that having the weight of the council behind me will make her see that she has no other choice. If she cannot agree, we will not support her plan. In that case we will hold her to her original oath of allegiance with no claim to Lieth." He sighed again. "Though I do hope it will not come to that. Lieth has been a burden for Bargia these last two years."

"That burden will remain for a time, even if she acts as regent, for she will need our support to rebuild the city."

"Indeed, but there will be fewer decisions on our part and that support will decrease as the city recovers." He rose from his chair. "Come, let us join the ladies and break our fast."

"I do so wish Merrist were here as I have something important to tell you all. Merrist ought to share this with me but I do no know when we will all be together again and this will not wait."

Gaelen sent her a questioning look, one eyebrow raised.

Liannis shook her head. "It will wait until we are together."

"Very well, then, let us join the ladies before my curiosity gets the best of me." The jovial tone did not completely hide the hint of worry underneath.

When the two joined Marja and Brensa and sat in the lord's chambers, each   platter full of eggs, fresh aromatic rye bread, aged sheep's cheese, mugs of steaming sage tea beside them, Liannis told them of her condition and that their daughter would be a seer.

Marja responded with delight. Gaelen congratulated her warmly as well, but expressed concern over her safety.

47

RUN!

Merrist let his mount have its head. Their progress was slow in the dark. What had taken only little more than a span when he had been an unwilling passenger in the wagon, now took most of the night. Fatigue and hunger warred with the need to stay alert and think. Since Whilsh showed no inclination to talk Merrist let his mind wander to Liannis. Not feeling any particular anxiety when he did so led him to the sense that she must be safe and well. Somehow he felt that if she were in dire difficulty he would know, though he had no reason to think so.

When the first grey hint of the coming dawn filtered through the trees, he urged his horse close to Whilsh and gave a low whisper to catch his attention. "Whilsh. Hssst. Stop a moment."

Whilsh moved to the side and waited for Merrist to edge beside him on the narrow path.

"What lies ahead?" Merrist asked. "I expect an ambush. We need a plan."

Whilsh nodded sagely, as if he had also thought of that possibility. "I thin' they be waitin' fer us t' come out. They dinna need t' stay hid."

"So what will we find, when we have to come out?"

"I 'spect they be waitin' where the trees end, on the road. The city gate be 'cross a big space. I 'spect they think we be comin' out at th' trail there." Then he grinned, teeth glowing white in the pale light. "But I be takin' us 'nother way. Those men hevna bin here long 'nuff t' know all th' trails. We be comin out jes' t'other side. 'At that be giv'n us a bit t' get ahead." He grew serious again. "No' much time, min'."

"So it is open territory between the trees and the gate?"

Wilsh nodded. "We bes' run hard."

"How close are we to the gate when we leave the trees?"

"Mebbe half a quire len'th. It be a stretch."

Merrist thought about that.

It meant a mad dash being chased by men with weapons, men who would not hesitate to use them. If they made it to the gate the guards would intervene and they might be safe. If not they

155

would most certainly be killed. Yet, he could think of no other solution. If they stayed in the woods they stood a good chance of being discovered, the option they had worked so hard to avoid.

"All right. We will have to run for it. How long until we reach the edge of the trees?

"I kin almos' see it."

"Then let us run for it now. Perhaps it will give us a few moments more since they will not expect us until there is more light."

When Whilsh nodded and began to turn down the trail again Merrist asked, "Which direction do we run when we emerge?"

Whilsh pointed to the left as he urged his mount forward.

Whish was correct about where the men would be waiting. They were alert and spotted the pair as soon as they emerged from the cover of the trees.

"There! Get 'em."

"Run!"Merrist yelled as he dug his good heel hard into his mount's flanks. He could see the city gate as a dark spot in the distance and despaired of reaching it in time to draw the attention of the guards. They would not be expecting anyone so early and in such a hurry, and would likely not have the gate open yet. His only hope lay in the horse under him. Lucky for him, Whilsh had made a good choice. Merrist rode two lengths ahead of Whilsh and his mount.

Behind him he heard the clamour of pursuit. "We got 'em," reached his ears amid the thunder of hooves. He dared not look back but knew it meant their pursuers must be gaining.

As soon as he felt he might be heard by the guards at the gate he set to shouting at the top of his voice.

"Help! Open up! Help!" Hope waned when he could detect no movement at the gate. He kept shouting and spurring his horse on, hoping against hope that the men chasing him would stop rather than be discovered. Surely the guards could hear him now, and hear the approach of galloping horses as well. "Open the gate! Murder! Treason! Open then gate."

The thunder behind him told him those after him had not slowed. Just as he felt he must surely need to turn to face his enemies, or run headlong into the gate, he spotted a crack of light growing between the doors of the gate that told him he had been heard. He changed his calls to "Traitors behind us. Get them!"

As he reached the gate, still at full speed, his mount's sides heaving under him with exertion, the opening widened barely enough for him to pass through. His boot brushed one door as he passed. By the time he slowed enough to turn around he saw that the guards had reached Whilsh and were dragging him roughly off his horse. Merrist turned and shouted, "Not him! Out there! Four of them. Do not let them get away."

The guards had wasted no time calling for help. Before he could tell them who he was, six mounted soldiers galloped out of the gate. At the same instant, rough hands yanked him off his mount and held him in a vice-like grip.

It dawned on Merrist that, of course, the guards might have no idea who he was and would hold him for questioning. He did not protest, letting himself be hustled into a guardroom and quickly tied to a chair next to one in which Whilsh already sat, also bound.

Merrist's next thought was for their horses. "Guard, please make sure those horses are walked before they are stabled. They have had a hard run and need to cool down."

That brought an astonished look from their remaining guard. He had apparently not expected such care from a pair of possible traitors. He seemed to think the request over for a moment then gave a curt nod and stuck his head out the door. "Keross, those horses are spent, walk them and rub them down before you stable them."

"Thank you," Merrist said, "Now can you tell me if Lord Gaelen's son, Lionn, is in Catania? He, Brynnell and Charest will all need to be informed of our arrival. We have much to tell them regarding the traitors your fellows are after." He could hear that they had captured at least some of their prey, from the sounds of their return and the protests of those captured. He gave silent thanks to Earth that the guards had been ready with fresh horses.

The guard looked about to question him, then seemed to think the better of it and simply stood silent, waiting. By his tunic, Merrist could see that he held a low rank. Before Merrist could repeat his request another guard appeared in the doorway, one with the insignia of a higher rank stitched on his tunic.

157

This one ignored the first guard and gave Merrist a searching look, taking in his wooden leg. "I know of only one man with a wooden leg such as yours. We have been instructed to watch for you." He jerked his head at the younger guard. "Untie him. I have instructions to escort him the council chamber."

"I think my friend, Whilsh, here, ought to come as well. He has information the council will want to hear."

"As you wish."

48

COUNCIL

Liannis sat with Gaelen's advisors around the council chamber. Nairin had been escorted there and now she sat facing Gaelen from the opposite end of the table.

The Advisory Council had agreed to Gaelen's proposal regarding the splitting of Wartin's years of education between Lieth and Bargia and had suggested an additional condition. They wanted a delegation to return to Lieth, without Nairin present, with two purposes.

The proposal had come from Janest, who sat, frail and shrunken, but still keenly alert, opposite Liannis. He had sent her a huge wink as soon as he had spotted her, to let her know he was well.

The delegation's goal would be to find out as much as possible about how the people of Lieth would receive Nairin's return and the regency for Wartin. They would also consult with both the men Gaelen had sent to assist Lieth with its recovery, and with those who had come forward from among the citizens of Lieth and formed the interim government.

Gaelen agreed. "We need to know if the men who have led the governance of Lieth will be willing to follow Nairin and Wartin, or if they will resent giving back the power they have gained. Two years learning to rule themselves under difficult circumstances may make them resistant to living under the old rulership again."

Gaelen believed the main reason the new structure of government had been somewhat successful, was due to the leadership from the men he had sent from Bargia to assist. As such, they still needed outside assistance. He hoped that meant they would accept Nairin back.

Liannis agreed. "I think the people will be willing to accept Nairin's regency because their own leadership is not yet entrenched. Your men still have a great deal of influence. And the reception the citizens of Lieth gave Nairin has, for the most part, been friendly, even deferential." She explained that those who had opposed her in the beginning had also lost a good deal of their resistance, due to the strength Nairin had shown and her words to them. "The delegation will be able to get a better sense of the true attitude of the people if Nairin is not present." Liannis agreed to be part of the group sent to Lieth.

The findings of the delegation would determine what form reinstalling Nairin would take - unless the response from Lieth showed so much animosity that Bargia could not support her claim without incurring rebellion. Then Gaelen would need to abandon the plan.

Nairin had remained seated, hands carefully clasped on the table in front of her while the proposal was presented to her, face composed, betraying nothing. When they finished she rose to address Gaelen and the council, standing tall, firm, even regal. "My Lord Gaelen, gentlemen … Liannis." She paused to regard each person in turn.

Liannis had to admire the control Nairin showed. If her judgement matched her ability to hold sway in the council chamber here, as she had in Lieth, she could become a powerful ruler. She acknowledged Nairin with a small bow of her head.

"I have made my wish to return to Lieth as regent for Wartin plain to you. I will not be swayed from this. My visit to Lieth confirmed two things. Lieth needs me. She has no strong, single leader among men there who could be chosen as lord." She looked around to see if anyone, notably Liannis, would object. When no one made to speak she continued. "Secondly, the reception I received from my people left no doubt that they welcomed me back." She raised one hand and waived it dismissively. "Yes, a few dissenters made their anger plain. Yet, they had no strong leader among them. I doubt they could organise an effective opposition."

The chamber remained silent when she paused, though all eyes remained trained on her. This was her time and they would not interrupt.

Gaelen sat with his hands on the table, fingers loosely laced in front of him, leaning slightly forward. Liannis recognized this as his listening pose. Afterward, he would be able to recall every word Nairin spoke. His ability to listen and later analyze a conversation had stood him in good stead in negotiations in the past. It was one of the traits that had made him such a successful ruler.

Nairin took a deep breath before continuing. Liannis wondered if anyone else had noticed the slight tremor in her hands before she leaned forward to place them on the table in front of her, a ploy Liannis saw gave her even greater control of the chamber – and hid her tremor. No one showed any reaction.

"Let me emphasize, once more, that I value my alliance with Bargia greatly. You have my firm pledge that I will not act in any way which would put that alliance in jeopardy. Bargia has been a haven for myself and my children. I can never repay your generosity. Without your assistance I and my children would, in all likelihood, now be dead."

Nods from some of the members of the council showed they agreed. Janest gave no outward reaction, but sat attentive, listening and watching.

"Let me address each part of your proposal separately. First, I agree, with gratitude, to the offer to continue to train Wartin in Bargia, and for the opportunity for him to spend the summer months in Lieth with me until his sixteenth year. I hope we can speak about having him spend longer periods with me before that, as I will miss him. Be assured that I will not shield him from the hardships of the people in Lieth. He must learn to live with less grandeur than he sees here. And I will have him attend council meetings with me to learn how decisions are made and to see what the people need and want. He will also learn that the people cannot have everything they wish for. A ruler must know when to deny certain requests."

Her dry smile at Gaelen let Liannis know that she understood the irony of that. In light of this meeting, it had not been lost on her. Nairin was not getting everything just the way she wished it, either. "Wartin will learn that strong leaders cannot please everyone. I wish Lord Merlost had understood that better."

That brought an approving nod from Gaelen and a few others. Once more, Liannis admired her. The more she listened and watched, the more she became convinced that Nairin would succeed in ruling Lieth. Whether Wartin would show the same traits and insight would remain for the future to decide. Liannis brought her attention back to Nairin.

"Secondly, during my visit to Lieth I paid attention to how decisions were made there, who showed leadership, who showed good understanding of what needed to be done, who could bring

161

others to his side, who followed, who let the decisions rest on the men sent from Bargia."

That brought more approving glances from the council members.

Nairin's smile took on a hint of triumph as she noticed. "I have not spoken of this ere now but I have given a great deal of thought to what I saw and heard. The old council of Lieth is gone. In any case, there would not be many among them able to do the work that Lieth requires."

Liannis saw that Nairin held the rapt attention of every man around the table, now. Even Gaelen had leaned further forward and looked less relaxed.

"I know I will need a new advisory council immediately upon my return as regent." Nairin no longer showed any hesitation. Her voice had almost taken on the tone of an accomplished orator. She now stood at her full height, erect and proud, all trace of tremor gone. "I have marked the strengths and weaknesses of those in charge in Lieth. None of them are the members of the old ruling families. They are citizens who have shown ability, men who have led the recovery of the city with the kind of leadership the old way would never have allowed. The needs of Lieth are different from that of other established demesnes. The destruction from the great fire and the rift was so complete that it needs to begin anew. It requires new ideas. As a result, I have in my mind the names of some from among the men currently guiding Lieth. I will choose my council from among these."

Liannis watched Gaelen's eyes relax and the crease in his brow soften. Janest remained as alert as ever, but some of the others also relaxed.

Gaelen spoke. "My lady, I am pleased to hear it. These men have shown ability, have become accustomed to the respect and power such leadership brings. They would be loath to give it up. And from what I have learned from the delegates who went there with you, and from Liannis, there are some among them who show the traits I look for in my own council. Choosing from these men will make for a smoother transition."

Nairin looked primly satisfied. "Very well, then. I ask you to make haste with sending the new delegation. Summer is already at its peak. I would like to be back in Lieth before winter. Lieth has suffered without proper rule long enough." With a nod that almost looked triumphant she reached down, smoothed her skirts neatly under her, and resumed her seat.

Gaelen rose. "My lady, I believe we have concluded our consultation with you for now. If you would leave us, we will consult on who we shall send to Lieth."

"Thank you, my lord." Nairin rose and swept to the door Gaelen held open for her.

When he noticed that the man who had brought her had not waited to escort her back again, he asked, "May I offer you an escort back to your lodgings, my lady? It may be wise to resume that practice, as word will spread of your plans to return to Lieth. There may be those who will try to prevent you."

Nairin bowed her head at him. "Yes, thank you. I do think that may be wise. I recall past attempts on our lives."

"Lennor," Gaelen called to the one of the two guards posted down the hall outside the chamber, "See that Lady Nairin reaches her home safely."

At the guard's crisp "As you wish, my lord," Gaelen turned back and closed the door.

"Liannis, I am pleased that you are able to return to Lieth with the delegation."

Liannis heard the unspoken *are you well enough?* She knew that to remain in Bargia would not relieve her fears for Merrist, so she said. "I wish to spend a few days with my mother. After that I will be ready to return to Lieth, my lord."

"That will be fine. Do you have any suggestions as to who might best accompany you?"

They decided on sending one member of the advisory council, two heads of prominent families to see about trade, and six guards. Gaelen wanted to send more guards. Liannis understood his primary concern was for her, and not for the rest of the party. She assured him they would be safe and that a larger group might be seen as a threat more than as a friendly delegation.

49

TAKE ME HOME

"Liannis, I want to go home. The babe must be born there. I will be nearer Klast there." Brensa's voice had taken a stubborn tone.

Liannis knew Brensa would not be dissuaded. Her mother had never been truly happy at court. Truth be told, she, too, would love to go back to their secluded cabin.

When Liannis said nothing Brensa added, "It is where we both belong."

"Mama, I will agree, but I have two conditions."

Liannis watched the set of Brensa's mouth ease and her shoulders relax, though she remained alert. "What conditions?"

"Mama, you are not strong enough to live alone in the cabin. Gaelen has requested that I return to Lieth with the new delegation. That will keep me away for four or five eightdays. I ask you to remain here until I return. And whenever it is necessary for me to be away from home for more than a day or two you will come to stay here where you will be safe and looked after." When Brensa did not protest Liannis went on. "The second condition is that you must be well enough and strong enough by the time I return from Lieth to make the trip and to see to some of your own needs."

"I am already able to do that."

"Mama, you have grown weak while I was away. You must work at regaining some strength."

Brensa bridled. "I am much stronger since you came back. I am well enough."

"Mama, you will not have all prepared for you, there, such as your meals and a fire. I will have other things to do as well. I must know that if I am needed for a day or two at court you will be able to manage on your own."

Brensa grew thoughtful for a few moments, then, more quietly, said, "I will be ready."

"That is good, Mama. I, too, look forward to going back. And when Merrist returns all will be well again."

Liannis hoped, fervently, that he would return before she came back from Lieth. Perhaps he would even meet her in Lieth

164

and accompany her home. She still did not know exactly what had happened to him.

That evening, when she and Brensa took their supper with Gaelen and Marja, Brensa announced her plans to return to the cabin with Liannis when she came back from Lieth.

"But Mama must be strong enough." Liannis hurried to interject this before Marja could voice her objections. "She has promised me that she will work on regaining her strength."

Brensa glared at her, but agreed. "Of course. I know I must be able to ride."

When Brensa grew tired Liannis took her to their shared chamber, lay beside her until she slept, then slipped out to rejoin Gaelen and Marja.

Marja wasted no time broaching the subject. "Brensa is not strong enough. She cannot go back."

"I have doubts, as well, Liannis," Gaelen agreed. "Whatever led you to agree to this plan?"

"I know it looks foolish. But I have never seen Mama more determined. It also gives her a reason to push herself to regain some strength. And I agree with Mama. I also feel our daughter must be born there. There is a peace there that cannot be found at court, much as you do your best for us. Besides, Mama thinks she will be closer to Papa at the cabin."

Marja still looked worried and shook her head. "Liannis, she will not be ready. What will you tell her when you return and see that it is impossible?"

Gaelen's response was less negative. "Perhaps this will encourage her to take a more active part in her health. She is a strong-willed woman, in spite of appearances. I see a change in her already. She has purpose. This may be just what she needs."

"But ..."

"My lady, if Mama is not ready we will not go. She knows this. It was a condition of my agreement. But I believe she will be, and by then I hope Merrist will be back as well. I do not believe Earth would deny him being present for the birth of our child." Liannis spoke with more conviction than she felt.

"Yes, you will be nearer your time when you return. Harvest will be upon us, then winter." Marja spread her hands wide. "Liannis, it will be harder to send help once the snows come.

165

You will be alone at the cabin. Do you not think it best to give birth here, where you will have a midwife to hand?"

"I thank you for your concern, my lady. But Earth needs this child, and I do not think she means to leave her motherless. I will be much more at peace at the cabin. I am not afraid of the birth." That was not entirely true, but she told herself it must be so. If that changed she could act on it when the time came.

"We will send someone every other day."

"That we will, my love." Gaelen took Marja's hand and gave it a squeeze. "Do not fear. They shall have everything they need."

"Thank you. I have no doubt of it." Liannis hugged Marja, then Gaelen. "I must return to my chamber, now. Perhaps Earth will give me news of Merrist."

50

CATANIA

Merrist found some amusement in realising this was the first time his wooden leg had been an asset. The guards hustled the pair to the council chamber with alacrity. They found Lionn, Charest and Brynnell already waiting for them.

Lionn rose to greet him with an enthusiastic grip on his arm, a relieved expression on his face. "Merrist! I am so pleased to see you unhurt." He stepped back and gave Merrist a closer examination. "You are unhurt, are you not?"

Merrist grinned back. "I am well enough, Lionn. A few bruises. But I am famished. Whilsh, here, too, has had nothing to eat for a full day." He cocked his head at the food and ale waiting on the table.

Brynnell broke in. "Come. Eat. Your news can wait a few moments more." He quirked an eyebrow at Merrist. "Or am I mistaken? Do we need to act immediately?"

Merrist shook his head as he and Whilsh took chairs and sat down. "No, a span or two will make little difference, but I fear we must act soon." He piled his platter with bread, cheese and cold venison, stuffing his mouth mid-way. With his mouth full, he grabbed the mug of ale Lionn handed him and took a deep draught. Noting that Whilsh hesitated, he said, through the next bite, "Whilsh, you are among friends here. Eat. Drink."

Lionn handed Whilsh a mug of ale as well, which he took with a deferential bow of his head, mumbling a shy, "Thank ye, m'lord."

Lionn laughed. "My father is the lord, Whilsh. I am only Lionn. And as Merrist names you friend that is how you must address me."

Whilsh acknowledged this with only a quick, nervous glance, his mouth too full too speak, then cast his eyes back down to the table.

When Merrist had relayed everything that had happened to him and what he had learned of the situation in Catania, Charest turned to Whilsh.

"Whilsh, what can you tell us? Do you know how many there are? Can you remember any names you may have overheard, anything about others in league with the traitors outside of that group? Are any others in need of rescue?"

"When they came they killt my master, Pellor ... an' th'gard'ner when 'e tried to pr'tec' 'im. I dinna see, but I hear Mistress Morna and th' young girls be locked in the big house. 'Less they killt them, too. Th' stable hand, they made him work fer them, tole 'im they be killin 'is sister in th' city if he try to run." Whilsh stopped to give Brynnell a pleading look. "'E be a good man. But 'e be 'fraid. 'E be no traitor."

"We will determine that when everyone is questioned, or when the seer can truth-read them," Lionn told him. "If he acts under duress that will be considered. Go on."

"Th' cook, Tellis, and th' maid, Lua – Lua an' me, we plan t' join – they be kep' in th' house but I dinna know how they fare." Whilsh ran one hand roughly over his face in distress.

Merrist could see the man's fear when he relayed that last piece and wondered if he thought the women had been raped. The cruelty these men had shown would not make that surprising. "Whilsh, we must hope they are all right. Go on. What of the prisoners in the cell next to ours?"

"That be th' hand an' 'is 'prentice and one more. I dinna know who."

Lionn asked, "What of their injuries? Did they hamstring them as well?"

"Nah, but they beat 'em bad. Pern, th' hand, he got hit on th' head and dinna wake fer a whole day. He jus' moan. I dinna know how he be. Th' young lad, he try t' care fer 'im, but I dinna know how they fare. It were'na safe te talk much. If they hear us, they come an' beat us."

Merrist saw that Lionn had gone very pale as Whish spoke. Lionn had his father's strong aversion to cruelty and his sense of justice. "They will see justice. Such cruelty merits worse than death." Lionn gripped the arms of his chair. Merrist saw his knuckles standing out stark white with the pressure.

Charest nodded soberly, holding Lionn in his gaze. "Indeed, they will be brought to justice. But we will do that according to the law and with proper trials."

The quiet in Charest's voice seemed to have a calming effect on Lionn. He took a deep breath and loosened his grip on the chair.

168

Charest turned to Whilsh. "If I bring a scroll and quill, do you think you can help make a map of the area, including the layout of the buildings?"

Whilsh hesitated, shifting uncomfortably. "I dinna read."

"You will not have to read or write. I will do that. But you must tell me where things are so that I can put them in the right place. Can you do that?" When Whilsh did not answer, he added, "Merrist has told us that you know the area very well. All you need to do is remember and tell us."

Whilsh gave a doubtful nod.

"Good man."

As he spoke Lionn lifted the top on the small scribe's desk in the corner and pulled out a roll of scraped leather, followed by a small clay bowl of black soot and a goose-feather quill. He set them on the table and mixed a small amount of water from the pitcher on the table into the bowl, making a black slurry to use as ink. When it was ready he drew a line at the bottom with a break in it and a line beginning at the break going upward. "Here, Whilsh, below this line is the city, with its gate and this is the road leading out of the city. You said there was a copse of trees. If you look out from the gate where would you see the trees on this map? Are they on this side, or that one?"

Merrist could see the excitement rise on Whilsh's face as he understood.

"Th' trees be on tha' side."

"Good, and does the road run beside them all the way, or are there trees on the other side at one point?"

"Nah, they be only tha' side."

A second scroll had to be added for the layout of the buildings, but when they finished Merrist agreed that, from what he had seen in the dark, they had a fair map. Because of the darkness, he could add nothing of the trails through the forest and Whilsh could not give an accurate description of them. Since they would not travel in secret, it did not matter.

Just as they congratulated Whilsh on his map a knock interrupted them. Lionn opened the door to one of the guards.

"Sirs, we have two of the men. They have been taken to separate cells so they cannot speak together. The other two disappeared into the woods and we could not take them. I am sorry, sirs."

169

"Is Strennock one of those captured?" Merrist knew he had been in the party that gave chase.

"I do not know. We have no names, sir. We had orders not to question them."

Lionn made ready to leave. "We will have that answer soon enough."

Brynnell stopped him half-way out the door. "Lionn, I think our interrogation can wait a span or two. It is too late to mount a party to the manor today and our friends are sorely in need of baths and rest. Let the prisoners stew a while. We can interrogate them before breaking fast in the morning."

Merrist grinned at Lionn. "We will smell much sweeter for it." He looked at Whilsh. "We will need to find some clean garments for Whilsh." His grin became replaced with concern as he addressed Lionn. "My clothes are in Warrior's panniers. I left him at the stables. Has he been looked after, do you know?"

After a brief look of embarrassment over his previous excessive enthusiasm, Lionn clapped Merrist on the arm. "Warrior is lord of the stable, my friend. That is how I knew you had returned to Catania. We have been trying to find out what happened to you, ever since."

"Good. Whilsh will share a chamber with me." He turned to clap a friendly hand on Whilsh's shoulder. "To our baths, my friend."

Whilsh blushed at this honour and mumbled something incoherent. Merrist paid him no heed as he and Brynnell followed Lionn out of the council chamber, Charest bringing up the rear.

It was almost full dark as they left for the castle. Lionn nudged Merrist. "Have you any strength left? We need to speak of other things."

"I will come to your chamber as soon as I am refreshed." Merrist understood the unspoken question. Lionn wanted to know about Lieth. "I hope for news from Bargia, as well."

51

EARTH

Once again, before going to sleep, Liannis stilled herself to seek out Merrist's aura. Instead of Merrist she found herself facing Earth in her woman form.

***

"Daughter." Earth smiled at Liannis, imparting warmth. "You are troubled."

"Mother, I wish to know what passes with Merrist. I miss him. I sense he is in danger."

"Merrist is past the greatest danger. He is with Lionn, now. Do not fear for him. He will return to you."

"Will he return for the birth of our daughter?"

Earth gave a gentle shake of her head. "It is not clear. But he will return to you. Our daughter must have her father."

The declaration puzzled Liannis. "Mother, what do you mean 'our' daughter?"

"Liannis," Earth chided, "do I not name you 'Daughter'? And now I name Merrist 'Son'. This child is also daughter to me. She is my gift to you and to the people." Earth gave Liannis a stern look. "And do you not understand that all creatures are my children? Lesser, perhaps, but still my children, nonetheless."

Liannis bowed her head, shamed, until Earth touched her cheek. "I am not angry, Liannis. No one can understand completely, not even you. Be cheered."

The touch banished Liannis's shame and her hesitation. "Mother, I do not sleep well. I miss Merrist so. Now Mama wishes to return to the cabin. Is this where our daughter must be born? I fear it for Mama, but wish it for myself. I cannot find peace at court. It can never be home to me."

"Go to Lieth. When you return Brensa will be strong enough to travel to the cabin. Ayliss must be born there."

"Thank you, Mother. Lady Marja worries that I will need a midwife and should give birth at court."

"A midwife will not be of use to you."

Liannis felt a weight lift. "Thank you, Mother."

171

"Daughter, Ayliss is aware of herself while she is unborn. Like you, she will have no memory of her special destiny once she is born. She will learn of her abilities in the course of time, as you did."

"Mother, will she be plagued by the press of thoughts and emotions of others as I am? Merrist does not suffer from this. Must I keep her away from court to protect her until she learns how to control barriers, as I do?"

"Ayliss will sense things as you do. She will need that ability. But she will learn very early how to control it so that it will not trouble her sleep, even away from home."

"How will she be different from us, Mother? What must I know to help her best?"

"You are her mother. You will understand her well, as will Merrist. Yet, even I do not know the full extent of her abilities. That is not yet revealed. I know that she will be very powerful and will have some abilities that differ from both you and Merrist. More I cannot tell you."

Earth turned as if about to leave when another question struck Liannis. "Mother?"

"You wish to ask about the mission in Lieth."When Liannis nodded she added, "Not all will welcome Nairin, but I foresee no great dissent. The suffering Lieth endured is still fresh in the minds and hearts of the people. They yearn for stability and peace. They will not cause great difficulty. Those few who dissent will be overruled."

"Thank you, Mother."

"Once you return from Lieth you will go to the cabin and remain there until after the babe is born. You will not be called away again."

"And Catania?"

"I do not see Catania clearly. There is much there I still cannot predict."

Before turning once more to leave she touched Liannis's left temple with one finger. "Sleep well this night, Daughter. Your dreams will be untroubled."

***

Liannis woke to the sound of the maid bringing a jug of warm water to wash their faces, and Brensa shushing her.

"I am awake, Mama."

"You slept too soundly. That happens so seldom I did not wish to wake you."

"Thank you, Mama. I did sleep well." She took the mug of tea Brensa handed her. "Have we missed breaking our fast with the others?"

The maid overheard the question and turned at the open door. "They have eaten, but Lady Marja said you must come to her chambers in any case. She has food there for you both."

"Thank you. We will be there in a few moments." She hurried to splash water on her face, pulled on her gown, gulping tea in between, brushed her hair and braided into a single thick braid down her back and turned to Brensa. "Are we ready to join Lady Marja, Mama? I am famished. I think I could eat a whole loaf of bread."

Brensa gave a gay laugh, the first such Liannis had heard in many moons. "Then come. Let us eat."

52

LIONN

The two friends shared ale and news of Lieth and Bargia. Since neither had anything of real consequence to say, Lionn brought the discussion around to what had transpired in Catania since he and Merrist had parted last.

"Father sent me here to assist with the transfer of power in Catania. If Grund had not escaped, or been sprung from prison, all would have gone smoothly. Brynnell is the only real candidate, in any case, after Frellick placed his support behind him." Lionn's tone was matter-of-fact. "Charest will remain as an advisor, as will Frellick. Brynnell and Charest are reviewing candidates to round out the Council. I have not added much to that process as I am not as familiar with the citizens of Catania."

"But you are content that they will choose wisely?"

"I am. Frellick is proving his worth in that area. His natural affability has made him popular with the merchants so he has much information about who is trustworthy."

"I am glad to hear it." Merrist waited for Lionn to go on.

"Most of the people appear well satisfied with having Brynnell invested as Lord of Catania. I think they want things to return to what they see as the proper way. While they are grateful for the governance Bargia has given Catania, the people want to be on their own again, with a proper succession, independent of Bargia. Were it not for Grund and his cronies one would have thought this to be a most natural outcome for Catania."

"And now we know Strennock has joined Grund and seems to have some authority. Have you any idea what their numbers are? Do they pose a serious threat?"

Lionn shrugged. "Grund is clever. The post where you were captured is one of several. We are not certain how many. Grund has spread his men out. We have managed to capture only three, not counting the two caught today. Those three know nothing of value, nothing that tells us where we may find Grund or locate the other places where his followers hide."

"But that makes it look like his numbers are few. Surely, more would have been caught if he had many followers."

Lionn ran his fingers though his hair in frustration. "That is the problem. We have no way of knowing. And even small numbers can cause a great deal of trouble. It takes only one man to assassinate someone. We have two guards each, posted to all four of us, Charest, Brynnell, Frellick, and now even myself. We do not feel safe. This rebellious faction must be stopped. As you have seen, these men are cruel and without honour."

"We will learn more on the morrow, when we interrogate the two new prisoners." Merrist's voice did not hold much conviction.

Lionn heaved a great sigh. "I hope you have the right of it. Brynnell's investiture is set for an eightday hence although that could be changed. I would feel much safer if it occurred with Grund and his men in the dungeons."

"Indeed."

Both men fell silent, having nothing more to add that could be helpful, until Lionn shook himself. "Merrist my good friend enough of this sober talk. I forget myself. You need rest and we must be about at dawn. Go and sleep." He rose and opened the door for Merrist. "But I must say I am much relieved to know that you are well. When we saw Warrior in the stable and could not find you I admit I feared for you."

"I think Earth has not done with me, yet, Lionn." Merrist laughed as he stumped out the door. "Earth will not leave Liannis by herself with our child on the way."

That cheered Lionn. He gave Merrist a teasing wink. "And you, almost three years younger than I. What am I doing wrong?"

"Hah!"

Lionn could see Merrist trying to hide a blush as he hurried away.

53

INTERROGATION

Rather than have the prisoners brought to the Council chamber for questioning, Lionn, Charest, Brynnell and Merrist met just after dawn at the entrance to the dungeons. By interrogating them there they could keep undue notice, and thus gossip and interference from possible enemies, to a minimum. The less Grund found out the better.

"I have ordered food brought to the council chamber so we can make plans while we break our fast," Brynnell told them.

"Good," Charest replied. "We will need to act with speed if we are to gain anything at all from what we learn. I expect the manor has already been vacated."

Merrist nodded. "I only hope they have left their prisoners alive. They will not want to move them."

"I thought of that, as well." Lionn looked grim. "I think the best we can expect is that we will find them alive but still locked away. It is another reason to act quickly. And if they have been taken along with their captors, we will need to follow and attempt a rescue."

"Lionn, I do not think the three in the cell next to mine will be able to travel." Merrist could still hear the one man's moans in his mind. "Especially the older man."

"We do not know the condition of the women, either." Brynnell added.

"Perhaps we erred in not sending a party out immediately." Lionn gave the others a questioning look.

Charest, who Merrist noted, usually inserted the voice of calm, made a cutting gesture with one hand. "It was well past midday before we had finished our consultation and made our map. It was too late." He followed the others as they filed into the dungeons. "We would have gained nothing in pursuing yesterday. We would not have reached the manor before dusk. They had the advantage of knowing the lay of the land and would have prepared for attack or already left."

No one answered him. They had reached the guard post in the hall.

Brynnell, as first in command, addressed the guard posted there. "Take us to the first prisoner brought here yesterday."

The guard touched a finger to his brow in salute, lifted a rusty ring of ancient keys from a peg on the wall, led them down the dank, narrow corridor to the farthest cell. He unlocked and unbarred it, and stood aside to let the men in. The keys reminded Merrist that Catania was the oldest demesne on the One Isle, the dungeon just as old.

Brynnell turned to him. "Thank you, Kort. I will take the keys. Return to your post. We will bar the door when we leave."

The guard looked surprised for an instant, then saluted again. "As you wish." He handed Brynnell the keys, turned and strode back down the corridor without looking back.

Merrist understood Brynnell took the keys as a precaution to prevent their being overheard. As he watched Brynnell take charge, it confirmed for him that the right choice for Lord of Catania had been made. Brynnell was steady, had a solid presence, and took leadership in stride. He would not be a man given to impulse or extremes.

A half span later the foursome emerged from the dungeons no wiser than when they had entered. The two prisoners had given up their names, and the names of three more, but it seemed even they did not know how many men had been at the manor, nor what had been done with the women other than that they had been locked up. It appeared Strennock, who was in charge of that location, had not divulged much to his men.

As the discouraged group broke their fast, Brynnell led the discussion.

"So we are agreed that a cadre of soldiers must be sent immediately. They must prepare for possible ambush, but our main hope is that this will be a rescue mission."

Merrist nodded. "I wish to accompany them. There may be injured that I can heal."

"But you are not yet fully recovered."

"I am well enough, Lionn. We will take food and drink for me in case I am called upon to do a healing. I am needed. I sense it."

Lionn gave an unhappy shrug. "Very well." Then he brightened slightly. "Perhaps I ought to go as well."

177

Brynnell stopped him. "Lionn, you are not needed there. It is unwise to put yourself in danger if it is not necessary."

Charest agreed. "Lionn, I think the rest of us need to continue to search out the other lairs of our enemies. You cannot add to the success of this party. And it will hamper them if they believe they must also keep the future lord of Bargia safe."

"I will be all right, my friend," Merrist assured him. "Earth will keep me safe."

A span later a cadre of twelve soldiers rode out of the city gate in the direction of the manor. Merrist, on Warrior, brought up the rear. In another span they would be followed by three more men leading four horses and pulling one wagon. These were for the prisoners they hoped to free.

Whilsh, at his own insistence, drove that wagon. "It be m' duty. I mus' go back t' m' post."

Merrist understood that his thoughts also went to Lua, his intended.

54

M'LADY

As soon as the party arrived at the manor Merrist could see that Strennock and his men had left in haste. Platters of cold meat, already taking on a reek of spoilage, and chunks of hard bread and cheese, sat half eaten on the table, along with unfinished mugs of ale and wine. A pall of abandoned silence hung in the main hall.

The men split up to search the other chambers. Merrist, slowed by his leg, followed two of them up the central staircase.

"Oh, Earth, in here," one called out softly, soon followed by a "Help, in here!" from another chamber.

By the time Merrist reached the top of the stair, a young guard rushed out of the first chamber, ashen, and vomited in the hall. He grabbed Merrist as he tried to pass him into the chamber and managed a choked, "She is so young."

As soon as he entered the chamber, Merrist understood what had caused the young guard's reaction. A girl, certainly not more than ten years old, lay splayed on the bed, wrists and ankles tied to the posts. Her skirt had been shoved above her waist, leaving her naked below. Blood and urine had pooled on the sheets between her thighs.

Merrist swallowed hard and hurried to her, pulling his dagger from his belt to cut her bindings. He placed on hand on the girl's throat. Though he could still feel a weak pulse his touch brought no sign from her that she was aware of his presence. Even as he examined her to determine the extent of her injuries, he sensed her pulse and breath go still and her spirit leave her body.

A part of Merrist felt relief that the girl would be spared further shame and pain. Another raged at knowing he had arrived too late to heal her. One of the guards entered as he stood up. "Merrist, the lady is alive. Come."

Merrist gave himself a mental shake to gather his thoughts, pulled the girl's skirts down to hide her shame, and hurried after the guard to the next chamber. There he found a woman in the same position as the girl. A glance about the chamber revealed another small body crumpled in a corner, her gown crusted with dried blood. He could tell she no longer lived so he turned his attention back to the woman on the bed.

179

"Lady," he murmured as he touched her throat to determine the strength of her pulse and pulled her skirt down to cover her legs, "we are friends. You will not come to more harm."

The woman groaned and turned her head weakly away from him. Before he could say more another guard hurried into the chamber. "We found two bodies in the pantry, their throats have been cut and they look to have been raped. I think they were the cook and maid."

"There are three dead bodies in one of the cells." Another guard who had just entered spoke from behind Merrist, his voice full of rage. "They had no need to kill them."

Merrist felt the woman under his hand shudder at the words. "She turned back to look at him, an anguished question in her eyes, "Maira?"

"Is that the girl in the next chamber, Lady?"

She gave a weak nod.

"I am sorry, Lady. She no longer lives"

"Good." The woman turned away again.

Merrist knew better than to ask the woman if she wished to be healed. Her shame and grief would make her say she wished to die.

Whilsh's voice made Merrist turn to the door. "Th' horses be gone." Merrist watched his expression change from disappointment to horror. "M'lady." He made as if to come forward, then halted, covered his face with one hand, as if not wanting to see the woman's shame, and hurried back out.

Merrist turned back to the woman.

He did not begin to minister to her immediately, at war with himself over what was best. The decision was taken out of his hands as he felt the healing trance overtake him. He heard no more as his hands gently probed the woman's body and mended her wounds. Through it all he could feel her despair and knew he could not heal that. When he could do no more for her he let his hands fall away, carefully arranged her skirts to hide her legs again and looked around. Only Whilsh, who had returned, remained in the chamber with him.

"Water." Merrist could barely get the word out but Whilsh understood and put the mug into his hands, placing a hand under Merrits's arm to steady him.

180

"There be cheese an' bread." Whilsh shoved the chunks into Merrist's hands and pushed one toward Merrist's mouth. "Ye mus' eat."

Knowing Whilsh was right Merrist forced himself to chew and swallow a few bites. When he could speak, he said, "Whilsh, your lady needs to be washed. She must have a clean gown and a clean bed. I have not the strength. There are no women to do it for her and she cannot do it herself."

Whilsh hesitated then gave a slow nod.

"She be my lady. It be my duty." He looked at the figure on the bed. "But I dinna wish to shame 'er more."

"She will remain asleep for some time. She will not know."

Relief flooded Whilsh's face. Without saying anything he reached down to help Merrist off the floor, led him to a large chair, lowered him into it, placed a pillow behind his head and a blanket over him. "Ye need t' sleep. I be doin' what ye 'said." He headed for the door, turned and added, "I be findin' water and such."

Already fading into sleep, all Merrist could manage was a half nod.

Merrist woke to full darkness. The only illumination in the chamber came from the glowing embers of a brazier that had been placed just inside the door. On it sat a pot of sage tea and a bowl of stew, Merrist thought it must have been the aroma of the food that woke him. He was ravenous. The recognition of where he was banished all remnants of sleep. He threw off the blanket and rose to his feet, wanting to reach for the food and tea. Instead he stumbled over something that produced a grunt then quickly scrambled out of his way.

"I be watchin' wi' ye. Mus' fell asleep. Sit. I be bringin' yer stew fer ye."

"Thank you, Whilsh." Merrist saw no point in berating Whilsh for sleeping at his feet. He knew the man had dedicated himself to his service since he had healed him. Changing that could wait until he had more energy. He sat back and accepted the bowl and spoon. "Some tea, first, please, Whilsh."

When he had downed one mug of tea and swallowed his first huge spoonful of stew he asked, "Where have they taken the woman I healed? Has anyone remained to see to her?"

"She be ta'en to th' cabin back o' th' house. One o' th' guards be settin' by 'er."

"Good. I expect she will sleep until morning but I do not think she ought to be left alone. Whilsh, what can you tell me about what was found outside the manor?"

"There be no' much. No men left here. The stables be empty o' horses. Foun' th' stall gates open, nose bags still lef' on th' pegs on th' posts. If they be ridin' hard th' horses be needin' their oats." He shook his head in sorrow. "The other two from th' cells be kilt. Throats cut, jus' like th' cook ... an' my poor Lua." He shuddered visibly. "I don' wan' te stay here. Nothin' lef' t' do here now. Feel the spirits, I do."

"Where are the others? I don't hear anything."

"They be sleepin' in th' stables. No spirits there. Figure t' track them monsters come dawn."

Merrist realised with a start that Whilsh had remained behind to protect him from the spirits of the dead in spite of fearing them. "Whilsh, you are a brave and loyal man." He downed another mug of tea, and swallowed the last of the stew. "Come, we will join the others in the stables. You will sleep better there and we will be ready to ride when we wake."

The look of relief on Whilsh's face almost made Merrist laugh.

"On our way, show me the cabin so I can check on the lady. What is her name?"

"It be Missus Morna. Now she be th' las' one lef'." Whilsh hung his head, his chin almost to his chest. "She be like kin' te' me and the res' o' the servants'. She be a good lady."

"Yes and her life will be difficult now, with the grief and anger she must bear."

A sad nod was the only response.

They had reached the door of the cabin, which had been left slightly ajar. A guard sat outside on the ground, smoking a pipe. "The lady sleeps. I have heard nothing from her."

"Good. I will go and check on her before we sleep."

Merrist made his way to the narrow bed by the light of the moon through the doorway. He knelt beside it, placing a hand gently on Morna's forehead. Reassuring himself that she slept peacefully, he withdrew back outside.

"She will sleep until we wake her in the morning."

182

The guard touched his forehead in salute and Merrist and Whilsh headed to the stables to sleep.

MORNING

"I will take Mistress Morna to the city. I do not think I will be needed as you track Strennock and his men." Merrist had already checked on his patient. She had awakened but refused to speak, eat or drink.

"I mus' go wi' my mistress. I be drivin' th' wagon."

"Good, Whilsh. That will allow me to give all my attention to the lady."

"Agreed," the captain of the guard said. "We will not be needing you, Merrist, and Whilsh is no fighter. We have two trackers with us. It ought to be easy to follow their trail. Looks like they went north, into the hills. With luck they will lead us to more traitors." The captain looked haggard but determined.

"I shall ask Brynnell to send more men. If you encounter others you will need more to fight."

The guard nodded, mounted, and turned his horse to join his waiting men.

Merrist asked Whilsh to support Morna on her other side as she was still too weak to walk. When he had her as comfortable as possible with blankets and pillows, in the bed of the narrow wagon, he ordered Whilsh to head back to Catania City.

Whilsh had shed a few silent tears and avoided making eye contact with his lady. Merrist understood that his grief was mixed with a good deal of guilt for his inability to protect her and her family. Knowing he could not help, Merrist said nothing.

They had gone as far as the edge of the first field when they passed the fresh mounds where the guards had buried the dead the afternoon before.

The groan Whilsh uttered at the sight roused Morna, as if she knew what had caused him to react so. She struggled to sitting. On seeing the row of fresh earth, she let out one long, keening wail.

Merrist noticed that each grave had a wooden marker at its head, but could not see what was written on them. He knew the guards could not have known the names of the victims and wondered what they had written. "Whilsh, stop." He need not have spoken, for Whilsh had already halted the wagon.

184

Morna clutched the side of the wagon to hold herself upright, her face a rictus of grief. When Merrist got down from the wagon she spoke. "I must see."

Merrist helped her down and he and Whilsh supported her as she approached the graves. On each maker had been written something that could identify its occupant; old prisoner, young prisoner, cook, maid, young child, older girl.

"Noooooo," Morna approached the grave of her youngest first, brushed off Merrist's and Whilsh's support and fell by the marker. Then she threw herself prostrate on the ground over the fresh earth. When Whilsh made to reach for her Merrist waved him back. Morna needed time.

Merrist had Whish step back to a respectful distance until Morna raised her head to look at the markers again. She turned to him and Whilsh with a pleading look. "They have names. This is my Selna."

Unable to find anything with which to add the names to the markers, Merrist untied Warrior from the back of the wagon and said, "Mistress, I will return and find something. We will not leave until they all have names."

When Merrist got back to the house it took him several moments to locate writing materials. It seemed the traitors had no use for them and had shoved them deep into a cupboard in the main bedchamber. It was not a room he relished re-entering, so he hurried back as soon as he found what he needed; a quill and a small jar of dried ink made from soot. He would add water to it when he reached the wagon again.

When Merrist had reconstituted the ink to a usable consistency he took it to Morna. "Mistress, do you wish to add the names of your daughters yourself?"

Once she got over her initial surprise at the offer, Morna said nothing but reached for the quill and ink, taking them from Merrist with shaking hands.

At the top of the first marker she wrote, in clear but unsteady letters, "Selna, age 8." On her other daughter's marker, which she reached on hands and knees, refusing assistance, she wrote "Maira, age 10", handed the implements back to Merrist and lay across that mound as she had the other.

"Th' others deserve names, too." Whilsh gestured at the other marker with a sweep of one arm. "Lua needs a name."

185

"Tell me their names. I will add them." Merrist dipped the quill into the ink.

By the time Merrist had written the names of the others Morna had raised herself to sitting, her eyes dry and face void of emotion.

Merrist looked at the sun. "Mistress Morna, we must go. Will you let us help you back into the wagon?"

Her response was a bleak nod. When Merrist had her seated in the wagon again and Whish resumed his seat on the bench, Merrist offered her a drink of water from the flask they had brought. At first she shook her head in refusal. "Mistress, if you are to assist us in bringing these monsters to justice you will need the strength to tell us what you know. I understand you would rather join your daughters but you can do more for them by living and assisting us."

Morna eyed him for a long moment, then looked at the cup and reached for it. She drank a few swallows, handed it back, let herself sink to the bed of the wagon, and turned away from him.

With her compliance Merrist sensed she would find the courage to live.

The sun had begun to lower in the sky, causing long shadows, by the time they reached the gate at Catania City. Morna had not moved and Merrist had not pressed her to drink or eat more. He believed she would when they had settled her into a proper chamber. But he decided he would not leave her alone until she had at least drunk some tea once they reached that destination.

The guard stopped them at the gate. "Who are you and what is your business here?" The question died on his lips as soon as he saw Merrist's wooden leg. "Sir, I will announce your return." He called to the other guard stationed with him. "I will be back. The man, Merrist, has returned. Brynnell must be informed. I will hail another to stand with you."

His partner nodded and came to stand at the open gate. One side had been closed behind them once they entered. Merrist understood it as an added precaution after the events of the last days. It would only be opened for wider wagons, and then only after determining the occupants had legitimate business in the city.

Whilsh drove the wagon past the gate and looked back at Merrist in question.

"Go to the stables, Whilsh." Merrist told him. "We need to pass them, in any case, and I will leave Warrior. Then we will proceed to the castle. They will find a chamber for Mistress Morna there."

Whilsh touched his finger to his forehead and urged the horse to keep moving.

At the stables, Merrist was in the process of untying Warrior and handing him to the groom when Lionn strode up to meet them. Merrist jerked his head in the direction of the wagon and Lionn hurried to have a look.

"Mistress Morna needs a quiet chamber in the castle."

Lionn did not question Merrist. "I will see to it right away. It will be ready by the time you reach the castle." He spun on his heal and headed back to the castle.

When the wagon reached the entrance to the castle Lionn stood waiting there with Joranna. Seeing her there with Lionn did not surprise Merrist but it was not until later that he remembered where and when he had seen them together before.

Whilsh climbed off the seat and went to the back of the wagon. "She be my missus. I c'n carry 'er in."

Merrist nodded and stepped back. Morna roused enough to move into a position that made it easier for Whilsh to lift her. Merrist took the woman from his arms only long enough for Whilsh to climb down and reclaim her. Merrist expected Whilsh believed this might be the last service he could offer his poor mistress. He was likely correct.

Lionn led the way to a guest chamber near the top of the grand staircase. A bed waited there, freshly made with clean linens, pulled back so Whilsh could lay his burden down comfortably.

"There is tea on the way, and I have asked for broth to be brought." Lionn gave the door an expectant look. The words had no sooner been spoken than a maid appeared with a brazier, followed by another carrying a tray with tea. Some fresh bread, butter and honey also sat on the tray. Merrist doubted Morna would touch it.

As soon as the maid had gone another appeared carrying a clay pot filled with beef broth and set it beside the tea on the brazier.

187

"Lionn, if you would ask Brynnell and Charest to meet in the council chamber I will join you as soon as I have settled Mistress Morna."

Lionn nodded and started for the door. When Joranna made to follow, Lionn placed a restraining hand on her forearm. "Joranna, if you would stay with the lady. She will need an attendant after Merrist leaves."

Merrist could not help but notice the proprietary gesture and the way Lionn regarded Joranna.

Joranna looked relieved. "As you wish."

Merrist turned to Morna. "Mistress, you will need your strength if you are to avenge your family." He handed Joranna a mug of broth. "This is Joranna. Please allow her to assist you to take some broth and tea. She is known to me and can be trusted."

Morna glanced at Merrist then looked Joranna over. Finally she gave a dull nod and tried to sit up. Joranna deftly placed an arm behind her shoulders for support and kept the other under the mug as Morna brought it to her mouth with shaking hands.

Satisfied that she would be well cared for, Merrist nodded a silent goodbye to Joranna and slipped from the chamber, closing the door behind him.

56

GRUND

His scout rode barely able to keep his seat on his horse. Grund noticed that he seemed fearful and knew immediately that something had gone amiss. "What are you doing here? Tell me what happened."

"It is Strennock, Sir. He has fled the manor. It has been discovered by guards and taken."

When the scout mentioned that they had captured Merrist but had let him escape, Grund flew into a rage. "Fools! I am served by idiots! You cannot even keep a man with only one leg captive? You knew how important he was!"

The man cringed and stepped back when Grund drew his sword and looked about to run him through.

Grund stopped just short of the thrust, knowing he needed the rest of the man's information.

When the scout informed him of the rapes of the women and that they had been killed or left for dead Grund almost lost control again. He reigned himself in with effort and went still. A cold fury became his armour. Within it his thoughts went to revenge, not against this messenger, but against the man who had caused the failure. Strennock.

Grund forced a smile upon his lips. "Did Strennock not tell you that the women were not to be harmed?"

The scout recoiled at the coldness in Grund's voice. "N..no, sir."

"I am destined to be Lord of Catania. A lord cannot have his women raped and tortured. And his men must obey him, do you not agree?" Grund kept his voice cold and flat, nor did he move a muscle. Watching the scout tremble in terror helped calm him, gave him a sadistic pleasure. He was fully in control again.

The man nodded vigorously, too cowed to speak.

Another thought struck Grund. "Were you followed?"

"N...no, Sir."

"How can you be certain? Bah! A man who cannot obey the simplest orders is too much a fool to make sure he is not followed. Useless!" He spun on his heel and called to a man posted by a tree several paces away. "Krynn."

Krynn hurried over.

"Take three men and check for strangers lurking. I need to know if this fool has been followed here."

"Sir!"

Grund turned and entered the manor, not waiting to see if Krynn obeyed, leaving the scout standing alone, a dark wet spot spreading in his breeches.

Inside, Grund marched into the dining hall where three others lounged at a table, enjoying platters of food and mugs of ale.

"That fool, Strennock, has lost the northern outpost and flees further north." Grund's rage at the men at the table for not anticipating him and being at the ready fuelled his tirade even further. "Gather all the men. We leave now."

The men merely gaped at him in surprise, not making any effort to rise.

"Now!" Grund roared and slammed his fist on the table, making them, and the platters, jump. "He has betrayed me. Go!"

The three rose in unison, one pushing his chair back so quickly it fell over. They rushed for the door, almost knocking each other over in their haste to exit.

A span later ten men rode north. The poor scout rode in the lead, having had no rest and only travel fare to eat while mounted. Grund did give him a new mount so that at least his horse was fresh.

When the scout made to head back the way he had come Grund stopped him with a chop of his hand. "This way. It is more direct." He thought he knew where Strennock would go. They had had a meeting at a large cabin hidden in a copse of trees just outside the northern border of Catania. Fury made Grund ignore caution and safety. He felt an elated, wild confidence so he made no attempt to hide their hasty departure.

They took no time to rest, eating as they rode and stopping only long enough to commandeer fresh mounts at the stables of a wealthy horse trader along the way. To prevent those good people from raising the alarm he had all the men tied up and barred the women in a shed. He made certain they were not seriously harmed, and that they would be able to free each other after he had gone. "Tell the people Lord Grund is just and does not harm his people needlessly."

The owner, silenced by terror, had bobbed his head up and down wildly in agreement.

The scout, having tumbled from the saddle in exhaustion, was thrown into the shed with the women. "You have less spine than a maid," he sneered as he shoved him inside.

Grund knew that his hold on his men was tenuous at best. Those who had sprung him from prison had not managed to muster more supporters. Aside from the post they had just left and the manor Strennock had held, he had only one other group of followers; roughly twenty men at an abandoned warehouse just east of the city.

The man he had sent ahead to scout out the trail rode back to fall into step beside him. "Grund...'

"Lord Grund!" The audacity of the man's familiarity made him scream it in rage. Yet he had a niggling sense that he had not demanded that form of address before now. He pulled his rage back in. "You will address me as Lord Grund." Then, louder, so that all the men would hear, "I am Lord Grund. That is how I will be addressed. Any who fail to do so will feel my wrath."

His men nodded, not even looking his way, eyes kept firmly on the reins and their horses' heads.

Grund turned back to the man who had scouted ahead. "Report."

"Lord Grund, I see signs that a mounted party has gone along this same trail not long before now, perhaps two spans. By the number of hoof prints it may be Strennock and his men."

Grund felt himself fill with an elated triumph. "We have them. Forward, men!"

He spurred his horse on to a reckless pace, leaving the others scrambling to keep up.

191

57

AFTER THEM

After the interrogation of the prisoners Brynnell called a hasty meeting in the council chamber. He sent another cadre of soldiers north to assist those tracking Strennock.

"They may need a healer. Perhaps I ought to go with them."

Both Brynnell and Charest shook their heads before Brynnell answered. "No Merrist. They have been trained for this."

Charest added, "You are needed here. Mistress Morna may need further help from you. We wish to speak with her as soon as she is able. We need to find out what she can tell us about Strennock and his men."

"And you look like you could use some rest and good food."

Merrist sent Lionn a grateful look. "That will be welcome, I will admit."

A knock called the attention of the men to the door, which opened to reveal Frellick. "Forgive my lateness. I have information that may prove useful." As he folded his lanky frame into the nearest chair he eyed the table with relish. "Ah, strawberry preserves. You remembered." He grinned at the others.

His ebullience lifted the mood. Lionn quipped, "It was not one of us. I think that dark haired maid has her eyes on you."

"And I a joined man. What will my wife say?"

Brynnell chuckled. "I expect that will depend on what you do about it."

Frellick laughed it off, blushing. "I have given her no need to be jealous. I would pity any woman who tried to get between us if she found out." Then he gave the others a sideways glance from lowered lids, a soft shy smile creeping over his face. "She told me just yesterday that we have our first child on the way."

That brought congratulations and much table thumping, causing Frellick's face to redden even further, though a proud smile wreathed his face.

"Now, what have you to tell us?"

Frellick swallowed hastily before answering. "I have just come from speaking with the owner of the warehouses in the east end, the ones just inside the wall by the river."

All ribbing forgotten, four rapt faces fixed on his. Merrist had no idea where these warehouses stood but the nods from the others told him they did.

"That man told me he has seen unusual activity in the ones nearby, the ones on the far bank of the river, just outside the wall to the left of the gate. Those have sat empty for two years due to the famine and poor harvests. But my informant tells me men have been seen coming and going and they are not bringing grain. He tells me no one knows why they are there."

Brynnell's brow creased. "How long have these men been there? Why was it not noted earlier?"

"I asked him. He said they have been there only two eightdays. Since the buildings are outside the wall, and not in use, no one had reason to go there or even near. At first they ignored it, thinking some poor bastard needed a roof over his head. What harm could it do? But afterward, when they saw more men, they became suspicious and thought it best to tell me. They knew I had been seeking information."

Brynnell looked around the table at each of them, including Merrist. "I think another cadre of soldiers ought to go and speak to these men."

"Indeed, and quickly." Charest said.

"I will go as well, as I can tell you who belongs there. I believe my informant will be willing to identify those he does not know."

"That is well, Frellick, but do not engage in the fighting. Remain inside the wall with the grain merchants."

Merrist thought he saw a flash of disappointment cross Frellick's face, but it was brief.

"I agree. I am no fighter. All know I am better with my head than my hands." Frellick gave a rueful smile and opened his hands wide to show soft palms.

"I have learned that we need not all be soldiers to serve, Frellick. It was a hard lesson." Merrist, sitting in the chair beside Frellick, gave him an understanding clap on his arm.

Lionn was quick to agree. "And we are most grateful for that difference, Merrist. Else Brynnell would not now be among us."

That brought murmurs of agreement all around.

"Oh, just so, just so." Frellick bobbed with enthusiasm again. Merrist saw that his youthful energy and cheerful outlook helped to keep the council from descending into discouragement. He was a good addition. Merrist was glad Frellick had agreed to support Brynnell's claim rather than pursue his own.

A span later a cadre of twenty soldiers had been dispatched to the warehouse district.

As they left the council chamber Merrist said to Lionn, "I think I will see how Mistress Morna fares."

"I shall accompany you."

Merrist gave him a teasing poke in the ribs with an elbow. "I thought you might."

Lionn blushed and looked at his boots. "Joranna and I have been seeing quite a bit of each other."

"I am not surprised. I recall seeing the attraction the last time I was here, when Brynnell had been attacked."

"You do not miss much, my friend." Lionn met Merrist's grin with one of his own. "And do you approve?"

Merrist laughed. "It is not for me to approve. What does her father think?"

"He has voiced no objections."

The pair had reached the door to the chamber where Morna lay, putting an end to further discussion.

Joranna opened quickly to Merrist's light knock. She put a finger to her lips and slipped out of the room to join them in the hall. "She sleeps."

"Has she eaten or drunk since I left?"

"Yes, she had taken almost a full mug of broth and some tea. I put a lot of honey in the tea." Joranna looked pleased with herself. "She said nothing but I could tell she liked that. I think the lady may be partial to sweets." This last was directed to Lionn, as though Merrist were no longer present.

Merrist smiled inwardly, noting the indulgent smile Lionn beamed back at her. "You two wait outside. I will go in and see to the lady."

194

By her regular breathing and more relaxed pose as she lay in the bed Merrist could tell that Morna was now in a healing sleep. He decided against feeling her neck to check the pulse as it might wake or disturb her. More than anything, sleep would help her recover best. Her ordeal would have left her exhausted even without the grief she suffered. He silently let himself back out of the chamber.

"I think she will be hungry when she wakes. Let her sleep as long as she will. But have some porridge and soft boiled eggs for when she wakes." He winked at Joranna. "And more tea with honey."

Joranna answered with a toss of her hair. Then, her hand already on the door handle, she turned back. "Oh, there is so little to do here. Will one of you wait while I fetch some mending? Else I will fall asleep."

Lionn answered before Merrist could open his mouth. "Of course. We will both wait."

Joranna flashed a bright smile and hurried off.

195

58

LIETH

The journey to Lieth proved uneventful. Even the weather cooperated by remaining sunny and dry. Liannis found the heat of high summer oppressive, however, even in the light, summer linen gowns she wore. She wondered what the reaction of the people of Lieth would be now that she could no longer hide her condition under her heavier winter wool robes. She doubted even those would conceal her growing abdomen much longer. However, her increased girth did not prove an impediment to riding. She was grateful for that.

Each evening before going to sleep she checked on Merrist's aura, relieved to find the grey pall had lifted and its clear blue had returned. Only a few orange sparks indicated any anxiety, which she deduced were worry for herself.

On the last night before arriving in Lieth, Earth gave Liannis a dream. It showed Sennia with a girth matching her own and two tiny beating hearts within it. Liannis woke the next morning elated. Sennia's twins would be born only a few moons after her own daughter. All during the ride the next morning, until she could see the gate of Lieth City, she smiled inwardly, imagining the three children at play together.

Those thoughts dispersed when the guard opened the gate to admit the party into Lieth City. It pleased Liannis to see the gate now hung straight again and looked solid. All the timbers had been replaced with fresh wood. It had not even gone grey yet.

"Welcome." The guard gave a formal, short bow. "We have sent word to the castle of your return. How many chambers will you require?"

Bennill, the advisor Gaelen had sent with them, took charge. "Only four in the castle. One for myself, one for each of these two gentlemen and one for Liannis the seer. The others will sleep at the barracks."

The guard looked the group over, his lips moving as he counted. "Six bunks in the barracks, then." He nodded crisply. "You may proceed to the castle. I will see to your lodgings." A short bow and he turned to seek out another guard to take over his post.

Liannis could see that more improvements had been made even in the short time since they were here last. The air had a sense of purposeful industry mixed with pride. Judging by what she saw, Liannis felt they had good reason to be proud. She wondered how that would affect the attitude of the people to Nairin's return.

One of the leaders of the governing group came to meet them as they approached the castle. Karel was his name, Liannis recalled. She liked him. He would make a good member of the advisory council, if Nairin kept her word about including some of these men.

"Welcome. Chambers are being prepared for you."

As grooms came forward to look after their mounts, Karel turned to Liannis. "I admit we had not expected you to return so soon."

Liannis caught the unasked question about what the motives might be, and the unease that caused him. "Nor had I, Karel, but summer will not last much longer and we have business with you and the other leaders that must be concluded before winter."

She saw the furrow between his brows deepen though he did not press her further. His restraint increased Liannis's sense that he would make a solid member of the council. She decided she would personally recommend him to Nairin on her return.

A maid hurried from one of the chambers overlooking the great hall and came down the steps. "Sir, we have the first two on either side prepared."

Karel nodded his thanks and faced them. "I expect you will wish baths brought up before you join us for dinner."

"That will be most welcome. I am Frennan, one of Lord Gaelen's advisors. You know Liannis, and these are Larsht and Jorrin, merchants from Bargia."

Karel returned the formal, short bows. "And I am Karel, head of the council here."

Liannis noted the emphasis on the word council. Would he be willing to step down for Nairin? He had grown accustomed to his position. Nairin had best offer him membership on her council if she wished to establish goodwill here. Karel would make a better friend than enemy. Liannis looked at Frennan. His slight nod and one raised eyebrow when he met her eyes told her he had noted it, too.

197

At the top of the stairs, Karel turned to Frennan. "Is your business with us urgent, or can it wait until morning?"

"It may wait, certainly." Frennan gave Karel a broad smile, but Liannis noticed it did not reach his eyes. They were playing cat and mouse.

"We will all welcome an evening of rest, Karel, thank you."

Liannis decided to test the waters. "Will you and your council be joining us at dinner? It would be good for all of us to become acquainted before we discuss more important matters."

"Indeed. Excellent suggestion," Frennan interjected before Karel could answer.

Karel hesitated for only an instant. "But of course. I shall send word that we have important visitors."

Binnell pressed further. "It would be pleasant to meet their wives, if the members are joined, and their children. They would be most welcome."

Karel's look of surprise almost made Liannis laugh. She hid her smile behind a discreet hand.

Karel recovered quickly and returned Frennan's affable smile. "Certainly. I expect they will be curious." He turned to spot the maids bringing buckets of hot water for the baths. "Ah, your bath water. Please, enjoy your rest. I must tell the cooks we have guests." He gave a curt nod and strode off.

Liannis suspected he was relieved to end the awkward conversation. Liannis chose the chamber farthest from the open stair as it would be quietest. As she placed her travel bag on the end of the bed the maid returned with the second bucket of water. Noting that the tub was half full she smiled at the maid. "Thank you. That will be sufficient."

She saw the maid bestow a long look at her abdomen and frown before she averted her eyes and hurried away. The news would be all over the castle before dinner. Liannis sighed, then shrugged, slipped out of the soiled gown, sank into the welcome warmth of the tub and put that concern from her mind.

Dinner was more a banquet than a normal evening meal. Liannis could see that the kitchen had been given orders to make this a special occasion. She suspected it was an attempt to show that the current leaders had learned how to treat important guests and to demonstrate that they had the skills to put on what was expected. The servers knew their roles well, keeping goblets filled with ale or wine and new platters arriving from the kitchen.

Frennan must have noted it, too. "We want to thank you all for this impressive welcome. You have made us very comfortable and this meal is wonderful, especially after several days of travel fare."

Karel confirmed Liannis's suspicions. "Yes, Lieth is recovering well. Crops are coming in, game is once more plentiful and most of the people are back into homes of their own and have returned to their chosen occupations."

It sounded to Liannis like a prepared speech. When Karel gave Frennan a meaningful look and added, "Of course we are grateful for the assistance from Bargia. But soon we will no longer have need of it, as you can see."

Frennan kept his voice smooth. "Indeed, Lieth is almost its former self." He turned to Karel's wife. "And I am enjoying the company. Mistress, have we you to thank for this repast?"

She looked flustered for a moment and glanced at Karel, who sent her a stern look. Gathering herself, she turned back to Frennan. "I have taken charge of the household, sir. The menu is mine, but I do not cook. We have servants and cooks who do that. I have other duties and run the castle household."

"But, of course." Frennan gave her his most gracious smile. "I see you have a talent for managing a large household."

Karel answered for her. "That she does, sir. We have found many talents among our people that would have remained undiscovered before."

Liannis decided to defuse the tension she could sense building. "Yes, and I think those talents will serve Lieth well in the years to come. Sometimes change is good and we must embrace it to become stronger." She hoped that they would make the leap to include the changes Earth had made regarding seers, as well. Her hand went protectively to her belly.

Karel's shoulders relaxed. "Just so, Liannis."

The talk went to lighter subjects as the children performed music for their guests and the women talked of more feminine things, such as the new fabrics that had arrived from the east. The mood remained festive and they all lingered until late into the evening. Even the ever proper and cautious Frennan relaxed and seemed to enjoy himself.

199

59

MEETING

Karel met them early next morning and broke fast with them in the dining hall where they had eaten the evening before. As soon as they had finished he led them to the council chamber for their meeting.

None of them had been in the council chamber since the great fire. Liannis looked around in approval at the sturdy table and circle of chairs, plain but well made. The chairs had cushions on the seats and had a comfortable curve to the back. She admired the smooth wood and thought that others might appreciate the simple lines as well. The customary furniture in the other demesnes was much more ornate, with intricate carving on the edges. The more Liannis looked at this new style the more she liked it. Perhaps it would catch on outside Lieth once more people saw it.

Liannis noticed, with approval, that refreshment had also been provided; cold ale and hot tea, sage by the aroma, as well as fresh honey cakes. Those were not as good as the ones at home in Bargia, but she relished them, nonetheless.

Karel invited them to be seated. "I have had extra chairs brought in so that the men sent by Lord Gaelen from Bargia to assist us may also sit in on this meeting. I hope no one objects." He looked at Frennan.

"Excellent foresight, Karel. They know Lieth well, having been here for more than two years."

Liannis counted; the four of them, as the guards that accompanied them remained in the barracks, the three men Gaelen had sent from Bargia to guide the rebuilding and governing of Lieth, Karel, and five others who formed the current council, two of whom Liannis had not met the previous time she had come with Nairin. Karel and Frennan had pride of place at opposite ends. The chairs all fit around the table but their occupants sat elbow to elbow. Liannis approved of that arrangement, as everyone would be able to see all the others equally well, but it did make her uncomfortable. She had to take care not to touch anyone for fear of being accused of reading someone's thoughts against his will.

Frennan noticed her discomfort. "Liannis, I am aware that it is difficult for you to sit so close to another. I am willing to trade places with you if you wish."

"Thank you, Frennan. As leader of our delegation it is important for you to remain where you are. But, as I am here primarily to observe, I will set my chair back behind yours. If I wish to speak I will stand." She looked around the chamber. "As a seer I have the ability to read others' thoughts if I am in physical contact. I do not wish to violate anyone's privacy."

At the startled looks from some of the men Liannis knew that not all had known of this. "Does anyone object?"

When no one else spoke, Karel said, "Thank you Liannis. We appreciate your candor."

When Liannis made to lift her chair the man next to her rose and took it for her, setting it behind Frennan's shoulder in a position that gave her a clear view. He looked familiar but she could not place his name.

Once seated the only face she could not see was that of Frennan.

As soon as everyone had settled, Karel introduced everyone by name. Then he got directly to the point. "We had not expected visitors from Bargia so soon after Nairin's stay. What brings you to Lieth?" He kept his expression neutral as he addressed Frennan.

Liannis detected some tension in his voice, but he kept his tone level, betraying no overt anxiety. She could see how he had come to be leader and spokesperson for this group. He was a natural.

Frennan acknowledged him with a bow of the head and launched into the prepared speech he and Gaelen had agreed on. "Gentlemen, only Liannis, the two merchants with us and I are fully aware of the purpose for our request to meet with you. Lord Gaelen asked me to convey to you how grateful he is for all the work you have done and with the well considered way Lieth has found its path to peace and recovery. He is pleased with the way you have conducted yourselves in the absence of a lord and official advisory council."

Liannis could see the tension in the men from Lieth increase from the set of their jaws and the way they leaned forward, stiff and wary. Even Karel, whom she could tell was

201

doing his best not to react, sat rigid in his chair, his eyes narrowed slightly and the crease between his brows more pronounced.

No one interrupted Frennan as he put forth the proposal that Nairin return as regent for Wartin. Frennan was careful to explain all the conditions regarding Wartin's training and Nairin's promise to choose men from the current group as members of her advisory council.

"Lord Gaelen sees this as a good solution to the situation here, as he has never wished to rule Lieth as its Lord, and no other solution has emerged that will allow Lieth to resume its independence."

When a couple of the members from Lieth made to speak, Karel held up his hand for silence. The two sat back but remained agitated, one gripping the arms of his chair and the other clenching his hands in his lap. Liannis made a mental note of their names.

She rose to speak before Karel could say anything. "Gentlemen, as the only one in this group who was also here when Nairin visited I know that there are those who will not welcome Nairin back." She saw five nods of agreement, including two from Bargia. "Karel, can you give us an impression of the strength of that feeling and whether you see that group posing enough opposition to cause serious fighting? Is that faction likely to be a true threat to Lord Gaelen's plan?" She hoped that the way she posed the question let them see that their plan was solid and not open to negotiations. Nairin would come back. The men from Lieth would not be given a choice. "Can you give us your sense of what we must prepare for in order for this plan to succeed?"

Karel sat forward as if to answer but one of the two agitated men began to sputter. "But .."

This time Karel did not interrupt him but let him speak. "But, we have been governing ourselves for over two years. We have no need of a lord. You can see what we have achieved." The man waved an arm about the chamber, as if to have Frennan take in all that had been accomplished.

Liannis resumed her seat and let Frennan answer. "We have already agreed that you have done much and that Lieth's recovery is remarkable." As he met the eyes of each man around the table and they could see he would not argue against this, Liannis could see them relax, ever so slightly.

202

"However," Frennan continued, "throughout that entire time Lord Gaelen has left some of his best men to assist you."

Liannis could feel the tension build again. The men from Lieth grew wary, while the Bargians Frennan referred to nodded.

Frennan stood before continuing. "Lord Gaelen wishes to make it plain that he has no wish to rule Lieth. Nairin has given assurances that she will include some of you, who have worked so hard to rebuild Lieth, in her council. Both Lord Gaelen and Lady Nairin are set on this course. We believe that this is in the best interest of both demesnes. It is our fervent wish that this be accomplished in peace and cooperation. That is why we are here. Not to ask your permission but to engage your assistance, so that this transition may be accomplished as smoothly as possible." He leaned forward to place his palms on the table. "At this time Lord Gaelen is ruler here. The decision has been made. You men will help determine, not whether it will happen, but rather how it can be accomplished."

Silence hung in the chamber for several moments. Frennan resumed his seat and waited.

Liannis stood again. "So you see, gentlemen, the reason for my earlier question. We need to know what kind of opposition we will face and whether we may count on you to see that it takes place with a minimum of conflict. Your support from the outset is crucial to maintaining peace here in Lieth. The people must see this as a measure that has your support." She paused, making sure she had the full attention of all there. "When Lady Nairin came to visit she had not yet decided she wished to return. But the welcome most of the people gave her, and the grief she feels for the losses her people have suffered, have helped her see that she is needed. She wishes to dedicate herself to the full recovery of Lieth as a demesne that can stand proudly beside its neighbours. I can assure you, in my capacity as seer, that she is sincere. She is aware of the weaknesses in her husband, Lord Merlost that led to the circumstances which befell Lieth. She is determined to show you that his errors will not be repeated." She remained standing, waiting for an answer.

Karel steepled his fingers, elbows resting on the edge of the table, and leaned forward, his face set. "First let me say this. It is true that Lieth has relied on the guidance from Bargia during our recovery. I admit that I lose sleep at night wondering what the next

203

step will be. Who will replace us? Who will carry forward the work we have begun when we are no longer able? How will those decisions be made? I have discussed these concerns with the men here."

Liannis saw almost imperceptible nods from three of the men from Lieth. She almost decided to sit down but thought the better of it and remained standing, waiting for the answer to her earlier question.

"But," Karel continued, "you cannot fail to see that we have done well here. We will not wish to relinquish all of the power we have rightfully earned. We have demonstrated that we act with wisdom and good leadership." It was Frennan he addressed as he spoke.

When Frennan nodded Karel turned to Liannis. "You assure us that Lady Nairin will not abandon us all in favour of others but will include us as members of her council, and that we will continue to influence decisions on Lieth's behalf?"

Liannis nodded. "That is so."

Karel held the gaze of each of the men from Lieth in turn. "You all know that our situation was never intended to be permanent; that we always understood that things would change, though we had no sense of what that change would be. I think many of us believed we would become as Catania did, with a governor appointed by Lord Gaelen to govern in his place once things returned to normal here." At their solemn nods of agreement he turned once more to Frennan. "Now we are informed that Lord Gaelen has chosen a different path for us. It appears well thought out. I do not see that we have any recourse but to comply. To refuse would mean war, something we are not equipped for at this stage in our recovery."

No one spoke, all faces intent on his words. "So, we must put a good face on it, trust that Lady Nairin will act as she promises, and give our support to her return." Before anyone could respond he turned once again to Liannis.

"In answer to your question, Liannis, after Lady Nairin's visit many people let it be known that they missed the 'proper way' and are nostalgic for a return of the old way. They have, for the most part, favourable feelings toward Lady Nairin. Since she refused to say what her intentions were, rumours have spread that she wishes to return. I do not see widespread opposition to her doing so."

"That is good to hear. Have you heard anything more from the faction that showed such anger when Lady Nairin was here?"

"It is a small group. Even some of the men who followed their leader previously have fallen away from him since Lady Nairin spoke with them. We do know who the leader is. His name is Krellin. If I may make a suggestion?"

Frennan nodded. "Certainly. That is why we have come."

"I suggest we ask him and possibly two of his followers to meet here so you may address him directly."

"Excellent. Can that be arranged for tomorrow morning?"

"I am certain it can."

"Good, then I think we have accomplished enough today."

60

CONFRONTATION

Krellin arrived mid-morning, flanked by not two, but four followers. When he entered the council chamber his eyes darted quickly about the room, as if looking for someone. Liannis thought he possibly expected Nairin to be present.

"Gentlemen, please be seated." Karel took the lead. "And avail yourselves of the ale and food. We will wait until you are all comfortable."

Liannis liked the way he tried to set things up so the men looked like guests instead of possible enemies. Krellin looked like it put him more at ease. His shoulders lost a little of their tension. He nodded and filled his mug with ale gesturing to his men to follow. Several moments passed before everyone sat with full mugs and platters, Krellin's delegation on one side of the table and Karel's and Frennan's men on the other. Karel, himself sat at the head and Liannis the opposite end.

Frennan spoke first, addressing Karel. "Sir, if you will, may I put forth the proposal to these gentlemen as we did with you yesterday?"

Karel looked momentarily taken aback, but recovered quickly. "As you wish Frennan. Please proceed."

Krellin clenched his fists on his legs, under the table. Liannis could see this but the men opposite him would not be able to. Liannis could sense the effort it took for him to remain silent and listen. He kept his eyes fixed on Frennan the entire time he spoke, never looking at the men with him. It was as though he had rehearsed the scene and he feared losing his self-control if he veered from his planned course. His suspicion was almost palpable to Liannis. She wondered if anyone else detected it.

When Frennan finished, Karel jumped in before Krellin could speak. Krellin had half raised himself out of his chair but caught himself and sat slowly back, his face a strained mask.

"Krellin, when Lady Nairin visited last, you made it plain that you did not welcome her presence. You said, rightly, that our current state of poverty and disrepair had been brought on by her husband, Lord Merlost. Yet, I think, even you and your men will

206

agree that the greater destruction came at the hands of the traitor Garneth and his cronies."

Krellin squirmed. Liannis assumed it was because he knew Karel had the right of it.

Karel continued. "Much has passed since the great fire and rift. Lieth has made great strides. We have rebuilt, have reopened trade and now our fields and pastures fill with new crops. Lieth is well on the way to becoming a fully functioning demesne again. But we lack a clear government that we all understand and agree with. Yesterday we made an agreement with this delegation to invite lady Nairin back under the conditions set forth to you. We ask, now, for your support." He sat back and folded his hands loosely on the edge of the table.

Krellin still did not look at his men. If he had, Liannis knew he would have seen interest there, perhaps some confusion. They had come likely expecting a fight. This reasoned proposal did not meet that expectation.

Krellin clearly decided he had to brazen it out. He sputtered for a moment then banged his fist on the table. "We do not accept this. Merlost ruined Lieth. Nairin is his wife. She will return Lieth to the old ways. Ye cannot believe she will allow any of you on her council." His voice rose higher as he shouted, spittle spraying from his lips, his face growing red, his whole body tight as a coiled spring. "It is all lies! She cannot be trusted. Ye are all fools." For the first time since entering the room he looked at the four who had accompanied him.

With his emotions so heightened, Liannis did not need to touch him to sense his thoughts. What Krellin read on the faces of his men was a mixture of surprise and confusion. His voice rose even higher, desperation lending a wild tone. "Men, can ye not see what is happening here? We are being duped! These men are lying to us. Have ye nothing to say? Do ye not see? Tell them. We cannot have Nairin and her 'get' back! She will ruin us all." By this time Krellin had stood up, shaking with fear and rage, his arms rigid by his sides, his fists clenched white.

Liannis could see the wild sense of defeat that drove him on. When not one of his men made to speak he stopped. After a long silence he looked around the chamber, back at his men again then slumped back into his chair. He made one, last, dejected plea. "Ye must see. She cannot be trusted. She cannot."

When he received no response he let his chin drop, defeated. He had lost and knew it. Liannis suspected he had already known this before he arrived, as his support in the city had, according to Karel, declined greatly since Nairin had visited.

Frennan, consummate statesman that he was, brought the confrontation to a close. "Krellin, we do understand where your concerns come from. We have not undertaken this path lightly. Lord Gaelen has had a clear promise that Lady Nairin does, indeed, plan to include members here at this table in her advisory council. There are guarantees in place to see that Lieth does not fall into the errors that caused its downfall. We have made every effort to gain assurance that Lady Nairin will keep her word. Her son, the future Lord Wartin, will be Bargian trained." He held Krellin in his gaze. "Sir, I ask now that you give your oath that until such time as you witness Lady Nairin break her word, you will not speak against this proposal and that you will counsel your men to act likewise."

When Krellin did not look up or answer, Karel added. "We will need men among the citizens to keep watch on this. If you agree to this proposal I think, perhaps, we may find a role for you as monitor. We will need a few strong men to keep their fingers on the pulse of the people."

Krellin looked up at that, a flicker of hope in his eyes, though his words belied the expression on his face. "I dinna believe ye."

Frennan nodded agreement at Karel. "Excellent suggestion. It will be difficult to have a clear sense of the wishes of the people from the members of the council. They are often too far removed." He turned to Krellin. "Sir, what say you? Do we have your word that you will not oppose us until such time as you have good reason to believe that Lady Nairin has broken her word?"

Krellin's men looked at him, hope and an almost expectant eagerness on their faces. He saw it, too. Looking at Karel, he said, "So ye'll make me and my men watchdogs? Ye'll make us part of this?" A thought seemed to strike him. "We will be paid?"

Karel looked uncomfortable for a moment. "Krellin, all I can promise is that I will propose this to lady Nairin. And I do give my word that I will suggest it to her."

"Very well. I will hold my tongue until I get an answer. But do not wait too long. I will not be fooled into silence for long."

208

The air in the chamber grew lighter. The tension dissipated. Soon all but Krellin were smiling. Another crisis had passed, at least for the time being.

Krellin rose and he left, followed by his men. Karel closed the door behind him and sat down again.

"Well...?" He addressed his question to Liannis.

"I do not foresee any difficulties at this time. I sense he knows he has lost and that he cannot recover. The offer of work as informant has given some legitimacy to him so that he can hold his head up and claim he has not been defeated. He will not fight you at this time." Liannis paused, thinking before she continued. "But I do think he must be given some role, as suggested, or he will fall back to his old position and could cause trouble. That was an excellent suggestion, Karel. It will keep him close so you will be able to keep an eye on him."

61

CLASH

The man he had sent ahead to scout hurried out of the forest to Grund's side, breathing hard. "There is a party just a half span's ride ahead. About ten men, I think. They travel the same direction we do. There is a fork just ahead. I think they turned there from the east. There are tracks on that path."

Grund's face grew red with rage, making the man cringe back. "Men, after them!" He addressed the scout. "You. Lead the way. Now!" But he did not wait for the poor man to lead and galloped ahead, whipping his mount to go faster.

The rest spurred their own horses to catch up kicking up a cloud of dust that would be visible for a great distance.

Less than a span later, with all their horses lathered and heaving for breath, they reached a place where the trail seemed to end. Grund galloped past it, not noticing.

The scout shouted to him, "Lord Grund! Look out!"

The archers among the Catanian guards had four of Grund's men before Grund even registered the warning. He whirled back just in time to see his men fall, three dead, one severely wounded. Their horses ran off, one back the way they had come, the other three disappearing into the forest.

Four more arrows flew, finding four more targets, this time aimed to disable rather than kill. Four more of Grund's men lay on the ground. The only man still horsed was pulled down and tied up, while the rest of the Catanians emerged from the trees and surrounded Grund's horse.

Grund let out a wild scream of rage, defeat and madness. He made his horse rear in an attempt to lash out at the Catanians but one man grabbed his boot and twisted him out of the saddle. The guard at the horse's head managed to step out of the way of the hooves and grab the reins. Grund found himself face down on the ground, with two men on top of him, one binding his wrists, the other, his ankles. His screaming invectives were cut off with a rag stuffed into his mouth and tied in place. They rolled him roughly into a sitting position against a tree, and left him watching helplessly on.

Two of the felled men's injuries made them unfit to travel. They were swiftly given the coup de grace. Their deaths gave Grund a grim, mad satisfaction. They had failed him and deserved to die.

The three remaining alive were trussed and set against other trees. Grund glared at them, wishing they, too, had been killed, nay, wishing he could kill them himself.

Two of the fleeing horses returned at the same moment as another scout joined the Catanians. Grund saw the man's face change to surprise as he took in the chaotic scene. He watched as the leader of the Catanians explained what had happened, and saw the scout give him an appraising, satisfied look. Grund could not hear all of the conversation but thought he caught the name "Strennock" from the scout, and the question "how many?"

A detached calm had come over him and he observed the exchange as though outside himself. So, he reasoned, Strennock was up ahead, just as he expected. No matter. It was over, now. He would soon be dead. None of it would make any difference. He would be gone. He no longer even cared what happened to Strennock and his men. They had failed him, too.

He watched one Catanian guard separate himself from the group and gather the returned horses. The injured men were thrown over their backs and tied on, their mounts' leads tied together in a string. Soon Grund found himself in the same position face down on his own mount, securely tied to his own saddle. The other three horses trailed behind his.

Grund could just see the rest of the party from Catania continue north on the trail as the remaining lone soldier took the reins of Grund's mount in his free hand and led the string back the way they had come, toward Catania City.

62

HOME

With arrangements as stable as could be hoped, and Nairin's return to Lieth accepted in principle, Liannis had little to occupy her mind on the trek back to Bargia other than Merrist and her mother. Both of them seemed well as their auras showed no unusual signs of pain or distress.

This was the height of summer, when grain swayed golden in the winds, heavy with seed. Certain crops, oats among them, already stood scythed and drying in neat stooks, almost ready to be separated from their stalks, winnowed and stored. The straw would find its way into corners and lofts in the animal sheds and stables. The heat of the sun stirred a fine haze of dust into the still air which caught the sunlight, sparkling.

This season the rains had come regularly, giving a plentiful harvest. The people felt optimistic that there would be some extra to replenish the storehouses which had become empty and barren last winter from two years of drought.

Liannis took to sending Kira to fly above them over the landscape. She would 'borrow' the little kestrel's vision to enjoy the scenery and reassure herself that all appeared as it ought to be. Earth had not visited her so she liked to see for herself that nothing looked amiss.

The rain held off for two days, then poured for the next two. Liannis was fortunate that the party found a small croft along the way. While the men in the party had to make do with sleeping in soggy tents, Liannis was welcomed into the crofter's home for the night and so was able to get dry and warm. On the last night before arriving back in Bargia she thought she might not be as lucky, but one of the men remembered there was a warehouse just off the trail. With the harvest not yet in, they found it empty, so the entire party slept dry that night.

While she felt no anxiety pushing her to hurry home, the closer they came to Bargia City the more eager Liannis was to see her mother. She hoped Brensa was strong and well enough to leave for their home cabin. More and more, Liannis looked forward to returning there. The castle and court had never appealed to her and these last moons she had had little time away from others. Her pregnancy had become recognizable to all, now, and she wanted nothing more than to remove herself from prying eyes and suspicious or curious looks. Even more, she wanted Merrist to return so they could live like a real family. Until now they had not had that opportunity. Duty had always demanded something else from them.

Imagining how they would spend the short time left until Ayliss was born kept her spirits up. The men seemed to understand that she wished to be left in peace and spoke very little to her on the way. Indeed, they did not speak much to each other. The heat, the sun, and even the rain had the effect of making the men contemplative.

The sun had returned when they emerged from the warehouse for the last lap of their journey. It rode high in a clear sky as they entered the gates of Bargia City and handed their mounts over to the grooms.

Cloud, having been under Liannis's personal care the past days, grumbled at being handed over.

Liannis lost patience with her. *Cloud, we have been through this many times. You know this is necessary. I am too tired to feel sorry for you. Go."*

"Want apples."

"There are no apples this time of year. You know that."

"Hmph." Cloud snorted and tossed her head in protest, but when Liannis resolutely turned her back and headed for the castle she could hear her being be led away.

Liannis had sent Kira off to hunt before entering the gate. Kira still remained outside the city at Liannis's insistence. She feared for her and did not wish her to be caught.

Marja met them in the great hall, a guard having already announced their arrival. "You look dreadful, Liannis. I have already ordered a bath brought to your chamber." She embraced her then drew back, keeping her hands on Liannis's shoulders and looking her over. "My, but you have grown." She lowered one hand to Liannis's belly. "Is all well?" She gave Liannis a questioning look. At the return smile she beamed. "Ah, yes, I see it is."

"Yes, all is very well, although I admit I am tired." Liannis turned to the stair and began to make her way there. "Is Mama well? Has she regained some of her strength?"

"Yes, she has, although I still wish she would remain here where we can care for her." Marja kept pace beside Liannis as they ascended the stairs. "I still do not like the idea of you all alone, so far away."

Liannis stopped to look at Marja. "My lady, it is what we must do. I sense that this is right. Ayliss must be born at the cabin, perhaps even spend some years there, as I did." She resumed her ascent. "And I know that Mama will never remain away if I am there. She belongs with me and Merrist. And she must be with us at the birth of her grandchild."

Marja sighed, reluctant agreement heavy in her voice. "Yes, I know you are right. But I do not have to like it."

That brought a small chuckle from Liannis. "No, my lady, you do not." She took Marja's hand and gave it a gentle squeeze.

Brensa met them at the door to the lord's chambers, rushing out, arms outstretched to hug Liannis. "You have returned. Oh, Liannis it is good to have you with me again." She drew back, just as Marja had, to look at Liannis's belly, then place both hands there and closed her eyes. A sweet smile softened her face. She opened her eyes and patted Liannis's belly. "She does well." Then Brensa changed her tone, speaking briskly. "Now, I see that you are fatigued and in need of a bath. Go. I have seen what I needed to see. You may join us for dinner after you have rested a span."

Marja, who had come to stand behind Brensa, facing Liannis, caught Liannis's eye and gave a small shrug. "As you can see, your mother is much improved."

Brensa crossed her arms, looking smug. "Did I not promise you I would be?"

Liannis managed a tired laugh. "Indeed you did, Mama. We will speak of our return home at dinner."

THE CABIN

"I wish I knew when Merrist is coming back." Liannis sighed as she stroked her protruding belly. "There is work to be done at the cabin to prepare for our return and for the birth. The gardens will be overgrown and we need to make space for you, Mama."

"I will manage in the loft, Liannis."

"No, Mama, I will not have you climbing that ladder. You are not steady or strong enough."

Her mother had that stubborn look she recognised so well but Liannis knew she was right. Brensa could fall trying to climb the ladder. Before Brensa could argue Gaelen broke in.

"I agree with Liannis, Brensa. But that will be taken care of." He turned to Liannis. "Are you able to travel to the cabin tomorrow to see what needs to be done? I will send three men with you. Tell them what you need and it will be done. I will instruct them to do whatever you request."

Liannis felt a weight lift from her. "Thank you, my lord. The main thing will be to build a sleeping space for Mama on the main level. The cabin is so small I fear it will need to be added to the side."

Gaelen grew thoughtful, then said, "Then tomorrow you must decide what will be needed. Make a list of supplies. We will begin building immediately. You will oversee it so all is done as you wish it."

"My lord, it is a lot to ask."

"Nonsense. You have more than earned it." His tone brooked no argument, although Liannis expected no less.

Brensa sat on the edge of her seat, her face eager. "How long, do you think, before we may go there to stay?"

"I remember when Papa built the loft for me. That took three eightdays, I think." Liannis thought back to when Klast had added the loft for her to sleep in. She had outgrown the table and her sensitive nature made it necessary to have some space of her own.

At the mention of Klast, Brensa's face took on a wistful look. Then she pulled herself back and asked Gaelen, "Can we not stay there while the work is done? Liannis and I can share the bed until Merrist returns."

When Gaelen began to shake his head Liannis suggested, "Perhaps we may stay a day or two, Mama. It will show me how strong you are and how well you are able to ride, but not until I have cleaned it. Perhaps in a few days, if you are well enough."

Brensa bristled. "Of course I am well enough. Surely you can see that."

"I will miss you, Brensa." The worried crease in Marja's forehead deepened.

Brensa softened. "And I you. But this is something we must do." She rose to embrace her friend and lady. "And you will visit often, I know you will."

Liannis took her cue and also stood up. "Mama, if I am to be rested to visit our cabin I must get some sleep. Are you ready to go to bed?"

***

The next morning, as the party of four entered the clearing where the cabin nestled at the far edge, Liannis knew she had come home. She felt a peace, a certainty that she missed anywhere else. She urged Cloud forward, edging ahead of the others. Kira, sensing Liannis's excitement, flew up from her shoulder and executed two joyful circles before making a bee-line for the cabin. The sight made Liannis laugh.

Cloud, too, seemed to understand. *Show me stall shed. Is mine again?* Then she looked around. *Where are cow and hens?*

Yes, Cloud, you will have your stall again, but not until we are ready to remain here. And our cow will also be returned when we come to stay. She has a new calf, did you know? But we will need new hens. The others no longer laid eggs.

At the mention of the calf Liannis sensed a change in Cloud, an attitude she had never felt in her before. Even though Cloud did not send the thought clearly, Liannis intuited what lay behind the change. *Cloud, do you wish to become a mother as well? Like Cow and like me?*

No horse here to mate with Cloud. Must be special horse. Warrior too stupid.

216

Then we must find one that is clever like you. This will be a good time. While Ayliss is tiny I will not need to leave here, I think.

Cloud will bear foal for babe if find a good sire.

How wonderful, Cloud. I would like that very much.

Hmph. Need find a sire first.

Yes, Cloud, you do.

By now they had all reached the cabin. Liannis dismounted and removed the bit from Cloud's mouth so she could graze on the lush grass.

The men followed her lead, but hobbled their mounts so they could not stray far. Cloud did not need that.

As Liannis entered the one room cabin where she had grown up, followed by the three men, and looked around, her mind flooded with memories. It seemed that the layer of dust which lay on everything merely served to preserve them for her, to polish and cherish as she cleaned the dust away.

"Lady?"

Liannis pulled herself back to the present, realising that one of the men had been calling her name more than once. "Forgive me, I was in deep thought."

She watched the men exchange uneasy looks. "No, this was not a vision. I am quite fine." Their faces eased.

She stepped toward the tiny window to the right of the door. "Could this window be enlarged into a door, do you think? Then a room could be added here for Mama, opening onto the main cabin. Perhaps you could add a small window for her in the front wall." She gestured as she spoke to demonstrate what she meant, her hands wide as if outlining the door.

"Yes, I think that is the best place." The lead man examined the wall. "I do think this wall will need to be replaced. It is too old and warped to reuse those beams." He took a closer look at the window. "But I think we can salvage this and put it in the new wall." He turned to Lainnis, looking decidedly uncomfortable. "Will you also be needing space for the babe?"

Liannis understood his discomfort came from needing to acknowledge aloud that a seer was going to have a child. She sensed no animosity, however, only confusion over how things were changing. "No, that will not be needed. When she needs to, she will use the loft, as I did." She made her voice as cheerful and

217

positive as she could, to reassure the men. "And will one of you please go up on the roof, to see that it is sound?"

"As you wish, Lady." A second man headed to the door.

"Please call me Liannis."

He turned to face her. "As you wish, La...er, Liannis." His face reddened as he hurried out.

"Let us have a look at the shed. The animals will need safe shelter." Liannis led the way. As she passed her mother's garden she could not help but groan inwardly at the weeds. The herbs had become entangled and overgrown and the patch Brensa had used for beans and squash needed to be completely re-dug. She could see not one patch of brown left between the green of the weeds. That would need to be done before she brought Brensa here or her mother would be trying to do it all herself. Brensa's health was still too frail to permit that. She decided to ask Gaelen to send a gardener for a few days to help.

Late that afternoon the group mounted their horses and headed back to the castle. Each man had a solid sense of what needed to be done and what tools and supplies they would require to do it. Liannis spoke little as they rode, allowing the men to talk among themselves as they planned their tasks. She had been pleasantly surprised when they informed her that all would be ready in only two eightdays.

64

CATANIA

An eightday after the capture of Grund the guards who had continued after Strennock and his cronies returned to Catania City with five captives and much to report.

Brynnell insisted the exhausted men, after depositing their prisoners in the dungeons, take the remainder of the day to rest and eat. The entire party convened in the council chambers the next morning with Brynnell, Charest, Frellick, Lionn and Merrist.

"We have already heard what happened up to the point where Grund was captured." After inviting the men to help themselves to ale Brynnell wasted no time. "We know we now have Strennock and three others in prison." He inclined his head toward the leader of the guards. "Hellor, please report."

"Sir, we had no difficulty following Strennock's trail. It appears he knew nothing of stealth. We first encountered one lone man, on foot, heading back in our direction. He could barely walk and had blood all over his tunic. He told us that he had argued about which way to go and that Strennock had stabbed him and left him for dead, accusing him of treason. The man confirmed the path Strennock had taken. When I examined his wounds I realised that he would never recover, as the knife had pierced his gut. Since he had told us all he could I gave him the coup de grace. We had no time to bury him, so left him in the forest for the scavengers, as we had the others from Grund's party."

Hellor halted, looking somewhat ashamed, as if expecting disapproval.

Brynnell cleared his throat. "I understand. It was necessary, as it was with those in Grund's party. Please continue."

The faces of the four others in Hellor's party mirrored the relief on his. He swallowed before continuing. "We came upon Strennock and his men just before dusk. We could tell he knew we were almost there as we could hear him shouting orders to hide in the trees and try to ambush us. The fool made no attempt to keep quiet. I told my men to proceed with caution, but we need not have. As we rounded the last bend I saw Strennock standing at the side of the forest, waving his arms, still shouting, 'Cowards, Grund will have your heads!' The men with him stood in the middle of the

219

path, their arms in the air and their weapons on the ground." Hellor looked perplexed. "I thought it might be a diversion at first. My men did as well, and we looked into the trees for archers." He held his hands out in disbelief. "There were none. Strennock had only these four and they had surrendered to us."

Merrist saw Hellor's men shake their heads as if they, too, could not believe it. He heard one mumble, "Cowards."

Brynnell leaned towards Hellor, fingers interlaced on the table in front of him. "And Strennock?"

"As soon as he saw us, sir, he stopped yelling, turned tail and fled into the trees on his horse. I left one man to control the prisoners and the rest of us went after him. It was growing dark, especially among the trees, so we followed him until we could no longer see. I sent Parst back to assist with the prisoners. Then I ordered Restin to light a torch so we could continue to follow Strennock's trail, which was plain in the torchlight. We found Strennock's horse, wandering rider-less. I thought Strennock might have given us the slip until I heard the crack of a branch and a yelp of pain further into the forest. Restin soon located Strennock's boot prints and we were able to follow them. Another crack of a branch led us straight to him. He turned to face us and then charged Restin with his sword out." Hellor turned to Restin. "Perhaps this part of the tale belongs to you."

Restin's face creased in a broad grin. "He was wild, sirs. But he could not run as he had hurt his ankle when he fell. That was the yell we heard. So Strennock lost his balance when he tried to relieve me of the torch by trying to cut off my hand. I was ready for him and kicked his sword arm out of the way as he fell. He still tried to kick the torch out of my hand as he lay on the ground. When that did not work he made a grab for my ankle and made me lose my footing. He made a last lunge for my torch and I thrust it into his chest." Restin looked embarrassed as he continued. "Not my most memorable fight, but we have our man ... and," he added, "he will recover from his burns to face trial."

Merrist could understand the man's chagrin and almost sniggered but managed to hold it in. This was not the way a soldier wanted to show his skill in battle. He looked around and saw Frellick and Hellor hold hands in front of their mouths. Hellor's other men studied their hands, sheepish looks on their faces.

Hellor could not hold himself in and let out a chuckle. "Not our proudest moment, sirs, but as Restin says, we have our prisoner."

"Indeed," was Charest's only response. It seemed he was the only one who saw no humour in the debacle. But Merrist could tell that even Charest's eyes crinkled slightly at the corners.

A few more questions filled in the details. Strennock's men had been hungry as they had fled without provisions. When questioned as to why they had surrendered, they said they knew they had no chance of getting away, that Strennock had become increasingly enraged and unpredictable. When he had stabbed the man who disagreed with him they decided they had a better chance to survive if they no longer followed him.

After determining that no one had any more questions Brynnell ended the debriefing and dismissed Hellor and his men.

As soon as the door closed behind the men Charest revealed his true feelings by snorting, "Not our proudest moment, indeed," and barked a short laugh. Then he sobered. "So, my friends. We have the traitors in the dungeons, at least those we know of; Grund and his men, Strennock and his, and the group from the warehouse outside the city. We have no knowledge of any other lairs, though that does not mean there are none."

"True," Frellick broke in, "But with Grund no longer there to lead them I think the threat is small."

"Agreed," Charest said. "But we now have other decisions to make. The first, as I see it, is whether to have the trials of the traitors before Brynnell's investiture, or to wait until after."

Merrist could feel the change in the chamber as the men shifted from the need to capture and contain their enemies to the plans that had had been put aside until they had dealt with the threat. Even though the mood seemed to lift, the chamber grew quiet as everyone gave their attention to Charest's question.

Lionn spoke first. "My friends. I think it would add weight to Brynnell's new position as lord if he held that title before the traitors come to trial. Then the people will see him as acting with the authority of lordship upon him. It will lend a finality to his position. The people will respond better to him in that role if they see him deal with treason as any lord does."

Brynnell raised an eyebrow as though he had not thought of that possibility. If he had seen any humour in the proceedings

221

earlier, that disappeared now. He sat back, his face a solemn mask as he regarded each of them in turn.

Merrist would later tell Liannis it seemed that the weight of Brynnell's position had finally come to sit on his shoulders and he found it heavy, indeed.

All eyes rested on Brynnell. No one spoke. After a weighty silence Brynnell sat up and squared his shoulders. "Yes, I see the wisdom of this. Nor can there be any delay or the people will begin to ask unwelcome questions." He took a deep breath, as if gathering courage. "Gentlemen, let us set a date for my investiture."

"It must be a grand occasion, one fitting a new lord." Merrist spoke for the first time. "The people will accept you better if they see you invested with all pomp and ceremony. The celebration must show that Catania is no longer merely a servant of Bargia. She will be a demesne on her own again, independent and strong." At the nods around the table he went on. "How long do you think it will take for the grand announcement to reach all the citizens? And what will be required to plan the day of celebration? We will need to declare a holiday, I think, so as many citizens as possible may attend."

They settled on an eightday hence. The decree was written, copies made and sent to all corners of Catania, banners ordered, food and drink decided on. For this short period they could put the tensions of the past difficulties behind them. Only Brynnell did not completely allow the buoyant mood to overtake him and remained quiet, though even he had lost some of the apparent weight from earlier.

65

LORD BRYNNELL

Rain had fallen overnight before the day of the investiture. Dawn found busy hands scurrying to dry the many chairs and benches set out around the perimeter of the central square. These would be occupied by designated honoured guests.

"Lionn, you will have to stand in for Lord Gaelen. He has not yet arrived." Charest had taken Lionn aside. A scout had been sent to Bargia with all haste to invite Lord Gaelen and Lady Marja in the hope they would be able to arrive in time for the ceremony.

Lionn opened his mouth to answer, but had no time to get the words out of his mouth when the two spied a lone horse and rider approach with speed - the messenger they had sent with the invitation. He halted in front of them, dismounted awkwardly in his haste and bowed.

"Sirs, Lord Gaelen and Lady Marja are on their way. I left them before dawn. They had already risen and instructed me to inform you that they expect to arrive shortly after midday. Lord Gaelen asks that you delay the formal investiture ceremony until he arrives but that the earlier festivities must begin as planned."

Merrist had seen the messenger arrive and overheard this as he hurried over to stand beside Lionn. He clapped Lionn on the shoulder. "That is excellent news, is it not, Lionn?"

Lionn's relief showed plainly as his face split into a broad grin. "Indeed." He addressed the messenger. "Sir, go to the stables for a fresh horse and return to Lord Gaelen to tell him how pleased we are with this news and that all will be as he requests."

As soon as the man had gone Lionn grabbed Merrist's forearm and began a short dance around him in glee, almost causing Merrist to lose his balance.

Laughing, Merrist stopped him. "Lionn, remember your dignity, my friend. What will the people think?"

Charest looked on, shaking his head in mock reproach. When Lionn finally stopped, Charest chuckled. "I will tell Brynnell the good news." Still smiling, he strode off in the direction of the castle.

Lionn could not contain his glee. "I must tell Joranna. Now we will be able to watch the proceedings together. I will not be required to act as my father's proxy." As he raced away, Lionn turned back long enough to shout over his shoulder, "Now I can forget that speech I had planned."

Merrist watched his friend race off. He understood how heavy Lionn's duties in Catania had been these several eightdays. Without Lord Gaelen to guide him he had learned to make the difficult decisions of a leader, even if only as proxy, but the toll on him could be seen in the haggardness of his face. Lionn had done well, in spite of his youth and lack of experience. Now he could rid himself of all the tension he had been holding in.

Merrist looked about the square before following Lionn to the castle. All around the perimeter bright pennants, in the orange and green of Catania, fluttered in the morning breeze. On two sides elevated platforms stood arrayed with chairs, benches lined up on the ground in front. Men hustled to erect canopies over the platforms in the event of a sudden shower during the ceremonies. Smaller kiosks filled the remaining spaces around the edge, all gaily decorated with bright banners and ribbons. Some stalls were designated for musicians and performers, the rest slowly filled up with every kind of food imaginable; baked treats - both sweet and savoury, meats of all kinds - some turning on spits over open fires.

By shortly after dawn very few stalls remained empty. The noise grew to a happy cacophony of voices, with men shouting orders as they added the last touches to the decorations, and children running about chasing each other as parents ignored them, having too much to do. The owners of the food stands shouted across the square in greeting. The air had a buoyant feel.

Merrist looked up at the sky and decided that even the sun had decided to smile on them. The clouds that had dampened the square earlier thinned, and a patch of bright blue grew in their place.

As Merrist made his way to the castle, he noted that guests had begun to arrive. From almost every opening between the stalls he could see families, couples and single men and women converging onto the square. Soon they would be shoulder to shoulder, jostling each other as they moved among the food stalls to taste as many of the treats as they could; foods that, for this one day, they would not be asked to pay for. After the investiture part of the ceremonies, ale would also be doled out at no charge. Then,

224

the music and dancing would begin. Yes, this would be a good day. Merrist could feel it.

By late morning invited guests had filled all the chairs on their platform, many with hands full of food and carrying pennants to wave after the ceremony.

At midday, Merrist took his seat at the edge of the smaller platform set up as a dais. Beside him Lionn and Joranna took their places. Frellick and his wife soon joined them. Only one chair on this side remained empty, waiting for Charest. A single, ornately carved chair, with an embroidered cushion on the seat, had pride of place half-way back in the centre, facing the square. Opposite Merrist, facing him, stood three more chairs, more ornate than his, with cushions on the seats. These waited for Gaelen, Marja and Brynnell.

Even though Merrist knew what to expect, as he had been involved in the planning and preparations, he could feel his own excitement build.

Precisely at midday, the sun high in the sky, Brynnell, followed by Charest, emerged from the castle, soberly but richly attired, and made his way to the chair third from the front, opposite Merrist and his friends. Charest came to stand at the front of the dais and faced the square. When he held up his hands a great cheer went up.

In spite of his advanced age, Charest still possessed a voice that carried to the far corners of the square. "My good people, please be seated so the ceremonies may begin."

The din fell to a thrum of murmurs as people looked about themselves, settled on the ground and turned expectant faces to the dais.

Silence fell when Charest raised his hands once more. "As you all know, today is an auspicious day for Catania, the day when we once more claim our heritage as an independent demesne. It is the day we once more invest our own lord." He paused to allow the roar of the crowd's cheering to fill the square then held his hands up for attention once more. "All such special celebrations call for feasting ... which I see you are enjoying." Another wave of cheering drowned him out until he gestured once more for silence. While he waited for the din to die down a messenger hurried onto the dais to whisper in his ear.

225

At the look of relief on Charest's face Merrist knew he must have announced the arrival of Gaelen and his party. The crowd had gone silent, regarding Charest with open curiosity. He did not keep them waiting. "My good people, I have wonderful news. If we can be patient for just a few more moments, Lord Gaelen will take his rightful chair on the dais and preside over the official proceedings."

Murmurs, hushed yet excited, rolled through the crowd like waves on water. Lionn gave Merrist an elbow in his ribs and sent him a relieved wink. He grasped Joranna's hand tightly in his, where he sat next to her. Though he held it low where the people would not notice, hidden behind the fold of her skirts, Merrist had not missed it.

Charest invited a group of musicians to play while they awaited Gaelen's arrival. When he appeared the crowd moved aside in haste to let him through, followed by Marja and ... Merrist almost jumped from the dais for joy. Liannis followed them. When she spotted him he knew from the expression on her face that she mirrored his joy. Then he looked down to her belly. Had he really been away that long? She had grown so much. No one could doubt that she was with child any longer. Her white linen gown draped softly over her rounded belly in proud display. When he met her eyes again she placed a hand on it and sent him such a look of love it almost made him weep.

But a chair for her had been quickly placed beside that of Lady Marja, so they had no chance to speak.

When the newcomers had taken their places, and been served food and drink Charest called the people once more to attention. He swept his arms wide to include all those on the dais, the platform across from him and the people below, laughing. "Good people, my work is done here. I defer to Lord Gaelen and turn these proceedings over to him."

Gaelen rose and came to shake Charest's hand before allowing him to retreat to the chair set aside for him.

Gaelen gave a speech explaining what had led to the decision to allow Catania, once more, to become independent, and what had led to choosing Brynnell as its new lord. The people listened respectfully, but Merrist could sense their impatience to get on with things. Gaelen kept his speech short and soon called Brynnell to stand beside him.

226

From a pouch embroidered with the colours of Catania, he drew forth a gold torque. At that gesture an expectant hush fell. The crowd grew so still that Merrist could hear birds chirping at the edge of the square. All eyes fixed upon the two men standing before them.

"Brynnell." Gaelen's voice rang with authority. "You have been acclaimed by the people, and confirmed by myself and my advisors to, henceforth, be the ruling lord of Catania. Before I place this torque, held in trust in Bargia since the overthrow of this demesne by my lord father, around your neck, I must request of you one oath. Are you ready to hear it?"

"I am, Lord Gaelen."

Though Merrist detected a slight tremor in Brynnell's voice it was so small that he suspected no one below noticed. The response had been clear and strong.

"Brynnell, do you swear to rule Catania and its people with honour and strength, and to uphold Catania's alliance with Bargia and her other allies? If you agree, the seer Liannis will truth-read you as you swear the oath."

When Brynnell once more agreed aloud, Liannis came to stand beside him, and placed a hand on one shoulder. Merrist knew the gesture was not necessary but agreed that it was a good decision, as not all the people would understand that Liannis could truth-read without contact.

Gaelen inclined his head to Brynnell to begin. "Please, swear the oath."

"I, Brynnell, do swear to rule Catania and its people with honour and strength and to uphold Catania's alliance with Bargia and her other allies."

As he spoke a soft green glow grew around both Brynnell and Liannis, unmistakable to all watching. The authority in Brynnell's voice grew such that it rang out past all the people and seemed to spread beyond the square. When he had finished the glow gradually receded. Earth had given her approval.

Liannis removed her hand, and with the voice lent her by Earth, declared, "Brynnell has spoken true," and stepped back.

Gaelen raised the torque above his head and held it there for all to see. "Earth has spoken." He turned to Brynnell, who stood rooted, awe still written in his face.

"Brynnell."

On hearing his name, Brynnell managed to draw his attention back to Gaelen.

"Brynnell, Earth has chosen you to be Lord of Catania." Gaelen placed the torque of office around Brynnell's neck and turned to stand beside him facing the people. "People of Catania, welcome your new lord, Lord Brynnell. May he live long and rule in peace." He took Brynnell's right arm and raised it high.

Merrist thought the cheering and shouting would never stop.

After some time Gaelen stepped back to sit in his chair, leaving Brynnell standing alone. Brynnell let the cheering continue a short time more before holding his hands up for attention. It took the crowd some time to settle before he could make himself heard.

"My good people. My gratitude to you, for your trust and honour, cannot be adequately put into words. Please know that I will serve you to the best of my ability as long as I have breath. I already have an advisory council that I respect and trust, who also wish nothing more than to serve you. May Earth send us her support as we stand, once more, as an independent demesne." When the crowd began to murmur again he held his hands up a final time, smiling broadly. "No more speeches. Let the festivities continue. Ale for everyone who wishes it!"

Another great roar went up as people rose and began to seek out refreshment and entertainment once more.

66

REUNION

As soon as Gaelen and Marja rose to indicate that they, too, would join in the festivities, Merrist and Liannis hurried across the dais and embraced. Liannis wondered what the people who noticed would think about this show of affection, but she had watched Gaelen and Marja publicly show affection for each other. She hoped this gesture would act as another affirmation of the change in her status.

Merrist finally stood back but held tightly to her hand. "Let me look at you. How do you fare, my love? How is our daughter? I am so surprised to see you here. Was the journey not too tiring?"

Liannis laughed at the tumble of questions. "I am happy to see you too, Merrist. Both Ayliss and I are well. But I will welcome a quiet chamber and some rest very soon." She took a moment to check herself and observed, "Hmmmm. The truth-read and Earth's visitation during Brynnell's oath have not tired me as they would have before. That is very curious."

Merrist placed his free hand on her belly. "Perhaps Ayliss has something to do with that."

"Yes, perhaps, or Earth has sent me extra strength." Liannis began to draw Merrist toward the steps leading from the dais. "Merrist, do you need refreshment? Or are you ready to go to the castle? The journey was hurried and I am tired. I feel my fatigue more, now that I need not be on my mettle quite so much, now that the ceremony is over."

"I need only to be with you. Let us leave here."

Liannis kept her senses open for disapproval from the people as she and Merrist made their way across the square to the castle. She sensed a few who were still not ready to accept them and looked at them with some hostility, but most people took no notice, and of those who did, many showed acceptance mixed with curiosity. Perhaps the optimism of the celebrations had made them more inclined to generosity.

Merrist gave her a sideways glance, one eyebrow raised in question.

"I sense no danger. Most of the people seem to accept us, or at least are not disposed to oppose us." She squeezed his hand. "It seems you have won many over. Most are in awe of you."

"I think word of my healing is spreading. And the guards I worked with when they went after Grund and Strennock are telling everyone about it."

"And I hear you have found a follower."

In spite of the teasing lilt Liannis had put into her voice, Merrist blushed in embarrassment. "You have heard about Whilsh already? I am not liking having so much admiration. He follows me about like a dog."

"Indeed."

"He has asked if he may accompany me back to Bargia. I do not know what to tell him. I have no desire to have a servant."

"Has he no other work?"

"He worked on the estate for the lady Morna, with the horses, but she is now here in the city. Her entire family is gone, murdered at Strennock's hands and those of his traitors. Morna barely speaks, even now. She will never need Whilsh again."

"Hmm." Liannis did not answer as they had reached the castle gate.

Merrist stepped ahead to address the guard. "Sir, we wish to proceed to my chamber. This is the seer, Liannis, my wife."

After a startled look the guard stood at attention and saluted Merrist smartly. "Of course, sir" He stepped back to admit them.

"This way." Merrist took the lead.

On the way he ordered food and tea brought. The maid he spoke to also gave a startled look before hurrying to obey.

"I see that your arrival has caused some questions." Merrist gave Liannis a crooked, wry smile.

"True, but I sense little serious animosity. I think Catania has decided not to oppose us, to wait and see." Merrist had unlocked their door and stood aside to let Liannis precede him. Before he could close it he spotted the maid bearing their tray and waited to take it from her. "Thank you."

Liannis sank into the lone chair. Merrist poured her a mug of tea before seating himself on the bed facing her. "Liannis, shall I leave you to sleep or shall we share our news first?"

"I will tell only a few things, now. Then, will you lie beside me while I sleep until dinner? I have missed that so much."

"That would please me." The tone of his voice told her he had missed it as well.

Liannis filled him in on the expansion to the cabin and the decision to have Brensa join them there.

"The rest of my news can wait until we are all together over dinner. Lord Gaelen will wish to hear from you and Lionn as well. That way we will all learn together." Her tea finished, Liannis ignored the food and lay down on the bed. She slept as soon as Merrist lay beside her and drew her head onto his shoulder.

67

NEWS

A soft rap on the door woke Merrist from his snooze. He extracted himself from Liannis and quietly opened the door to a maid.

"Sir, you requested that you be told when dinner was ready. Lord Brynnell suggests you all meet in the council chamber, as there are too many of you for his chambers and you will wish for some privacy."

"Thank you. Tell him we will come shortly." He went back to the bed and placed a light hand on Liannis's belly before trying to wake her. Ayliss rewarded him by moving under his touch, which filled him with awe and tenderness. Then, he gently shook Liannis by the shoulder. "Wake up, my love. We are called to dinner."

Liannis opened her eyes, found his gaze and gave him a sleepy smile. "I am ready." She drank another mug of the now cooled raspberry leaf tea before smoothing her gown and following Merrist out. They were the last to arrive at the council chambers. The table was laden with all manner of foods brought in from the festivities, as well as ale, wine and two kinds of tea.

Merrist noticed that Joranna had joined them. That was fitting, as she was Brynnell's daughter, but she stood out as she sat beside Lionn rather than Brynnell. Merrist took a second look at the pair and decided they looked apprehensive. He did not have time to wonder why.

"Liannis, Merrist, please find chairs and help yourselves to food and drink." Brynnell indicated the pair of empty chairs at the corner of the table. "I regret we are not able to meet in the greater comfort of my chambers, but space will not permit it."

Over the next few spans everyone reported on what had occurred while they were apart. Much of it confirmed the consensus that they faced no major new crises. Only the last item dampened the mood – the pending trial of the traitors Grund, Strennock, and their men.

"We waited until after the official ceremony today," Brynnell explained to those who had newly arrived, "to lend authority to the trial."

232

Gaelen agreed. "That was wise. Now that you are lord there will be fewer to challenge you. Yet this must be dealt with swiftly, lest you be seen as weak and unable to make the difficult decisions."

Brynnell gave a grim nod. "True. I thought to begin the trials in two days time."

Merrist could not help but notice how fatigued Brynnell looked, now that he had dropped his jovial mien. "I think that is wise. I know that your other advisors feel the same. The sooner this is dealt with, the sooner life can resume its proper pace."

"Do you wish that I stay to see it through with you, to lend support?" Gaelen asked. "Or do you think it best handled without outsiders involved?"

Merrist noticed that Lionn and Joranna kept looking at each other and fidgeting more as the evening wore on. Lionn did not seem focussed on the discussion. Merrist also noticed that Brynnell and Gaelen seemed to be deliberately ignoring them. Since he had some idea as to the cause of the couple's anxiety he took some pleasure in their discomfort. Let them squirm a little longer. When he brought himself back to the discussion he realised he had missed something. If he had sat close enough he would have given Lionn a teasing elbow in the ribs.

"I am relieved that you will not need me to truth-read the prisoners. Their guilt is plain. I am not at all certain I could manage it in my current condition. I also worry about the effect on our daughter." Liannis had placed both hands protectively on her belly and stroked it as though calming a child.

"That is well, then. Marja and I will depart tomorrow and leave you to deal with this on your own." Gaelen, too, seemed relieved. He turned to Marja. "Pehaps we can visit Gharn and see Sennia and Dugal before we return to Bargia?" When Marja answered with an eager nod he turned to Liannis and Merrist. "Will you accompany us?"

Merrist was about to agree when he saw Liannis shake her head.

"No, my lord. Mama is alone in Bargia. I know the ladies will look after her but she is anxious, as am I, to see our cabin and return to it. I, too, am weary and feel the need to settle and rest as we await the birth of our daughter. Please give Sennia and Dugal our love and best wishes for the arrival of their twins."

233

Everyone gaped at her. Merrist found his voice first. "Liannis? What are you saying?"

Liannis's eyes widened in surprise then changed to delight. "Yes, it appears Earth has sent a message in a most unusual way. I know that Sennia is with child again, two children, in fact, a boy and a girl. I saw it in a dream a few days ago. Now I have permission to tell you all. Oh how wonderful." She clapped her hands in glee. Soon everyone joined in with congratulating Gaelen and Marja. The mood had once again become joyous.

Everyone quieted after Lionn had loudly cleared his throat at least three times. When they turned their attention to him he stood, drawing Joranna up beside him and grasping her hand for all to see. "Joranna and I also have happy news. I know custom would ask us to do this with each family in private, but we decided to create our own custom. We wish to announce our decision to join. The summer is well past its midpoint and we wish it to take place before travel becomes a problem."

Merrist knew that Lionn had, indeed, broken custom. A union such as this required the permission of all living parents. This was more than a simple union of a man and woman; it also created new bonds between two demesnes. It ought to have been discussed privately. He wondered for a moment, in the silence that ensued, if Lionn would be reprimanded for his impetuosity. But Liannis rose to speak before anyone else found their tongue. And she had the mantle of power on her, the aura that let all know it was not she, but Earth, who spoke.

"Let all rejoice in the union of these two servants of Earth. Their joining will bring strength and stability to both demesnes, which will influence their neighbours and deter their enemies." When she finished she sank back into her chair, spent. Merrist hastened to place a mug of tea into her cold hands.

The startled responses of the others soon changed to delighted congratulations.

Lionn and Joranna beamed as everyone came to embrace them and wish them well.

When Liannis had recovered enough to do the same she turned to Merrist. "I need to sleep, now. Will you come with me?"

"Of course, my love."

68

RETURN TO THE CABIN

Lionn embraced Liannis as she and Merrist stood holding the reins of their horses by the city gates. Merrist looked at Brynnell, catching his eye. "Brynnell, please convey my gratitude to Charest and the others for finding a place in the stables for Whilsh."

Brynnell nodded. "He wished to follow you but I understand that your lives have no place for a servant. Whilsh now has a respected position. I am certain he will be happier here among his own people."

"Indeed."

Lionn spoke, disappointment thick in his voice. "It is most unfortunate that you will not be with us for the joining. I had always thought you would be present to celebrate that with me."

"I, too, wish I could be there, Lionn, but my time is near and Mama waits for me to take her home. I am torn, but I know this is what I must do."

Lionn looked forlorn. "I do understand."

Merrist clasped Lionn's forearm, and followed it with a hug. "Promise us you and Joranna will visit as soon as you return to Bargia."

Lionn managed a smile as he turned to catch Joranna's eyes. "You may depend on it. At least my parents will return here to Catania for the joining." He gave Gaelen and Marja a brave smile.

"You may count on it. Perhaps we can even persuade Dugal and Sennia to return with us." Marja put an arm around Joranna's waist and drew her close.

Liannis could tell this reassured Joranna. Her shoulders relaxed and her face lost its slight apprehensiveness as she returned the gesture, exclaiming, "Oh, I do hope so. I have never met them but by all accounts they are wonderful."

Gaelen and Marja, even Brynnell, had come to see them off. They all delayed several moments, with repeated embraces and admonishments to be well and happy, before Liannis and Merrist could finally mount and ride out, waving back at the group watching in the open gate.

235

"I do wish we could have remained for the joining ceremony," Liannis told Merrist once they were no longer in sight of the gate, "but that would have meant I would be there during the trials and executions. I do not think I could bear that, now. And it is not necessary, as their guilt is so plain."

"I am certain they understand, Liannis." Merrist sidled Warrior close to take Liannis's hand. "And Brensa waits for you. I, too, am glad to be going home, to have some peace before the arrival of our daughter. I hope Earth has no further need of us for a time." He grew quiet for a moment, as if in reverie. "I have no sense that we need to be anywhere else, do you?"

"No, this is what we are meant to do. I think our work is finished for the moment."

"You do not sense any unrest in Bargia or Lieth? Catania has accepted us, I think."

"No, I sense no danger. But that can change, of course." Liannis let her awareness expand, hoping for a message from Earth. When she sensed nothing, other than the peace of the terrain they travelled in, she turned back to Merrist. "Earth is silent. I think this is a time for rest."

Each night, before sleeping, Liannis checked the auras of her mother, of Gaelen and Marja and of Dugal and Sennia. She regretted not being with them and this was the only way she had to feel connected. On the fourth night she wistfully confirmed, "They have reached Gharn. They are all happy and well."

"Can you see if Dugal and Sennia will return to Catania for the joining?"

"Oh, yes, I am certain of it, even without a message from Earth. As long as Sennia is well, nothing will stand in her way. Lionn is her brother after all, and she has not met his intended. She will wish to see if she approves." Liannis laughed. "She will be furious that Lionn has not sought her approval before anyone else."

The laughter lifted their spirits.

While it was possible to travel from Catania to Bargia in four days, Merrist insisted they travel more slowly, so Liannis would not overtire.

Liannis did not argue. She did tire more easily, now, and sensed no urgency to return in haste. The slower pace allowed them to enjoy the trail and the surrounding land. They crossed crofts where happy farmers and their families brought in wagons

236

piled high with heavy harvests of spelt. The sheaves were then beaten to dislodge the grain and the straw stored in lofts for bedding for the livestock. They admired the development of fat ears of maize, to be ready for harvest in another moon. Beans weighed heavy on their vines, some already hanging from rafters to dry before shelling and winnowing. Cabbages sat outside cabin doors, waiting for the slicers. After slicing they would be mixed with salt and pounded into great glazed crocks and weighted down with platters and stones to ferment into sauerkraut.

Gardens trailed vines of winter squashes around rows of fat carrots and turnips. Onions and garlic hung in braided strands in the sun to dry.

They passed orchards where early apples had already been picked and later ones weighed the branches low, almost to breaking. These would soon be picked, sliced and strung in long garlands, to be added to winter cakes. Others, those that lasted well, would be stored in wooden bins, beside the carrots and tubers, in cool cellars dug into the earth and covered with sod to keep them from freezing.

Everywhere they went they shared the optimism of people looking forward to a winter with abundant food.

Liannis made an effort to be seen by the citizens, in spite of her penchant for privacy. They managed to get lodging with crofters on every night but one. She wanted to see to it that as many people as possible would be exposed to the changes in her position and role and to see Merrist. She wanted to get a sense of how the people received them.

The first reaction was often surprise, puzzlement, and occasionally suspicion, but almost everyone had already heard about their joining, so their hesitation soon turned into frank curiosity. The bountiful harvest seemed to reassure them that Earth approved. These were simple folk who did not question as much as their city counterparts, and so the couple found welcome, once their hosts recovered from their initial hesitation.

The journey found them at the gates of Bargia castle at midday on the seventh day. Someone had alerted Brensa of their arrival and she came to meet them as they entered the castle grounds.

"Mama, you look well." Liannis returned her mother's hug, then let her go to receive one from Merrist.

"Merrist, I am so happy to see you have returned with Liannis." She let go, stood back to give Liannis's belly a measured look. "You have grown, I see." She placed a hand on Liannis's abdomen and gave a girlish giggle. "Oh, my, yes. Soon, now, soon," at which both Liannis and Merrist laughed.

Brensa turned and hurried to the castle doors. "Come, I have ordered tea and cakes."

Merrist sent Liannis an indulgent glance, took her hand and followed.

"So, Mama," Liannis asked when they sat enjoying their tea, "have you had news on the work at the cabin?"

"Oh yes indeed. Just yesterday one of the men came to tell me that all is ready for us. The work is complete. They also made sure the roof was tight and patched the sod where it had become thin."

"Then," Merrist said, "we will go there tomorrow to see that all is ready. Perhaps we will all be able to return there to stay in a few days."

"Oh, it is ready, now. And I am ready as well."

Her mother's eagerness stopped Liannis from urging patience.

When Liannis saw Merrist begin to shake his head and raise his hand as though to urge caution, she broke in. "Well, then, Mama, I think we will all leave after breaking fast tomorrow." When her mother beamed, she added, "I am anxious to be home as well."

Merrist frowned. "Do you not think it wise to be certain that Brensa will be comfortable before having her come? Her bed may not be ready and there may be no wood for the fire to prepare food."

Brensa gave Liannis no time to respond. "Oh, I am well enough to sleep on the floor, if needed, and we can take cold food with us."

Merrist capitulated. "Very well, then, but it is I who will sleep on the floor, if that is necessary." He grinned at Liannis. "Truth be told, I am eager to be home as well."

Brensa clapped her hands. "Good. It is settled then."

The trio left the castle soon after breaking fast the next morning, each horse carrying panniers laden with food. An additional pack horse followed, carrying a full load. Liannis tried

238

to protest that they did not need so much, but her mother insisted and the women in the kitchen agreed. Merrist had checked on their cow and received assurances that she would be delivered to them, along with her calf, in two days, as they would need to travel more slowly. Chickens had also been purchased and delivery assured for the next day, as well as a supply of oats and other grains.

They rode into the small clearing at midday. Liannis stopped at the edge to enjoy the feeling of homecoming. There it was, their cabin, nestled at the back against the trees.

"I will go ahead and see to the wood and a fire." Merrist kneed Warrior forward.

Liannis looked at her mother. She sat stock still on her horse, her gaze fixed on the spot where they had buried Klast. "Mama?" She kept her voice soft but it broke her mother's reverie.

"He calls to me." She urged her horse toward the spot.

Liannis followed several paces behind, alert but not sensing any need to interfere.

When they reached the spot Liannis helped her mother slide from the saddle and braced her until she found her feet. She had not ridden so far in a long time and needed assistance for a few moments.

When Liannis released her Brensa tottered to the grave and knelt beside it, placing reverent hands on the shallow mound. After a few moments she turned to Liannis. "Leave us, I will be fine."

Liannis nodded, and took her mother's mare's bridle to lead her to the shed, where she removed it and the saddle, and hobbled her in the clearing to graze. She could not lift the panniers. They would have to wait until Merrist could take them down.

Cloud made her impatience known. *Why is nag more important than me? Take this off. Want to graze.*

I am sorry, Cloud, but she does not know what to do and needs help. Come, it is your turn now.

Hmmph. Want carrots. Tell Merrist take things off. Heavy.

Perhaps later. I need to see to the cabin first, and to unpack. I hope there are some carrots in the panniers. If not, grazing will have to suffice. Merrist will remove the panniers soon.

Cloud gave a loud snort to show her displeasure and butted Liannis's behind with her nose. The nudge was not hard enough to make Liannis lose her footing, so Liannis knew Cloud had not forgotten her condition. She laughed and patted Cloud's flank before taking a last look at her mother and entering the cabin.

"There is a pile of wood already chopped at the back." He looked over his shoulder at her as he coaxed the kindling into flame.

"We have been well looked after." Liannis went to the doorway to the new room her mother would occupy. "Oh, Merrist, have you seen this? Mama will be very comfortable here. The bed already has a mattress and blankets. It seems our needs have been well anticipated."

Merrist blew on the flames before answering. "Yes, I had a quick look before I went out back for wood. I think once we have emptied the packs and panniers we will be set. There is nothing more to do." Seeing that the fire had taken well, he rose and came to stand beside Liannis. "We are home, my love." He drew her into his arms.

Liannis sighed with contentment. "Yes, we are home."

As Merrist went out to retrieve their supplies from the horses' backs Liannis asked, "Please, check on Mama. She visits Papa's grave."

She watched the back of his head bob as he left, looked around, and sat in the rocking chair Klast had commissioned for Brensa when they had first come here. She closed her eyes, as she rocked gently and stroked her belly. Home at last.

TRIAL

A relieved Lionn agreed quickly when Brynnell suggested that he need not be part of the trial except as a witness. The advisory council, which Lionn still sat in on, wanted to move forward quickly with the trial. Keeping Lionn as only a witness, without influence or power in such an important procedure, would be a strong first act for Brynnell.

"I wish to proceed without delay and put this unsavory business behind us. It has hung like a pall over Catania for far too long."

Brynnell looked grey with fatigue but kept his head erect and shoulders back, showing no sign of hesitation.

"The interrogations are complete," Brynnell agreed. "We are ready to begin with the public sentencing and executions as soon as the platform is built. We can choose hanging or beheading. May I suggest hanging?"

Frellick gave a thoughtful nod. "I agree. It is less bloody and so less likely to provoke strong reactions from the crowds."

"If these crimes had been less known I would have kept the executions private." Brynnell ran his hand through his hair. "But everyone is aware of the situation and will see a private execution as leniency for the traitors and their families. The people expect a public trial and executions. I cannot show such weakness so early in my rule."

Lionn shuddered. "I understand. My father, too, deplores the necessity of public executions. Fortunately he has had few to see to. I also know they cause Earth pain. Liannis has made that plain on more than one occasion."

The atmosphere in the council chamber could not be more grim. No one ate from the platters of cold food on the table. Even the ale sat almost untouched. The sage tea, brought in hot when they began, sat cooling, unnoticed, in the pot.

"I am glad to see I have a council that is not bent on blood and spectacle. Thank you, my friends." Brynnell's gratitude was almost palpable.

"You will need to add two or three more to our number soon, Brynnell."

241

"Indeed, Charest. I will welcome suggestions. One member must come from the traders and one from the guards. The third may wait yet a while until we find a good candidate."

"I have a suggestion for the guards, my lord," Charest said, "but let us finish with this trial first."

Brynnell heaved a weary sigh. "The platform can be ready by the end of the day. I propose we set the date for dawn the day after tomorrow so the people will not have time to gather in great numbers. The fewer present, the less bloodlust we will see ... and perhaps that will spare Earth at least a small measure of pain."

"The executioner will be told as soon as we leave here." Frellick offered. "I will take the message myself."

"Thank you, my friend."

Dawn, two days later, proved cold and wet. Lionn was pleased to see that the crowd was thin. He suspected both the weather and the busy harvest season helped to keep many away. He hoped that some stayed away because they had no desire to see the spectacle but wondered if that were an idle wish. His thoughts went to Liannis and Merrist. Thank Earth they were spared this. He wished he could avoid it as well, but duty dictated that he be present to witness. At least Joranna could stay away. The thought of Joranna allowed him to forget his gruesome duty for a moment. The date for their joining would arrive in only seven days.

"Lionn...."

Hearing his name brought him back to the present with a lurch. Brynnell looked at him, as if waiting for an answer.

"Forgive me, my lord, my thoughts were elsewhere."

"Yes, I could see that." Brynnell managed a thin smile that did not reach his eyes.

"What were you saying?"

"Will you know what to say if the verdict is challenged?"

"Yes, I am prepared to tell what I saw and know, and to repeat the evidence presented to the council."

"Good, please sit here. I will give the signal for the prisoners to be brought out."

Lionn looked at the other side of the platform. There stood the wives and some of the children of the men about to be hanged. They clung to each other, some weeping, others as though frozen past all feeling. What future would they have, tainted by the stigma of their association with traitors? He suspected that they would also

242

lose their homes and be unable to find work. How would they provide for themselves and their children now? He remembered long discussions with Gaelen and Klast about the injustice of confiscating the homes of traitors and decided that he would speak to the council after the trial to see what, if anything could be done to ease the families' way.

It seemed that the council members were not alone in wanting to get the proceedings over with quickly. No one questioned the verdicts or the sentences. For each prisoner, after hearing a summary of the evidence against him, Lionn was asked to rise and declare that he agreed with it, whereupon each man was sentenced and hanged without delay, his body taken down and placed in a waiting wagon, to be buried outside the city walls in an unmarked grave.

Lady Morna had insisted on witnessing the trial and sat two chairs away on Lionn's left. She said nothing, seeming unaware, until Strennock appeared on the platform. As his sentence rang out and she watched the noose placed about his neck she gripped the seat of her chair, knuckles white, her face a mask of hate. When he fell through the platform she almost rose out of her chair then sank back again, silent, until they took him down. Only then did the tears flow. Lionn heard her whisper, "It is not enough." Her eyes remained closed for the remainder of the proceedings, silent tears coursing down her wrinkled cheeks. She seemed oblivious.

By midday the wagon with the bodies had left. When Morna made no move to rise, Lionn went to her. "Lady, do you require assistance back to your chamber?"

Her head came up when he took one of her hands, but Lionn could see no comprehension on her blank face. He placed an arm under her legs and the other behind her, lifted her gently from the chair and carried her back to her chamber. She showed no sign that she was aware of what he did, sagging limp in his arms. He could not help but note how frail and light she felt.

Lionn knew Merrist had not been able to heal her. The only thing that had kept her alive had been the desire for justice for her daughters. Now that her captor and his men no longer lived she had nothing to keep her here. Lionn believed she would not wait long to follow her daughters into Earth's embrace.

As he laid her gently upon her bed something made him bend down to place a tender kiss on her forehead. "You may rest, now, my lady. It is over."

He stood and watched her breathing for several moments before tiptoeing out and shutting the door behind him. He paused before leaving just long enough to ask a maid to bring some tea and sit with Morna, though he knew Morna would not drink it.

When he joined the men in the council camber the next morning he was not surprised to hear that Morna had not wakened. She had stopped breathing and slipped away in the night.

"May Earth offer her peace." The others murmured assent.

70

INTERLUDE

"I do not understand what has come over Cloud," Merrist came into the cabin about a moon after they had settled in. "She will not let me touch her at all. I thought we had gone past all that."

"What were you trying to do?"

"I gave her her ration of oats and tried to pat her neck in greeting, as I always do. She has accepted that for moons, now, but not today." Merrist sounded both hurt and puzzled.

"Hmmm, that is strange. I will go to her later and see if she will tell me what the trouble is." Liannis also found this puzzling but gave it no more thought as she added carrots to the stew pot over the hearth fire. "Mama, those biscuits smell wonderful."

Brensa set the tray she had just brought in from the outdoor oven on the table to cool. "Yes, it looks like I took them out before they burned this time. I suppose I will never be a good cook."

"We never starved from your cooking, Mama. I don't suppose we will start now." Liannis gave her mother's shoulders a quick hug. "Tomorrow is bread day. I will do the kneading as it is too heavy for you. Merrist has to go into the city for salt and flour."

"Good. I must finish the little gowns for Ayliss or she will have nothing to wear." Her mother sent Liannis a teasing look. "If I had known you would one day become a mother I would have taught you needle work."

Liannis grinned. "I fear my needle work would have been worse than your cooking."

"Hmmph," came the good natured retort.

Merrist, who had gone outside to chop wood for the coming winter burst in the door. "Look who I found!"

"With honey cakes," Marja followed him in, Gaelen close on her heels. She handed Brensa the linen cloth that held the cakes. "I made these myself, as our cook still has not quite mastered them as old Cook did in Catania."

"What news?" Liannis set the kettle on to boil for tea.

Gaelen held back allowing Marja to speak first.

245

"There is so much to tell. We only arrived back home yesterday." She sat at a stool by the table and reached into the cloth for one of the cakes. "Let me see if I got these right."

"I thought those were for us," Brensa quipped.

"True, but I must test them to make sure they are acceptable." She closed her eyes. "Mmmmmmm, yes, I do believe these are just as Cook made them."

"You are keeping the children in suspense, my love." Gaelen winked at Liannis. "Shall I be the one to tell them everything?"

Yes," Liannis urged, "tell us all about Lionn and Joranna and about the joining. Did Dugal and Sennia attend? I could not tell, though I admit checking on their auras."

Marja's glee showed clearly. "Of course, they both attended. Do you seriously believe anyone could keep Sennia from it? Oh, I do wish you had all been there. It was hastily put together, but no less lavish or joyous, for all that." She gave a wicked laugh and looked at Gaelen.

Gaelen joined in the laugh, "All right, my love, you have had your fun. Let us not keep them waiting any longer." He nodded at Merrist, who had stood back in silence.

Merrist flashed a grin and opened the door. Several voices chimed at once.

"Surprise!"

There stood Lionn and Joranna, their grins about to split their faces. Lionn rushed in ahead of Joranna and gave Liannis a huge hug. Joranna wasted no time following his example, though she still seemed a little shy.

Amid excited chatter and exclamations they looked for places for everyone to sit down. Lionn and Merrist had to bring in three uncut logs as there were not enough places to sit even when the bed served as a sofa.

Next Lionn took Merrist out to the horses to bring in the feast they had brought with them. They even brought apples for Cloud, Warrior and Brensa's mare.

Darkness had fallen long before the festivities ended. Lionn thought he could guide them back safely in the dark, but Brensa prevailed on the party to bed down for the night and leave in the morning after breaking fast. The men went to sleep in the

246

shed, with blankets and extra straw. The women shared the beds in the cabin, Joranna and Marja going up to the loft.

The next morning, as the party mounted their horses and made to leave, Lionn declared, "So, my friends, you could not be there for the joining, so we brought a celebration here to you."

"Indeed, you did, Lionn." Liannis gave him a last hug before he leapt onto his mount. "We will never forget this." She went to stand between Gaelen's and Marja's horses. "And I want to tell you how grateful we are for the addition to the cabin. I certainly did not expect glass windows. We will have much more light, now. Thank you."

Gaelen brushed off her thanks. "We cannot have our seers and healer living with oiled leather for windows."

Liannis, Merrist and Brensa stood together watching them ride off. Just before disappearing into the trees they turned to wave back. The air felt empty in the silence that followed.

"What a wonderful surprise." Liannis took Merrist's hand as they walked back the few steps to the cabin. "When did you know?"

"When they rode into the clearing."

"That was Lionn's doing, I just know it."

"I expect so. It is the kind of thing he would do. Though I would not put it past Gaelen or Marja, either."

"We do have wonderful friends." Liannis buried her head in Merrist's shoulder, resting there for a few moments in his embrace until Brensa broke in.

"Come, we have much to do. Winter will not wait for us, nor will Ayliss. We must be ready."

Merrist gave Liannis a last squeeze and chuckled, "Mama has decreed."

"I suppose I had best see what is making Cloud so grumpy." Liannis followed Merrist back out the door.

71

CLOUD

Cloud?

Cloud lifted her head to regard Liannis and answered with a quick snort but no mind-speak. She stood still, waiting for Liannis to approach but made no move to meet her part way.

Cloud, what is the matter with you? You are acting strangely.

Cloud still did not answer, nor did she move, but Liannis caught some amusement from her mind which puzzled her even more.

When Liannis was almost within reach Cloud sent *Catania has strong, clever stallion.*

What are you saying?

You left me in the corral in Catania.

Yes, I wanted you to be free to graze and to get some exercise.

Handsome stallion there, clever. More clever than Warrior. Not a war horse. Smaller. Very clever.

Liannis thought she was beginning to get the meaning of Cloud's amusement. She recalled Cloud's desire for a foal and her remarks that an acceptable sire would be hard to find. But Cloud was having some fun, so Liannis did not let on that she sensed where Cloud was leading. Instead she decided to play along and tease Cloud a bit.

I agree. Catania has many beautiful, clever horses. Though, none as clever as you are, I imagine. None worth your attention.

Liannis sensed Cloud's amusement grow. She said nothing at first, just tossed her head and stepped further out of reach. Liannis decided to push her a little, to needle her into revealing herself. *Surely there is none that can meet your high standards. I am sure no such stallion can be found, not even in Catania.*

Cloud gave her head another toss that looked almost coquettish. Liannis had to bite her lip to keep from giving herself away and laughing aloud.

Hmmph. Perhaps one.

One what?

One stallion, of course.

Liannis continued to act as though she had no idea what Cloud was talking about. *What stallion? In Catania? Do stop avoiding me. I am becoming annoyed with you, now. Come, what are you hiding from me?* But she could no longer keep up the charade and a laugh escaped her.

Cloud knew she had been caught out and gave up on the game. *Cannot keep thing from you.* Cloud stopped dancing out of the way and came to rest her chin on Liannis's shoulder. *Found one stallion in Catania. Too small for war horse, but strong and very clever. Can mind-speak. Sired foal. Will be your daughter's mount.*

Oh, Cloud, how wonderful. We shall be mothers together.

Cloud's response was a deep, satisfied snuffle into Liannis's neck. *Daughters grow together.*

How do you know you carry a daughter, Cloud?

Know.

Liannis did not press, knowing she would get no more from Cloud. *I see, and what will she be called?*

No name, yet. Will come when she meets babe.

So, tell me, why would you not let Merrist touch you, earlier?

Would know. Is a healer. Want you to know first.

But why could he not tell before now?

Because I did not know.

That explanation did not make sense to Liannis, as she knew Merrist often sensed things about the people and animals he touched that they were unaware of, but she decided to drop the issue. Perhaps Merrist had simply not looked for anything untoward and missed it as a result. After all, Cloud still allowed Merrist only limited access to her. It seemed as if Cloud felt Merrist might be tainted by Warrior's lack of intelligence. It caused Cloud to continue to regard him with a certain disdain.

So Ayliss will be born at the beginning of winter and your daughter at high summer. This is a good time for you to be with foal as I will not be riding much until after your foal's birth. This is wonderful news for both of us. Congratulations, Cloud.

Cloud spotted Merrist over Liannis's shoulder, coming toward them. *Merrist leg comes.*

May I tell him?

Yes, you know first.

Thank you.

"Well, what is the matter with Cloud?" Merrist asked with mock anger.

Cloud's response was to butt him in the chest with her head, sending him sprawling on the grass.

"Cloud! You are naughty. Now help poor Merrist up." Liannis sputtered with laughter as she chided Cloud.

Cloud sent Liannis a mind-speak laugh back and went to stand beside Merrist so he could grab her mane to pull himself up, which he made a great show of needing, though they all knew he could manage very well on his own. As he stood he let a hand rest on Cloud's flank. "Ah, I see, now."

Cloud stood still and let Merrist examine her. "So, Cloud, who is the sire? Not Warrior, surely?"

Cloud gave a loud snort even Merrist could not mistake for anything other than disdain, making him laugh.

"It seems she met a suitable candidate while we were in Catania. A small stallion, she tells me, but strong and *very clever*."

Merrist's eyebrows went up at the emphasis on clever. He narrowed them again and quipped, "I always knew Warrior was too strong and brave for you. A small stallion, you say. I should have expected no less."

Cloud seemed to catch the ease in Merrist's voice and gave him another playful nudge.

"Cloud, you must let Merrist see to you and make sure all is well."

Cloud indicated her assent by leaning her forehead against Merrist's arm, then asking Liannis, *Apples? Are fresh now. Smell them.*

"Hah, now she is asking for fresh apples." Liannis grinned at Merrist. "I think she expects to be spoiled now that she is with foal."

"If it will make her less inclined to bump me off my feet I will be happy to oblige." He patted Cloud. "But you will have to come to the shed for them. I will not chase you all over the clearing just to offer you apples," and began to walk away.

"You win, Cloud." Liannis gave Cloud a solid slap on the rump as they both followed Merrist back toward the shed.

Cloud's answer was a low, contented whinny.

72

AUTUMN

Liannis had grown too uncomfortable to ride into the city for the Harvest Festival but that did not prevent her from urging Merrist to take her mother. "It will be the last time Mama can see Marja. The winter will make riding into the city too difficult."

Merrist looked at her over the rim of the basket between them, into which they were placing the last of the fresh herbs to be hung and dried for winter. They had not had time to put in any vegetables, but Gaelen and Marja had seen to it that their shed and pantry were well supplied.

"Do you not think it will tire her overmuch, even now?"

"She always loved the festivals. I think she will miss it if you do not take her, though she will not suggest it herself. No, I think it will do more good than harm. If she is too tired to come home wait an extra day. I will be well enough alone for a few days."

"I do not like to leave you so long so near your time."

Merrist had resumed his cutting of the sage and kept his eyes on his work, but Liannis was not fooled. "Merrist, you know as well as I that Earth will not let anything happen without you present. Please, go and enjoy yourself."

"In any case, I shall attempt to bring Brensa home the next morning."

"As you wish. Mama will be well enough."

The following morning a delighted Brensa left the clearing followed by a reluctant Merrist. Liannis waved them off and went back inside.

***

Merrist and Brensa stayed overnight with Gaelen and Marja and headed back to the cabin after breaking fast the following morning.

When Brensa expressed eagerness to get back to Liannis, Merrist felt relieved.

251

"We will visit soon," Marja declared as she embraced her friend at the castle doors. "You know a little snow will not keep us away long."

Once again, both horses carried panniers laden with supplies and treats, many from the festival. If Liannis could not be there, she would still enjoy its tastes.

"I wonder what Liannis will think of that new cheese, the one from the sheep's milk?" Brensa chattered as they rode.

"She will like it, but I think her favourite will be the cakes with the fruits and nuts in them. She loves sweets."

"Now you will not allow her to pound the cabbages for the sauerkraut, will you?"

"Now, Mama, do you not think I will do what is best for her?" Merrist teased. "Besides, she likes to keep busy and perhaps pounding cabbage will prevent her from taking her impatience out on me."

Brensa caught the tone and retorted, "Merrist, you are impossible."

***

Liannis met the pair as they entered the clearing. She came out of the forest from the other side. "This has been a peaceful time. I do love to walk in the forest at this time of year. The air is so fresh and I love the scents of the earth. I saw you coming through the trees as the leaves have almost all fallen."

Merrist had dismounted so he could walk beside Liannis but Brensa remained on her horse until they reached the cabin, where Merrist helped her down. Once he had unloaded the panniers he came into the cabin and gave the rafters a suspicious look.

Liannis laughed. "No, Merrist, I did not hang them."

Liannis had tied the sage and oregano they had gathered into bunches. Merrist had forbidden her to climb the stool to hang them, fearing she would lose her balance. She had set them side by side across their table so they would have air around them and not become tangled with each other. Now she waved an arm at the table. "See? They are all still here."

Brensa busied herself with unpacking the sweet buns and treats. "Here Liannis, taste this." She handed Liannis one of the fruit buns.

"Oh, Mama, this is delicious." Her words could hardly be made out as her mouth was full.

When Merrist brought out the four huge cabbages Brensa said, "Liannis, you must let Merrist make the sauerkraut. The pounding is too heavy for you to do."

"Mama, I am fine. I can do my share." When Brensa made to protest she said, "Perhaps we can take turns. I will stop when I tire, Mama, I promise."

Merrist sent Brensa a 'did I not say so' look as he lifted the now empty pannier to take it out to the shed.

By the time the first light snows remained on the ground preparations for both the winter and the coming birth were complete. Each visit from the city brought more supplies and gifts, so that before the winter solstice arrived the threesome had more than they needed. Merrist spent his time snaring rabbits and checking and rechecking the soundness of the shed, the roof and the animals. Both Brensa and Liannis teased him about it but he simply could not sit still. The closer the date of the impending birth came, the more he needed to work off his nervous energy. Knowing that all would be well still did not calm him.

73

AYLISS

I am coming, Mama. You will hold me before this day ends. I love you but will not remember this after I am born.

Ayliss had been quiescent for some time, but she sent that last message to Liannis just before labour set in. Before Liannis had a chance to ask her anything more Ayliss retreated again.

This was the winter solstice, the day Ayliss chose to make her appearance into the outside world.

Liannis lay awake for several moments, letting the news settle. Then she woke Merrist. "Merrist, it is time. Ayliss just told me she will be born this day."

Merrist shot up to sitting, instantly wide awake. "Have your pains started?"

"Shhhh. There is no reason to wake Mama." Liannis put a finger to her lips. She shook her head. "Not yet, though I expect they will begin soon."

"I must stoke the fire ... and get water on to heat." Merrist made to get out of bed but Liannis put a hand his arm. "Not yet, my love. There is time. I feel nothing. And you have already had things prepared for some time." She pulled him gently back down. "Let us enjoy these last moments alone."

As Merrist reluctantly lay back down Liannis settled her head on his shoulder. She could feel him relax as he pulled the blankets back up and placed his arm around her. "I suppose I will know when it begins." Merrist gave a wry chuckle. "It seems that when it comes to you I forget I am a healer and can sense such things."

Liannis gave his chest an understanding pat. "Indeed."

They lay entwined until the first light crept over the horizon, throwing long shadows into the cabin. The first twinges began, far apart at first, then closer together as the cabin grew lighter.

Brensa woke, as was her custom, as soon as the first rays of morning light fell upon her bed through the tiny window in her chamber.

Liannis put a cautioning finger on Merrist's lips, so that Brensa would not know they were awake.

Brensa's daily routine saw her throw on her cloak and shoes and leave the cabin to visit Klast's grave. She always stayed there for some time, seeming to gather comfort from the visit, before returning to the cabin to begin the regular day.

Liannis and Merrist watched her go. When the door closed quietly behind her Liannis said, "Let her have this time. She will be calmer the rest of the day for it. I think if she knew what is happening she would not have gone and would feel the loss all day."

They both got up, Liannis to drink some fresh water and Merrist to stoke the fire in the hearth and put on a kettle to make tea. By the time Brensa returned Merrist had set out the bowls and spoons for porridge, the mugs for tea, bread, butter, cheese and honey.

Brensa needed only one look at Liannis, still in her night-shift and rubbing her back, to know. "Liannis, has it begun?"

"Yes, Mama. Ayliss will be born this day."

Brensa came to place both hands on Liannis's belly, eyes closed in concentration. "It will be some time yet, I think."

"It will," Merrist confirmed. "The pains are still mild."

"Are you afraid, Liannis?" Brensa searched Liannis's face.

"No Mama, I am quite calm. And the pain is mild." She turned to Merrist. "But when we have broken our fast I would welcome having my back rubbed."

"Let me do it, now."

"No Merrist, we all need to eat first. It can wait." She grinned at him. "Besides, I am hungry and need some porridge." She looked at the table. "Though I think I will forego the cheese. That may be too heavy."

"That is wise." Brensa hurried to fill the bowls with the porridge, kept warm overnight in the pot on a ledge just outside the hearth's flames. She gave Liannis a questioning look. "Shall I add a little more honey this morning?"

At Liannis's nod of assent Brensa added another generous dollop to the bowl, along with a knob of butter, before gesturing to Liannis to take her stool and handing it to her.

Liannis sniffed the steaming mug of tea. "Ah, raspberry leaf this morning, for strength. Good." She reached behind to rub her lower back at the onset of another pain.

Merrist gave her an appraising look. "They are coming closer together now."

"Hmmm," Liannis agreed as she took another spoonful of porridge.

By midday the pains had begun to come closer together. Liannis continued to pace the length of the cabin in between having Merrist rub her back and sitting to take some more tea or small amounts of bread and honey. As the day wore on and Liannis grew more fatigued, she began to feel chilled. Brensa added a second pair of socks to her feet and wrapped a blanket around her shoulders. Liannis hardly noticed. Her thoughts were on Ayliss. But she uttered no complaint. Her pains did not trouble her more than she could manage.

Since Ayliss had chosen the shortest day of the year to make her appearance, it was almost full dark outside before Liannis felt the urge to push.

"It is time."

Merrist had procured a birthing chair on one of his visits to the city and now pulled it into position. "Sit, now, Liannis. And let me examine you once more." He knelt in front of Liannis and probed. Brensa had come to stand behind him, her small hand on Merrists's shoulder.

"Merrist?" Brensa's whispered question needed no more words.

Merrist kept his eyes closed, but relaxed and nodded. "All is well. Brensa, would you light the rest of the candles and the other lamp, please?" Brensa hurried to comply then returned to take up her position with her hand on Merrist's shoulder.

Liannis understood that her mother was trying to add her small healing strength to that of Merrist and had not the heart to tell her he did not need it. "Mama, will you hold my hand?"

Brensa came to sit on the edge of the bed and took Liannis's cold hand in both of hers. "I am here, Liannis."

Liannis took five deep breaths and pushed as she let each one out.

Merrist placed two fingers between Liannis's thighs once more, to check on her progress. "I feel hair."

Then he blanched. "No!' His hoarse whisper held panic.

"Merrist, what is it? What do you feel?" Liannis tensed, making the next contraction much more painful.

256

"She is being strangled. The cord – it is around her neck."

Brensa went white and let go Liannis's hand to move behind Merrist. "What must we do?"

"Push! Hard! We must get it off so she can breathe and I cannot reach it here."

A profound silence came over the chamber and a blue glow filled every corner. It seemed as though the entire world had come to a halt. Earth had come.

Two more pushes and Merrist held the tiny, wet body in his waiting hands. Three anxious faces peered at the blue body, looking for breath. There was none. Ayliss still did not breathe.

"Merrist! Do something!"

Brensa's panicked cry roused Merrist out of his shocked inertia. He placed his mouth over the tiny blue one and blew a puff of air into it. Nothing. Ayliss lay limp, her skin even darker, not moving.

Liannis looked on in immobile disbelief. Earth had promised. Ayliss was needed. What had gone wrong?

She watched as Merrist took a thumb and began to massage the little chest. A small amount of fluid leaked out of Ayliss's mouth. When Merrist saw that he placed his own mouth once more over the tiny one. This time, instead of blowing, he sucked, drawing out more sticky fluid. He spat it out and repeated his first action, blowing a small breath of air into Ayliss's mouth. When he withdrew they saw the little chest contract, fill, and a small cry escaped the tiny mouth. Ayliss's skin rapidly lost its blue hue and turned a bright pink.

Merrist quickly tied the cord, which he had not yet done, cut it, wrapped Ayliss in a soft, warmed blanket and handed her into Liannis's waiting arms.

The light in the cabin began to pulse.

***

"Daughter."

"Mother? Why?!"

"Do not fear, Liannis. All is well."

Liannis felt a cool hand on her forehead and watched as Ayliss's breath became regular and she felt her daughter's body relax into her.

257

"All is well." Earth repeated the words before lifting her hand away.

***

The pulsing stopped and the glow Earth surrounded them with began to recede moments after the afterbirth slipped from Liannis's body. Earth returned to her invisible realm.

Merrist came back to awareness of himself. "Liannis! Is she well? Are you well?"

Liannis came out of her trance and looked around her, at the two people she loved and then at the babe sleeping in her arms.

"Yes, Merrist. All is well, now."

"Thank Earth!" As the reality sank in he heaved a great sigh and joined Liannis and Brensa in admiring Earth's gift.

Ayliss had a shock of curly hair, lighter than Liannis's but darker than Merrist's that shone red where the firelight fell on it. They silently counted fingers and toes and touched her tiny, strong body with awed feather touches. Ayliss took the examination with aplomb, eyes now wide and solemn, regarding them each in turn, not making a sound.

After these shared moments Merrist took Ayliss from Liannis and handed her to Brensa. He washed the blood from Liannis and helped her into bed. Once he saw she was comfortable he took Ayliss once again from Brensa and nestled her in the crook of Liannis's arm.

Brensa broke the silence first. "Oh, Liannis, she is beautiful." She reached out and stroked a downy cheek with one finger. Ayliss had gone back to sleep and did not stir.

"Indeed she is, my love," Merrist breathed as he gazed, rapt, upon their daughter, their very special daughter.

"Are you certain all is well?" Brensa still looked anxious.

Liannis gave her a tired smile. "Yes, Mama, Earth has assured me of it."

Ayliss stirred and turned to nuzzle Liannis, searching for milk.

The spell had broken.

BRENSA

Time passed.

With the crises in Lieth and Catania behind them, peace settled on the lands. Weather and harvests returned to normal, leaving the people well fed and healthy. In Gharn, Sennia gave birth to a healthy boy and girl. By the following year she quickened again and bore another son. Dugal now had two heirs, his succession assured.

At the height of that first summer after Ayliss's birth Cloud gave birth to her foal. Liannis took little Ayliss out to the clearing to meet the new arrival. Though only a few months old, Ayliss placed a chubby hand on the foal's nose and laughed.

Cloud whinnied her pleasure and mind-spoke Liannis. *Daughter has name.*

Well, don't keep me in suspense.

Name is Dancer.

Dancer. What a perfect name. Thank you, Cloud.

Liannis placed an arm around Cloud's neck. Ayliss reached out and grabbed a handful of her mane and pulled. Cloud stood very still until Liannis pulled the tiny fist free. Dancer came to nurse, but before she did, she reached up to nose Ayliss, eliciting another happy laugh from her.

Ayliss began to ride Dancer when she was not yet two. Being so small the weight was not too much for Dancer. Dancer seemed to intuit how to help Ayliss balance. They became inseparable companions.

***

Each day, as she had done since her return to the cabin, Brensa communed with Klast at his graveside. Slowly, so slowly that it hardly seemed worthy of note, she seemed to fade, appearing more distant and less aware, though she remained close to Ayliss.

Ayliss thrived, a happy, cheerful and affectionate child. As expected, she proved to be precocious and sensitive. She seemed intuitive with others, understanding, without effort, their feelings and concerns.

Once, when only two years old, she put her arms around Brensa's neck and told her, "Do not be sad. He knows you must wait." Liannis understood that to mean that Klast did not want Brensa to hurry to join him.

While these could not yet be called fully developed abilities, they gave some indications of what was to come. Ayliss possessed a calmness of spirit that would help her cope with the difficulties her abilities would bring when they blossomed as she grew.

She seemed, especially, to have an empathic understanding of Brensa and a knack for bringing her out of her reveries. She developed a close affinity for Brensa, even as an infant, that fostered a deep bond between the two. Her patience with her grandmother had an ethereal, serene quality to it that spoke more of Earth than this earth.

At times Ayliss would reveal, in her child-like way, things about Brensa that Liannis, herself, could never have discovered. It gave Liannis a measure of reassurance that her mother was well, as she spoke so little even when she engaged in the daily activities of the cabin and gardens. While she appeared content and never complained, Liannis still worried about her.

Ayliss favoured her father in her trait of patience and slowness to react. But she had Liannis's keen mind and soaked up knowledge like a rain-starved root. By her second winter solstice she spoke like a four year old and had a level of insight and understanding well beyond that.

The second autumn after Ayliss's birth Brensa seemed to retreat further and further into herself. Ayliss took to watching her from the cabin as she sat by Klast's grave, or, if the weather was mild and dry, would sit outside, a short distance away, as if guarding her. If Liannis tried to distract her she would fuss until her mother let her return to her vigil.

Over time, Brensa's visits to the grave grew longer. But whenever Liannis would inquire if she needed a warmer cloak, or if the rain did not chill her, Brensa would say that when she was with Klast she felt no other need. Since she never became ill, Liannis saw no reason to press her. On rainy days she would simply follow her out to place a cover of oiled leather over her, or in cold weather, a warm cloak. Brensa seemed oblivious to these

260

kindnesses, sometimes letting the coverings slip off her as she stood up and leaving them behind when she returned to the cabin.

Each day, after watching Brensa, Ayliss would turn to Liannis and say, "Nona is still here. She will not leave us yet," and go back to her play. It became a reassuring ritual to Liannis. As long as Ayliss told her Brensa was all right she could relax about her.

Three days after that second solstice, as the first heavy snow covered the ground in a soft, thick blanket, Ayliss pulled on her little boots and cloak and slipped out the door after Brensa. Liannis did not worry overmuch, as she knew Merrist was out back chopping firewood. Also, Ayliss understood danger far better than children her age, so Liannis was confident she would not wonder off.

Liannis continued to knead the bread on the table in front of her, but a slight unease began to tug at her awareness. Just as she decided to check on Ayliss she heard a light rap at the door.

Ayliss could open the door from the inside but still needed help getting it open from the outside. When Liannis pushed the door open Ayliss stood waiting there, a strange far-away expression on her wee face. Liannis recognised Earth's presence in her even before she spoke.

"Nona is at peace. She is with her love again." The smile she gave Liannis was filled with Earth's love and wisdom.

Liannis stood still, in shock, until the aura around Ayliss faded. As understanding came to her she whispered and anguished, "Mama, no." She looked past Ayliss to Klast's grave. There in the pristine snow, lay Brensa, gently curled as if in repose, as new snow fell softly over her and covered her with the beginnings of a white blanket.

"Do not be sad, Mama. Nona is where she wants to be. She is at peace."

Ayliss's eyes, so much those of a small child, so full of innocence, now also showed the knowledge gifted to her by Earth. Brensa did not lie in the cold snow; she had returned into the embrace of the goddess and of her love.

Ayliss took Liannis's hand and they made their way silently to where Brensa lay. When Liannis dropped to her knees beside Brensa, Ayliss patted her shoulder and said. "I will go and tell Papa," and toddled off.

261

Moments later Liannis looked up toward the cabin to see Merrist rounding the corner, carrying Ayliss on his arm.

Merrist soon knelt beside Liannis, with Ayliss between them. Somehow it seemed right that they remain silent for a time.

Ayliss broke the silence. "Mama, she wants to be beside him. Do not take her away."

"You are right, Ayliss. We will bury her here, facing Papa." Liannis gave Merrist a pleading look.

"I will get the shovel." Merrist rose and Ayliss came to sit closer to Liannis and leaned into her, offering comfort. "Nona is happy again, Mama."

"Yes, she is, but I will miss her." Liannis reached over and stroked back one of Brensa'a curls that had always stubbornly refused to remain in its braid, a last gesture of affection. The touch confirmed that Brensa had indeed flown. No response remained in that shell. It brought Liannis to full awareness. She put her arms around Ayliss and drew her onto her lap. "But we will not forget her."

Ayliss snuggled into her chest. "Yes, Mama, we will not. We will remember how she made us happy."

By now Merrist had returned with the shovel. "How shall we place her?"

Liannis stood and set Ayliss down beside her. "Just as she is, Merrist. That is what she chose, facing Papa."

Together they lifted Brensa's body and placed it to the side so Merrist could dig on the spot where she had lain. The soil had not yet frozen solid for the winter.

A span later Merrist had a trench the right depth and size to receive Brensa's body.

They placed Brensa in it, facing Klast, just as she had chosen.

Soon the low mound of dirt that covered her blended with the one beside it as more snow made it indistinguishable from the earlier one.

While Liannis and Merrist stood hand in hand beside the new grave, Ayliss moved forward to place both small hands at the head of the mound. After a long moment she rose to face her parents, a small smile on her lips. "Nona is home."

262

Liannis picked Ayliss up and she and Merrist trudged back to the cabin. In spite of her loss, Liannis felt a calmness and peace that told her all was well. One look at Merrist told her he felt it too.

75

THE DREAMT CHILD

Winter deepened. Liannis spent her time cooking, mending and seeing to their chickens. Aside from putting out snares, looking after the animals and chopping wood there was not much for Merrist to do. Winter provided a rest from the constant demands of the other seasons.

Their homely routines were broken only by the less frequent visits from the city. Gaelen and Lionn still managed the trek through the snow, bringing welcome news and treats but the women, Marja and Joranna, rarely came after the first sad visit to Brensa's grave.

Evenings would find the pair sitting in front of the hearth fire, Liannis with some chore in her lap, Merrist oiling or repairing some strap of leather, or whittling a toy for Ayliss.

On one particular evening Merrist had just put the final touches to the doll he had carved for Ayliss, with moveable arms and legs attached by thongs of leather through the hips and shoulders. Liannis, knowing the doll was almost complete, had found some scraps of linen and fashioned a night-shift for it.

Merrist handed the doll to Liannis so she could dress her. Ayliss played at their feet on the braided rug in front of their two chairs, with a toy horse Merrist had also carved for her. She seemed unaware of what her parents were up to, though Liannis knew she sometimes simply did not let on what she sensed.

When Liannis had dressed the doll she said, "Ayliss, see what Papa has made for you?"

Ayliss looked up and squealed with delight. Liannis handed the doll into her waiting hands as a grinning Merrist looked fondly on.

As they both watched, Ayliss found another larger rag, carefully wrapped the doll in it and began to rock it in her arms. She lifted her head to beam up at them. "See, Maya is sleeping."

"Is that her name ... Maya?"

As she heard her own question Lainnis had the sensation that this had happened before. She met Merrists's eyes and saw the same awareness on his face.

"The dream."

"Yes. She was ours all along." Merrist reached over and took Liannis's hand. They sat like that for some time, watching Ayliss play with her new doll, just as the dream had shown them.

76

JORANNA

Six year old Ayliss stood at regal attention, hands on her hips, and mocked, "Joranna, will you permit me to truth-read you?"

Joranna made a pretense of fright, shrank back and said, "But Ayliss, why would you ask me that? I have nothing to hide."

Ayliss, throwing herself fully into the game, gave her head a haughty toss. "Then you will not object."

Joranna threw her hands up in surrender. "Very well, then."

"Are you hiding something from me?"

"No."

"Aha. You do not tell the truth. I can sense it." Ayliss chortled with delight. "What are you keeping from me?"

Joranna put on her most guilty look and reached one hand under the cloth that covered the basket beside her on the floor. When her hand became visible it held a string of fresh water pearls with a gold clasp.

Ayliss squealed with glee before urging Joranna to place it around her neck.

"You are old enough now to care for this, I think." Joranna said, as Ayliss gave her a great hug.

"Oh, yes, thank you, Joranna, I will," Ayliss tossed over her shoulder as she danced over to her parents so they could admire her present.

Merrist shook his head. "You spoil her, Joranna."

Ayliss, suddenly serious, turned back to Joranna.

"Oh no Joranna. I will always understand the love behind the gifts I am given. You need not fear that I will come to expect them." Her empathy had caught the fleeting thought from Joranna that Ayliss might see these gifts as her due.

Liannis broke in. "No, Merrist, I have no fear of that. Ayliss has never asked for anything more than what she requires."

At that moment Martel, Lionn's firstborn, burst into the chamber, followed on his heels by his younger brother, four year old Janest. Janest had been named after Gaelen's old advisor, who had returned to Earth's embrace shortly before Martel's birth.

266

Behind them trailed Lionn, looking happy but tired. "We have learned the names of all the horses in the corral," he grinned, "and walked into the forest to bring back these." Lionn held out a handful of wilted wildflowers to Joranna. "The boys said they were too tired to carry them."

Joranna took the flowers and reached down to give each of her young sons a squeeze. "Thank you. These are beautiful." She poured water into a cup and placed the bouquet into it, setting it on the table next to her chair.

When she turned her attention back to the children she noticed the entire chamber had gone eerily silent. She followed the direction of everyone's gaze to find all eyes fixed on Ayliss. Ayliss stood facing Janest, both his hands held in hers. Her expression held power, and showed none of the innocence of childhood. Janest stood transfixed.

Ayliss spoke with Earth's voice, the mantle of Earth's power over her. "We will be together always. We will have a child. You will acquire the ability to sense danger before it happens, to protect me. And you will mind-speak with certain animals and with me."

When the trance broke she looked at Janest, who, having no idea what Ayliss meant, gawped at her, eyes wide, mouth half open.

His expression made Ayliss laugh. "Close your mouth, Janest." She let go his hands and looked for Liannis. "Mama, I am thirsty and hungry."

Liannis handed a cup of warm tea, into which she had already added a generous amount of honey, into Ayliss's now trembling hands, steadying it a she drank. When she had gulped the entire cup, in hurried swallows, she leaned against Liannis. "Mama why am I so tired?"

Liannis helped Ayliss fold herself into her lap, resting her head on Liannis's shoulder, and accept a piece of bread from her.

"Because it takes so much strength when Earth shows you something important, Sweeting."

Joranna caught Liannis's eyes over top of the curly head and gestured her astonished question wordlessly. Hands spread wide, eyebrows raised, eyes wide, she mouthed "What?"

"Ayliss has had her first vision, it seems." Liannis shook her head sadly. "I had hoped she would have more time to be just a child."

Joranna could not hide her distress. "But Janest? He's almost still a babe. How can this be?" She brushed away Lionn's attempt to put a comforting arm around her. "What does this mean? What is to become of my little son?"

Lionn placed a hand on her forearm. "He will fulfill his destiny, my love."

Joranna whirled on him. "How can you say that as if it is easy? How does this not alarm you?"

Liannis broke in before Lionn could respond. "Lionn has known me all his life, Joranna. He has become accustomed to such unexpected revelations."

Ayliss squirmed out of Liannis's lap and took Joranna's hand. "Do not be afraid, Joranna. Janest will come to no harm. It is Earth's wish. He will be given a great gift. But he does not feel his abilities yet, and will not for many years. He has time." She looked earnestly into Joranna's face.

Joranna saw Earth's wisdom and power in Ayliss's eyes. A small measure of calm settled on her, sent from Ayliss. She managed a deep breath. "It appears I will have no say in this matter."

"I am also surprised and have some concern, my love," Lionn said.

Joranna could see his worry in his furrowed brow.

As he pinched the bridge of his nose in the mirror of his father, he added, "But I have come to accept that Earth acts with wisdom."

Joranna looked at her small son, now tugging at Ayliss's skirt.

"Are you still my friend?"

Ayliss nodded. "Yes, Janest, we will always be friends. I promise."

"Good." Janest looked relieved as he let go, eyes sliding to the table. "I am hungry."

That normal reaction broke Joranna's tension. She gave a nervous laugh as she took a small platter and placed meat and bread on it, handing it to her young son. "Of course, you are. You have been playing all day with Papa."

77

PEACE

Seasons passed upon seasons. Minor disputes and individual crimes, always present where people live in groups were dealt with by the laws of each demesne. With crime at an all time low the demesnes carried on brisk trade with each other. The weather held steady, with no major droughts, floods, or unusually bitter winters. The people, without the privations and diseases such events precipitate, settled into a steady and predictable rhythm of life.

Throughout the lands there appeared more and more youngsters with abilities or gifts, though most showed only one, and then with only modest or minimal strength. Nevertheless, the awareness that anyone could and might show signs of having a gift helped to gain acceptance for the changes Earth brought. These gifted people joined and had children, some of whom also showed these traits, but most of whom did not.

In a remote corner of Catania a young girl was found who could truth-read. The discovery of that ability came quite by accident. Her father ran a small inn. One day a customer arrived, looking for lodging. When the girl brought him his stew, she accidentally brushed the man's sleeve as she overheard him tell another guest that he was a trader from Gharn.

"No, you are not," she blurted out. "You are running from the guards in Gharn because you have a pouch of coins in the pocket of your breeches that you stole from an inn there."

When the man tried to laugh it off the girl touched him again, then pulled her hand away in haste. "And you plan to rob us, as well."

The man tried to deny it and hurry away, but the other customers stopped him and asked him to empty his pockets to prove he had no coins hiding there. When he refused, they held him for the guards. They found far more coin than a man of his status would ever carry. The next day a couple of guards arrived from Gharn, hunting the thief, now being held in the dungeons. The prisoner was duly handed over to the guards who took him away, back to Gharn.

When she came of age, the girl became Brynnell's official truth-reader.

269

In Gharn a stable hand tried to help one of Gaelen's best mares give birth. To his distress he felt for the foal and knew that it sat sideways. His training had taught him that such cases inevitably ended in the death of both mare and foal. While he had his hand still inside the birth canal the lad discovered that he knew how to turn the foal and bring it safely forward. Earth guided his hands to the forelegs. As he took first one then the other in his hand and pulled it into position he murmured to the mare to calm her.

"There, Kenna, there. All will be well. There, there."

He kept up the litany until he found the nose of the foal and guided it forward until it pointed correctly over the forelegs, in the correct position for birthing. Throughout his efforts the mare had not had a contraction, a result of his telling her with his mind to hold back. At first, when he came out of his trance to see the foal nuzzling his mother for milk, the astonished lad did not understand. Later, he discovered that he could heal other horses, and calm them as well during training. The young man became a valuable addition to the running of the lord's stables.

In Lieth two children with abilities were discovered. The first was a young man who could sense danger and could read minds if he was in physical contact, with both people and animals.

The second was a young woman with a strong healing gift. That girl became the castle healer and mid-wife. Lady Nairin kept her close, allowing her to help only those within the castle Nairin deemed worthy, in spite of the girl's requests to help others.

When Wartin came of age and was made Lord of Lieth, the young woman appealed to him.

"My lord, people have heard that I can heal. They come to ask me for help but I have been forbidden to go to them. Please my lord, I swear that I will not neglect my duties within the castle if I am allowed to assist those who come to me." She wrung her hands as she went down on one knee. "Please my lord. I can help so many."

Wartin agreed that she must be allowed to work outside the castle, a decision that made him popular with the people and allowed him to stretch his hand to other issues without the expected resistance. He also became adept at avoiding Nairin's tight rein.

Most of the children displaying gifts came from the general population, although occasionally a child with a gift arose from among the ruling families. Little Janest was one of these.

270

As time went on, more children appeared to have various gifts in small measure. Gradually this became accepted as Earth's wisdom. At the same time, possibly as a result, most of the people's resistance to the changes Earth had wrought faded.

However, none showed the diversity and strength in abilities that Ayliss did.

By the time she reached her fifteenth year, the accepted age of maturity, her reputation had spread to the corners of the One Isle. She also remained the only one who had visions from Earth. Occasionally, someone would appear who claimed to have this gift, but when put to the test, was always found to be a fraud. These were punished by being held to public ridicule, after which they usually slunk away and disappeared into obscurity.

One thing that Liannis was most grateful for was that Ayliss did not need solitude or isolation to sleep as she did. The barriers that Liannis had found so difficult to keep in place were not necessary for Ayliss. She heard and felt the feelings and thoughts of others only when she chose to.

Ayliss travelled extensively throughout the demesnes, where she could determine whether a claimant had gifts, what those gifts were and in what strength. This proved of great value. It kept fraudulent claims to a minimum. It also reassured the parents of children who displayed abilities that their offspring need not be feared, nor indeed, revered. Ayliss could convince the people that those who showed gifts could lead ordinary lives, and that their abilities would enrich them as opposed to being a burden.

The friendship between Janest and Ayliss blossomed into much more once Janest reached his eighteenth year. As he was two years younger than Ayliss it gave her a few extra years to establish her reputation before the people were once more challenged to accept a seer who wished to join and bear children.

Joranna deemed both the cabin where Ayliss and Liannis grew up, and that of Liannis's mentor Liethis, as unsuitable for her son and someone as important as Ayliss. "My son must not live as a pauper. Nor so, ought Earth's best servant to live so." Instead she and Lionn had a more comfortable home built for Ayliss and Janest close to the city, yet still outside its borders. Ayliss insisted on the latter so she could be more accessible to citizens beyond Bargia City and outside the demesne. The location also allowed them a modicum of privacy.

Liannis and Merrist remained in their own cabin, preferring the isolation it provided.

AYLISS

Soon after Ayliss and Janest joined, but before they expected their first child, Earth came to Ayliss in a dream, appearing in her woman form.

***

"Daughter."

"I am here, Mother."

"The period of rest, of peace and balance, will not last for all time. Nothing remains in balance forever. The pendulum does not keep still. Chaos will come again."

Ayliss gazed into the ancient eyes of Earth, looking for answers there. *"How will I recognize when this comes?"*

Earth reached out and stroked a cheek with one finger. *"You will know when strife sets demesnes against each other. Then you must prepare for the effects of the weakness such events bring me."*

"Mother, how can I prepare? What must I do?"

"You will be given time to let your children reach their coming of age. The time of chaos is not yet. It comes when people grow complacent, and grow to want more than they need, when they become dissatisfied with what I provide for them. Your task is to prepare those with abilities, so that they learn to use them wisely. And you must teach the people to trust my chosen sons and daughters, those with gifts both large and small. Janest must do the same."

"Children, Mother? Am I to bear more than one?"

Earth smiled. *"Indeed, daughter, you shall have two, a son and a daughter. They will both be given abilities."* Earth grew serious. *"You and Janest must teach them all you know, must travel with them and acquaint them with the other gifted ones. And they must learn as much as possible about the customs, history and politics of each demesne. That knowledge will prove invaluable."*

"Two children." Ayliss let the words breathe over her lips.

"Your daughter will be as powerful as you, perhaps even more so. Your son less so but he, too, will have gifts."

273

Realisation struck Ayliss. "That period of rest you speak of. Do you know how long my children will live and grow in peace? How soon will they need to deal with the coming chaos?"

"Not before they are ready. More I cannot tell you, for even I do not know."

Ayliss remained silent, thinking, for a long time. Then she lifted her eyes to face Earth once more. "My poor children. I will do my best, Mother."

"Remember, Daughter, you are never alone. That is even more true now than before, for now you have Janest, and the others with gifts. And I am always with you."

"Thank you, Mother." A thought struck Ayliss. "Mother, will Mama see this chaos? She has suffered so much already."

"No, Ayliss, she and your father will be spared. They have both done enough."

When Ayliss made to ask another question Earth placed a hand on her forearm. "No more, I must go."

She reached up and touched Ayliss's temple with one forefinger as she began to fade away. "Remember the pendulum. All things ebb and flow."

***

Author Biography

Yvonne Hertzberger is a native of the Netherlands who immigrated to Canada in 1950. She is an avid student of human behaviour, which gives her the insights she uses to develop the characters in her writing. Hertzberger came to writing late in life, hence the self-proclaimed label 'late bloomer'.

Her first Old World Fantasy novel "Back From Chaos: Book One of Earth's Pendulum" was published in 2009. The second volume "Through Kestrel's Eyes" is available currently. The third book "The Dreamt Child" completes the trilogy. Hertzberger has contributions in "Indies Unlimited: 2012 Flash Fiction Anthology" and "Indies Unlimited: Tutorials and Tools for Prospering in a Digital World".

She is a contributing author to Indies Unlimited.

LINKS

Website ~ www.newfantasyauthor.com

Twitter ~ YHERTZBE

Facebook ~
http://www.facebook.com/EarthsPendulum.YvonneHertzb
erger.author

Email ~ yvonne.hertzberger@gmail.com